Falling Into Fate

J.M. DRAGON

Falling Into Fate

ISBN 13: 978-1-935216-17-9

First Printing: 2010

This Trade Paperback Is Published By
Intaglio Publications
Walker, LA USA
WWW.INTAGLIOPUB.COM

Credits

Executive Editor: Tara Young
Cover design by Tiger Graphics

Dedication

For my dad, I wish the fates had been kinder.

Acknowledgments

Thank you, Kay, for the original inspiration of this storyline. May your exploits into the paranormal be fruitful.

Mel, as always, my enormous thanks for using you as a sounding board and helping with drafts whilst writing this story. I'm eternally grateful for your continued friendship and support.

Thanks, Tara, for the help in the final editing and the useful information. I appreciate the assistance.

Chapter 1

"Where the hell is Stark?" Brian Johnson bellowed as several heads shook while others hid behind their work cubes. They knew too well that Johnson, the managing editor of the *Daily Post*, wasn't a nice man to be around if he was upset. Right now, his double chin hung low and determined. A full day's stubble was evident, although it was barely eight in the morning. His piercing dark blue eyes gave everyone in the vicinity a glare as he hunted for his quarry.

He made a full circuit of the floor area, then back to a cubical that was empty. A half-empty coffee cup was on the desk and the computer powered up and ready to go. A brown leather jacket hung on the back of the chair and keys were next to the computer console. Johnson leaned over the barrier that separated each work area and snarled at the man there. "George, where has she disappeared to now? And don't give me that guff that you don't know because I know you two are attached at the hip."

George Irons frowned in consternation. He pulled at his bow tie covered in tiny daisies and gave his boss a smile through thin lips. "She was tracking down Daryl. How's the ulcer, boss? Giving you a hard time today?"

"My ulcer hasn't anything to do with you, Irons. Why the hell is she chasing down Daryl? Hasn't she been putting in her expenses properly again? God, give me strength. If it wasn't that she had talent, I'd fire her ass." Johnson grimaced. "When she gets back," he said, lifting his eyebrows, "tell her my office, pronto." He stormed back to his office and slammed the door so hard that the glass in the window shook.

George didn't say anything but sighed heavily, then picked up the phone and called his boyfriend. Once he heard Danny's voice, he began a long conversation about the interior design of their new apartment.

Ten minutes later, Susan Stark returned to her desk and sank heavily in her chair, muttering inaudibly.

George, still chatting amiably with his friend, peeked over the cubical and waved at the well-built woman who was taller than he was. He guessed her height to be around six feet. Her Titian hair was held in check by a ponytail.

"What is it, George? I'm not happy. That fraud Luke Daryl is trying to screw me over again in more ways than one." Her hazel eyes focused on her good-looking associate. He at least was harmless, and she didn't have to be anything other than who she was with him.

"Tell that to the boss. He wants to see you. His word was *pronto,* and he wasn't happy, Suzy. I think he's having trouble with his ulcer again. He's way grouchy today."

"Shit, as if my day wasn't bad enough." Susan frowned. "Did he give any indication about why he wanted to see me?" She knew that her last serialized articles had been good—even better than good. There was talk of a possible merit award later in the year, but that could change with the next good story out there.

"Sorry, Suzy." George gave her an apologetic smile, then wailed, "Oh, no, not purple, Danny!"

Susan shrugged, knowing that George was lost in a conversation that definitely wasn't part of her life—settling down. Opening the desk drawer, she pulled out her purse, then applied more of what the cosmetic company called *dashing red* to her lips. She flicked her ponytail for moral support and strode confidently to Johnson's office.

When he gruffly said, "Come in," she breezed in.

"Sorry I wasn't around earlier, boss. I had to see Daryl. There was a little mistake about my last expense account."

Johnson glared at her and shook his head. "If I hadn't promised your father… What have you done wrong this time with your expenses?"

Susan felt like shouting, "Nothing as usual," but having done that in the early days, she knew her explanation would be ignored. Luke Daryl was the nephew of the newspaper's owner, and that said it all. For the past five years, she'd put up with the man's sleazy passes. When he wouldn't take no for an answer, she'd appropriated a football jock as a trophy boyfriend to help her cause. It hadn't. All it had done was make the man more meticulous when it came to her expenses. One day soon, she was going to deck the guy and say to hell with the job.

"Are you listening to me?" Johnson bellowed, and Susan winced. At times like this, he could use a voice suppressor.

Susan answered quickly, "Always, boss. What can I do for you?"

The man snorted. "I've a new assignment for you. Occasionally, someone interesting is released from the sanatorium. Have you ever heard of Lorna Hirste?"

Susan contemplated the name, and it didn't ring any bells. "Sorry, I can't say I have. What exactly did she do to end up there and warrant a news feature?"

Johnson flipped over a folder. "She's an interesting case."

Susan picked up the folder and ran a quick glance over the contents. The word that hit her first was *manslaughter*. Then she noted that the case was fifteen years old. "What angle do you want?"

"You decide."

Susan flashed her boss a quizzical look. He sounded different. She couldn't put a finger on what it was, but it was definitely different. "Okay."

"Good. In exactly two hours, she'll be released. What are you waiting for?"

"Apparently nothing." Susan left the room with the file under her arm.

Lorna Hirste impatiently walked as fast as her feet would take her up and down the corridor that led to the locked door leading to the reception area and her freedom. As far as she was concerned, it couldn't come fast enough. Her pale grey eyes hooked magnetically to the locked inner door, certain that the next person to open it would allow her to fly from her enforcement into a new world. One that her lawyer had assured her would be more willing to understand her gift.

A buzzing caught her attention, and her gaze shot to the man in white overalls opening the door. He closed it immediately behind him.

"How long now?"

Orderly Arnold Dawson shook his head. "As long as it takes for the formalities to be taken care of, Lorna. Don't worry, you'll be having a steak with your folks in no time."

Lorna didn't appreciate the man's cheery grin that accompanied his remark. He didn't have to endure what she had over the last fifteen years. She was innocent of the claim that she was a mental time bomb. It was that false accusation that committed her to the Llewellyn Sanatorium. Over the years, she'd watched people come and go. Some walked out voluntarily while others had to die to taste freedom.

"What's it like out there these days, Arnold?"

The man frowned slightly, then smiled. "Probably much the same as it was when you were last out." He shrugged. "Faster maybe." He moved away towards the administration office. "You take care out there. We'll miss you."

"Miss me? Well, I won't miss this place," Lorna muttered under her breath as the door buzzed again.

"I see you're impatient to leave us, Lorna." Dr. Isla Gerardo smiled, making her oval face beautiful. Her small mouth seemed to bring her countenance alive.

Lorna drew in a deep breath, suddenly nervous about what was to happen next. Then she walked towards the woman and nodded.

The doctor gave Lorna an assessing look. "You know why I wasn't sure about this, don't you? You've never fully faced what happened to you with that young man. I still feel that we could help you."

Lorna gave a cynical smile. "Thankfully, my lawyer doesn't have your doubts, nor did the judge at the codicil hearing."

Resolutely, the doctor said, "If ever you find you need to talk, you know where I am. Promise me that if things begin to get on top of you, you'll call."

"I'll call." Lorna gave lip service to the doctor. No matter how many times she insisted that her version was the truth, Dr. Gerardo hadn't believed her and thought her delusional. Everyone thought she was mad, and perhaps after all the time of living with the mentally unstable, she was—a little.

"Good. Now let's get you out of here, shall we? Your lawyer is waiting for you."

Lorna walked through the normally locked door and felt her body heave a sigh of relief. *At last, I can go home.*

Lorna's lawyer, Jenny Price, had signed all the necessary forms to have Lorna released into her custody and waited much as her client did—impatiently. Her blond hair, like a golden sheen around her head, had bangs that partially covered the deep blue eyes, which focused on the door of Dr. Gerardo's office. She'd taken the case two years earlier. At first, because her boss had insisted, and later, because she felt an injustice had been done to Lorna.

The woman wasn't delusional. Whenever they met, she was perfectly lucid. Other than a silly notion about protecting gravestones, nothing appeared amiss. Over her years as a lawyer, Jenny had come across far more people who had escaped a term as long as Lorna's for worse crimes. It galled Jenny that Lorna had remained in this place for the full fifteen-year term the courts had imposed after the original trial.

The trial, as far as she was concerned, had so many big holes in it that someone could drive a truck through them. To her standards, the Hirste family was relatively poor, having enough to get through each week with no extras. She speculated that was why Lorna had to suffer incarceration. If her parents had been financially able and had a reasonably competent lawyer on their case initially, Lorna would probably have served no more than five years.

Sam, the senior partner in her legal firm, considered it his duty as a fellow human being to help others from time to time. Everything they did legally for Lorna was pro bono.

As she thought about Lorna's family life, Jenny's family too demanded attention. Her father was a noted judge, her mother a celebrated society charity organizer, with the added power of being part of one of the founding families in the area. Jenny was the eldest of three. Her sister was married to a Royal Canadian Mounted Police officer and had two kids. They rarely came back to the States except for special celebrations. Her younger brother was a professor of physics at Merit University. They lived a comfortable lifestyle in Merit, never going short of anything, which she suspected was unlike her client.

Jenny's aspirations of becoming a prima ballerina ended when she suffered a permanent ligament injury to her calf. Her parents were supportive of any career choice she made, and when she took up the family legal profession, her father was pleased. At thirty-eight, she could have had partnership in the family's prestigious firm but opted instead to carve her own way through the profession. Eventually, through hard work and staying power, she had convinced Sam Wallis, a noted legal eagle for the downtrodden, to take her on. She'd been there for eight years, and a year earlier, Sam took her on as his partner.

Jenny was pretty sure that Sam's heart attack was the reason he finally allowed someone else to take the reins of his firm. Plus Jackie, Sam's wife, had been delighted since she looked on Jenny as the daughter she never had.

Her thoughts, interrupted by the door opening, had Jenny focusing on Dr. Gerardo and Lorna, who were walking into the room.

Jenny smiled warmly at Lorna. "Hi, Lorna, how are you? It's a big day for you."

Lorna blew out a heavy breath and returned the smile. "I'm good…all the better for being on this side of the building."

Jenny reached out and squeezed Lorna's shoulder. "Well, in a few minutes, you'll see more than this side of the building." Jenny looked at Dr. Gerardo. "Right, Doctor?"

Dr. Gerardo nodded curtly and reluctantly said, "If you'll sign these papers, Lorna, your lawyer can take you home."

Jenny saw Lorna's face change to one of wonder. She knew why. In that word—home—there was hope.

Lorna moved to the desk and with a shaking hand, reached for the pen. Seconds later, she watched as ink drew out her name.

Chapter 2

Susan Stark, in her black Jeep, mounted guard over the entrance of the gated building of the Llewellyn Sanatorium. From what she gathered, the only other exit from the grounds was a small tradesman's gate, and that was hardly fitting for a free woman after all this time.

She chose to wait in front of the perfectly preserved building. It was an old colonial style that was built in the 1850s. The original owner had been a wealthy entrepreneur whose descendants lived there through three generations. The Llewellyn family lost almost everything, including the eldest son to suicide, in the Wall Street stock market crash of 1929. That left the eldest daughter, Mary, who had become a nurse and had a minor fortune of her own, to salvage what she could. Eventually, she opened the house as a sanatorium. At the time, there never had been anything like it in the surrounding area, and over the years, the local government had taken over the running of the establishment.

Susan glanced at the beautifully kept gardens, suspecting that most of the plantings were from earlier days. She pondered what it would be like to own such a large and prestigious property and live, unlike the individuals there now, voluntarily.

The gates opened, and a red BMW coupe shot out of the entrance and into the virtually empty road. The glass was tinted, but she could see two figures inside the vehicle. Susan had done a little research in the short time she had and recognized the vehicle as belonging to Lorna Hirste's lawyer, Jenny Price.

Knowing what she had to do, she put her car in gear and followed the BMW at a discreet distance.

"What do you feel so far?" Jenny flicked her gaze from the road for a second and turned to Lorna for her reaction to the outside world.

Lorna shot her a hesitant smile. "Bewildered."

Jenny chuckled. "Great word. There have been a lot of changes over the years, especially to some of the buildings."

"Arnold was right…it is faster," Lorna mumbled.

"Arnold? What's faster?"

Lorna frowned. "He's an orderly, one of the nicer ones. He said life was faster today." Her fingers trailed the leather upholstery as she looked at the walnut dashboard with all the flashing lights. "Take your car, for instance. I bet it's expensive."

Jenny had the grace to look sheepish. "I confess it's my weakness. I don't smoke, drink much, and haven't a family to look after, therefore I can indulge this passion of having a snazzy car."

"It's beautiful."

"Oh, yes, she is. Maybe soon you'll be riding around in a car of your own."

Lorna didn't answer, and Jenny wished she hadn't said that. The woman was barely out of incarceration and had no job or any means of getting one. They hadn't trained her over the years to become a more productive member of society. Prison would have at least helped reintroduce her to the outside world. All she had now was her family to support her until she could be educated for some sort of employment.

"Your parents are looking forward to this. They wanted to come and get you, but I insisted it be me."

"Why?"

Jenny hadn't wanted to mention anything that might upset Lorna. That day was special, and she wanted Lorna to remember it with pleasure since she had so little in the last fifteen years. "I found out from a source that perhaps the newspaper might be interested in talking to you." More like hounding the woman, she suspected. That seemed to be the norm these days. She heard that the *Daily Post* had sent out a reporter. Her eyes narrowed as she once again saw the black Jeep that had trailed her since they left Llewellyn in her rearview mirror.

Lorna, with a narrowed glance at Jenny, asked fearfully, “Reporters? Why do they want to talk to me? I’m old news.”

Jenny momentarily glanced in Lorna’s direction and saw the look and heard the trepidation in Lorna’s voice. She was clearly upset. Jenny stopped the car abruptly, ignoring the one-finger salute from a couple of drivers who were irritated at her sudden action. Moving in her seat so that she could be in direct eye contact with Lorna, Jenny smiled reassuringly.

“It’s going to be okay, Lorna, I promise you. You have the right to deny them access on your property and don’t have to say a word to them. I can deal with it if you want.” In retrospect, Lorna had every right to be wary of the newshounds. They’d created such frenzy about her years ago, particularly with that nickname they gave her. It was Jenny’s opinion that the media was primarily the reason why they had been so hard on her at the trial.

There was silence until Lorna gave Jenny a weak smile. “Thank you. What will I do when you go? You won’t always be there with me, will you?”

Jenny hadn’t thought of that. She grinned before saying, “Yeah, I will…just as long as you need me. We’re friends, right?” She knew when she saw Lorna beaming, she’d said the right thing.

“Friends…I like that.”

“Great, now let’s go or your parents will start worrying.”

The BMW stopped in a less well-to-do neighborhood where once-fashionable houses had long since fallen into dilapidation. There was the odd house on Shannon Street that held some of its former glory—the Hirste home for one. Its well-tended garden was brimming with daisies and a glorious and colorful array of pansies. The exterior of the house had fresh paint. The curtains at the window appeared shabby but clean. A twitching of one corner in a window indicated that someone was watching and waiting.

Seconds later, the door flew open and James and Trudy Hirste stood in the doorway. Smiles wreathed their faces when they saw

Lorna swiftly exit the car and run towards their waiting and loving arms.

Jenny watched the reunion from her car with a feeling of pleasure seeping over her. This was one of the reasons she loved working with Sam. It could so easily have been more years down the track before Lorna was able to leave Llewellyn, especially if they hadn't contested the doctor's application for an extension of the enforcement order. A vehicle stopping behind the BMW had her sighing heavily. Lorna wasn't out of the woods yet. Jenny suspected the damned paparazzi had just pulled up behind her.

Jenny watched the longest legs she'd ever seen emerge from the Jeep, and a woman in black slacks and shirt get out. Her powerfully built proportions had Jenny wondering if she really could handle the situation. Climbing out of her own vehicle, Jenny moved to face the woman who was eyeing the tender reunion scene with a bland expression. Her cell phone was flipped open.

"Are you taking photos?"

The stranger flicked her gaze from the cell to the short woman who came up to her shoulder. "It's a free country."

Jenny felt slightly intimidated by the woman's size. Her five-foot-four height made her appear pint-sized in comparison. "For the most part, you're right. Are you a reporter?"

Susan idly replied, "I prefer journalist myself. You are?"

"I'm Ms. Hirste's lawyer. She doesn't want to give interviews."

"Did I ask for an interview?"

"People like you don't ask. Instead, they gatecrash and bully."

Jenny watched as the reporter's body language changed. It seemed to gain another couple of inches, and she didn't need that further disadvantage.

"You'd know that how? Have you ever seen me before or read any of my work?"

"I've had years of experience with you people. You're all out of the same mold."

Susan gave a cynical laugh. "You people? You've included me in with all other reporters good or bad. Really? I must tell my parents they brought a clone into the world. I'm sure they never thought of it that way." Susan shook her head, and her ponytail bounced back and forth. "Look, think of it this way. If I don't get the interview, someone else will. At least Lorna gets to tell her side of the story. For the record, I don't bully anyone."

Jenny remained belligerent as she asked in a less harsh tone, "Why not just let her be? Hasn't she suffered enough?"

"Perhaps you might think that being her lawyer. However, have you considered the parents of the young man she killed? Their suffering is forever."

Jenny accepted the point and drew in a deep breath. She was about to counter with something glib when a card was thrust towards her.

"Here, take my card and have Lorna call me when she's ready to talk. The sooner the better, so she can get on with living her life how she wants. You know what it's like in this business, don't you?"

Jenny gave her a blank look.

"You're old news as soon as the ink is dry."

Jenny glanced down at the card. *Susan Stark, journalist, Daily Post*. When she looked up again, the woman had left and was climbing into her vehicle. Maybe she'd been wrong about reporters. This one seemed to be different, not so pushy. On the return to her office, she'd check out Stark's work and her background. She knew in this day of computers and the Internet, it wouldn't be difficult.

As the black Jeep swung away from the curb and into traffic, Jenny saw Lorna watching her anxiously. With a reassuring smile, she walked towards the family, and they all entered the house.

"Photo! You have one measly photo, and they call you the star reporter around here! Give me a break, Stark," Brian bellowed.

Susan waited out the tirade. When he'd finally finished, she said, "I'll get that interview. It just wasn't the right time. For god's sake, the woman is finally free from the loony bin after fifteen years of confinement. Couldn't she at least have her family reunion in peace?"

Susan watched as Brian pulled at his tie, which twisted halfway around his thick neck.

"If someone else gets that interview before you, Stark, you can say goodbye to your reporting spot and say hello to features. Irons is always complaining he needs an assistant."

Susan had a feeling he wasn't joking. George might find it funny, but she certainly wouldn't. "I'll get that interview, and it'll be exclusive," Susan said through gritted teeth.

"I'll hold you to that. By the way, was it Sam Wallis or Jenny Price who took her home?"

"Price, why?"

"Oh, just wondered. Price might be worthy of a story sometime. She's from the ideal background of privilege and now she helps the poor. Maybe you can kill two birds with one stone."

"Maybe I could," Susan said shortly as she headed out the door.

One thing interested her when she saw the cozy family reunion. Why hadn't the parents done more to free their daughter? Why had it taken so long for her to integrate back into society? *I guess I'll find that out when I get the exclusive.*

Crossing her fingers, she hoped that Hirste would call. Otherwise, she might have to consider finally confronting Daryl on her terms by telling the idiot she was a lesbian and he didn't have the right equipment to jingle her bells. It was a wicked thought but then her career in this city would be over. She let out a small grin—it would be worth it to see the look on his face.

Lorna peeled back the bedclothes of the room she had called her own fifteen years earlier. It still held faint memories of a happy childhood. Though the bedclothes, wallpaper, and curtains were new, she recalled the posters of Nirvana and other grunge items of the era. Her glance fell to the CD player in the corner and her modest collection of CDs, which reflected her moods at the time. At Llewellyn, they didn't allow her to have anything personal. Their reasoning—something had triggered her psychosis, and she needed to be free of anything that might have influenced her mental instability.

Drained, she sat heavily on the bed. Her pale eyes stared almost unseeingly around her as she allowed the precious moments of newfound freedom to settle in. Still, she expected that at any moment someone would lock the door of the room as they had for the last fifteen years.

Then her mind traveled to her parents. It had been good to see them smiling. A testament to their love and devotion was the fact that they had visited once a month for fifteen years. Never once had they lost faith in her or her in them. She gazed at the mirror on the dresser and touched her pale skin before tracing her short snub nose and the thin lips. She wasn't beautiful. The only aspect of her that could be called that was her shining brown hair, which had luster to it. Well past shoulder length, it swung remarkably tidily around her long face.

Lorna opened her fist that clutched the card that Jenny had given her—*Susan Stark, journalist, Daily Post.* Her thoughts traveled to the trial and how the newspapers, the *Daily Post* in particular, had rallied around the deceased. They made her out as some kind of bitch from hell. They'd even given her that nickname—Gravekeeper. The name had given the stories they had engineered in the media more effect. Unfortunately, she had been too naïve and traumatized by the whole event to protest. At the time, no one had wanted to hear her side of the story, not even the judge or jury. She felt they had convicted her before the trial had begun. If the young man she had inadvertently killed hadn't come from a socially well-connected family, the case wouldn't have been newsworthy.

A sound outside her door had her closing her fist over the reporter's card. Her mother popped her auburn head around the door. Her smile was all Lorna needed to make her feel good inside again and eradicate the churning dark memories.

"Hi, Mom."

"How are you doing, dear? Do you need anything? I was thinking that maybe I could send your dad for takeout. I bet you haven't had one of those for a long time," Trudy said lightly.

"That would be great. Anything you and Pops would like is fine with me," Lorna said with a slight curve of her lips. "It's good to be home…I've missed you." Tears that she held in check for years flowed freely as Trudy rushed forward and cradled her only child close to her breast.

Lorna heard the soothing words of comfort flowing over the prematurely greying locks of her hair. "It's going to be okay now, Lorna, I promise."

Lorna knew the words were genuine but wondered how the sentiment could be true. No one could promise that everything would be okay—no one.

Chapter 3

Jenny flicked on the light over her desk and removed the large manila file that held everything about the Hirste case from her ongoing tray. They included the original police interviews, prosecution and defense transcriptions, and the final nail in the coffin—the trial verdict. In a separate folder were details from Llewellyn that were sketchy but gave her a glimpse into the treatment that Lorna received over the years. It made fascinating reading even now. Knowing the hard part was over, Jenny felt that there was still something unfinished with the case but couldn't quite grasp what it was.

The door to her office opened slightly and Sam Wallis placed his balding head around the door. His large handlebar moustache was the part of his face that her eyes immediately focused on.

"Hi, I saw the light. How did it go today?"

"Good. Lorna's home safe with her family. You were right to warn me about the media. Some woman from the *Daily Post* was trailing us." Jenny smiled at her business partner who was looking better each day. That was good for their client base. They loved Sam.

"Who was it from the *Post*?"

Jenny watched as Sam moved, allowing his lean body to wedge easily in the doorway.

"Hmm, I gave the reporter's card to Lorna. Thankfully, I only had to ward off one of those pests. Either the others aren't interested or haven't connected the dots that Lorna is out." Jenny looked perplexed, then her smile widened. "Stark, that's the one... Susan Stark. Do you know her work? She said I should check her out before flaming her."

Sam frowned. "You haven't been assuming things again, have you, and saying them out loud? One day, it will get you in trouble."

Jenny shook her head. "No…well, not exactly. Do you know her work?"

"Sure, I know her work. From what I've read, she's fair, and most have a good word for her. She wrote that article about the kids trapped in the house that the parents set on fire." Sam's voice took on an angry tone as he shook his head. "If it hadn't been for her cajoling of the oldest child, I doubt they would have convicted those bastards. They didn't deserve those kids."

Jenny pondered his quiet admiration for Stark. She had seen the article and knew it had prompted many to have varying opinions of what went on in that home—none of them good from the story's point of view. "Isn't that what they did to Lorna? Report it in such a way that a conviction was a done deal?"

"I never said that, and Lorna admitted she killed the boy. She deserved some penance, though fifteen years was harsh, which is why we took it on pro bono. To be frank, we never helped, really. Her release fifteen years to the day of the sentence wasn't a good result. At least now we can shelve that case and move on. As you can tell by your inbox, there's a mountain of others in crisis waiting for us." Sam sighed and moved to close the door.

"Sam, this mumbo jumbo the *Post* reported about the Gravekeeper aspect…do you believe any of it?" Jenny closed the file on her desk.

A low rumble of laughter greeted her question. "It was a gimmick at the time and a poor reflection on the whole situation if you ask me. Therefore, the answer is no. Why the interest?"

"Oh, nothing." Jenny stretched. "It's been a long day. I think my body is saying it needs sustenance."

Sam grinned. "No date tonight? I thought you and Sheila West were getting on great."

Jenny frowned. "I thought so, too. Alas, I'm afraid I was replaced by someone more reliable—a doctor. Hey, I ask you, who could be more reliable than a lawyer?"

"Don't worry. One day, there will be someone who arrives in your life completely unexpected, and *wham* you're done for." He looked at his watch. "Take me, for instance. If I don't get home soon, dinner will be ruined, and Jackie will kill me." He winked as he shut the door between them with a wave.

Jenny glanced at the file on her desk, picked it up, and was about to toss it in the closed tray when she changed her mind. Instead, she opened her briefcase and placed it inside. She didn't know why she felt compelled to do it and decided not to dwell on it. Besides, it was Friday and the weekend waited along with a grand family reunion for her mother's birthday the next evening. No doubt, it was going to be one of the social events of the calendar for Merit society. She smiled at the thought and switched off the light. With briefcase in hand, she walked out of the office, locking the door behind her.

Susan peered inside her refrigerator. The sight that greeted her had her nostrils flaring at the fact that once more she had forgotten to shop for groceries and her pantry was bare. She found a piece of cheese that looked very old, and the smell was overpowering. There was a half container of milk, so she supposed a bowl of cereal could be an option. Nothing fresh or edible was in the refrigerator, that was for sure. Closing the door, she ambled over to the TV and turned it on.

Usually on a Friday evening, she was either working or out on a date. Remarkably, she was doing neither. Her mind focused on work. She'd call Lorna Hirste the next day if the woman didn't call her first. She fervently hoped that she wouldn't have to make the first move. She had been ethically serious to Jenny Price when she said she was honest.

The memory of the aroma of Price's perfume seemed to permeate her senses and Susan laughed at the absurdity. "I could have put a hand on her shoulder and bulldozed her pint-sized body out of the way in her defense of Hirste. If I had been a male journalist, that probably would have happened. I know a few who indulged in the tactics the Price woman said were typical. It just doesn't apply to me, and I'm proud of it."

The more she thought of the lawyer, the more her emotions did a somersault. Susan's lips moved into a cynical smile. There was no way she was attracted to the woman. *God, I need to get laid.* Maybe that was what her subconscious was telling her.

Tonight was the night to go out on the town and have meaningless sex with a stranger. The more she thought about it, the more it appealed to her. Relationships were not her thing these days, especially after Leigh. Maybe when she hit geriatric status, there could be an advantage in reconsidering, but not at this time in her life. Leigh had burned her badly in that department, and it wasn't going to happen again.

Moving towards her bedroom that led to her small bathroom en suite, she grinned. "Yep, I deserve it tonight. Sex will be my reward for a crappy day."

Jenny showered, made chicken salad for herself, and contemplated the evening ahead of her—boring. Fridays with Sheila, who she'd dated for over three months, had been enjoyable. The bubbly woman, ten years her junior, certainly knew how to have fun. On reflection, they must have visited every nightclub in Merit in that time. Though nightclubs had never been a big part of her social entertainment in the past, she'd actually succumbed to the bug, at least while Sheila was with her. She pushed her empty plate away and stood as a thought occurred to her. *Didn't we get tickets to a new nightclub opening this weekend?* Sure enough, when she rummaged through the purse she'd last used with Sheila, the tickets were stuck in a side pocket. She glanced at the date, noting it was VIPs that night and exclusives the next. They were VIP tickets, so it was that night or never.

The next day was her mother's birthday bash, and she wouldn't be welcomed home for months if she missed the event of the year in her mother's social calendar. The only reason her sister was able to do so was because she was due to deliver her third child in two weeks, and it was unsafe for her to travel. Jenny didn't have that certain delicate condition and hadn't until fairly recently wanted the responsibility. When she began to coach a local Little League team made up of neighborhood kids, having a child took on a strange sort of appeal. She reasoned that it was her biological clock giving her a nudge.

Tickets in hand, she returned to the comfort of her living room and pondered her quandary. Should she stay home and watch TV or be adventurous and go to the club opening? No contest. She threw down the *TV Guide* she'd picked up and headed for her bedroom to find something fitting for a night out on the town.

Music seemed to pour onto the sidewalk from the newly opened club aptly called Crescendo. Though it was a lesbian club, numerous people, both male and female, jostled to get inside as the queue grew like a conga line.

Susan thanked God that she had a press card that opened doors on these occasions. She exited the bar across the street where she downed a couple of beers before taking on the excitement of the nightclub brigade. Heading towards two bouncers who were filtering people waiting to go in, she noted that they could be poster girls for the butch community. Susan flashed her card and caught their attention. After giving her the once-over, the bouncers allowed her to enter. The street buzz had been correct for once. The place was the best of the best. The lighting was garish on the dance floor but subdued in the more intimate booths that circled the floor. The main bar had an almost comfortable ambiance about it that made you forget the hundreds of gyrating bodies on the floor. Someone had gone to a great deal of trouble to accommodate as many tastes as possible. From her first impression, she was going to come back, which was all the club owner hoped to achieve.

Standing at the bar, she placed her elbows on the polished counter and waited for the bartender. Susan had found in other similar bars that the wait for a drink usually took a while. Surprisingly enough, after the woman next to her got her drink, the bartender asked, "What'll it be?"

"What do you have on draft?"

"No draft beer. Bottles and you can pretty much name any kind. The boss has a fetish about beer."

Susan smiled warmly at the young woman who had a vivacious grin. She was worth considering at the end of the night if she failed to hook up with anyone else. The woman had a flat chest, but the look she'd been giving said it all—willing.

"I'll have a Stella Artois and you can name your poison."

The bartender giggled. "Oh, we don't take those kinds of tips."

Susan gave the woman a rakish grin. "Really? Now what kind of tips do you take, I wonder?"

The bartender slid the beer bottle to her, and Susan paid the exorbitant amount demanded in clubs these days. She took a long swig. Her gaze rotated around the room. *Hmm, lots of nice eye candy here. I could be luckier than I thought tonight.*

The bar stool next to her was drawn up and a petite woman whose back was to Susan sat down, waiting for service.

"I'll have a glass of Shiraz. Do you have Pierpont?"

Susan's eyes crinkled at the corner in concentration. She'd heard that voice recently. Swiveling in her chair, she looked directly at the woman who had spoken and chuckled silently before theatrically announcing, "Well, as I live and breathe, someone else who likes to live dangerously."

Susan didn't get a reply but saw the shift on the bar stool, edging it a few inches away. Moments later, the bartender returned, and Susan watched as she placed the drink in front of Jenny Price, who passed over a small card.

The bartender smiled. "Enjoy."

"You're not the most sociable person on the block, are you, Ms. Price?"

At her name, Jenny turned abruptly. Susan almost laughed when she saw Jenny carefully school her features into a bland mask to hide her surprise.

"Ms. Stark, what brings you here? Is there a story for you to follow?"

Susan's eyes narrowed at the remark and she shrugged. "Believe me, Ms. Price, there's a story in every experience. However, they allow me a little pleasure hunting now and again. What about you?"

"I have tickets and I thought I'd check it out."

"Hmm, so this could end up being your usual haunt." Susan gave Jenny an appraising once-over and saw the tinge of red on her cheeks that had nothing to do with makeup. "You don't look the clubbing type. Not that I have you pinned as any category because I don't know you well enough." Susan felt that raw physical attraction drawing her in as it unconsciously had at their first encounter.

Jenny scowled. "I'm not interested in your opinion of me. Now if you'll excuse me, I'd prefer to enjoy this drink in private. I won't say it was a pleasure to see you again."

Susan chuckled as her head threw back in a highly amused way. "You don't mince words, do you? If you have tickets in the plural, does that mean I'm cramping your style?"

Susan heard Jenny give a heavy sigh before fishing in her purse. "Here, take the spare. You can have two drinks on me." Jenny slid off the bar stool and headed towards the rim of the dance floor.

Susan laughed even louder but pocketed the ticket anyway. Then with beer in hand, she followed Jenny, allowing her a few seconds of alone time. "Thanks."

"You're welcome."

"Dance with me?" Susan knew by Jenny's rigid stance that the offer wasn't welcome. However, it didn't hurt to ask. Besides, Jenny had been pretty judgmental earlier in the day, and it made for an interesting payback—annoying her.

"Okay, one dance."

Susan placed her beer on the table she'd commandeered from two woman who were about to sit down, her presence alone intimidating them. Jenny followed suit, and Susan guided Jenny onto the dance floor.

One dance had extended to four. When a slow song started, Susan moved closer, pulling Jenny's body until it molded perfectly into hers. During the song, Susan allowed her hands and lips to do the talking. Jenny called a time-out.

"I don't get that friendly on the dance floor with a stranger. What made you so confident you could try it with me?"

Susan allowed her hands to fall, ignoring the question. "I'll fetch us another drink." Her long legs traveled fast towards the bar before Jenny could protest.

A few minutes later, Susan returned triumphant. "Pierpont

Shiraz, right?" Then she settled down on the chair opposite Jenny. Finding that not to her taste, she moved it closer.

"Thanks. Look, I'm okay on my own. I didn't come here looking for a friend, only a good time."

Susan pulled a face at the comment. "Oh, now please, Jenny, anyone would think that you didn't like me. Besides, a good time and a new friend surely go hand in glove. Aren't you having a good time with me?"

Susan saw Jenny roll her eyes, and she almost laughed at the comical expression—was it loathing?—on Jenny's face while she sipped her drink instead of replying.

"I haven't heard from Lorna Hirste yet."

"She's hardly been home more than six hours. I think you need to learn patience." Jenny growled. "In more ways than one."

Susan considered the advice. "I can do that. Although, my boss isn't a patient man and worries others might get the story before me. Is anyone else sniffing around?"

"Exactly why does your paper want the story? Didn't you crucify her enough the first time around?"

"I told you I won't do that. I just want Hirste's version. Besides, that was fifteen years ago and things change." Susan had read the original articles and had to admit they were damning.

"Do they change? I doubt it. You coined the nickname Gravekeeper. What the hell was that about?" Jenny's voice rose an octave or two. "I've read the articles several times over the two years I've been on the case. They never made any sense to me. They were more like smears on Lorna's life and questioned her sanity."

Susan leaned so far back in the chair that it looked like she would topple over. "Come out on a proper date with me and I'll tell all."

Jenny's chair scratched the floor as she stood. "I'll take you out to dinner. Will that be enough? You can name the restaurant."

Susan pondered the tempting offer. "Okay. How about tomorrow night?"

Jenny shook her head. "I can't. Tomorrow is my mother's birthday and there's a party."

Susan chuckled and it seemed to rumble all around the table. "Oh, you mean I'm not invited, and we're dating…shame on you, Jenny. Don't your parents approve of your lifestyle?" Susan quipped, her lips tugging into a wicked smile.

"I need to go. I have an early start tomorrow." Jenny opened her purse. "Here's my card. Call me at the office with another evening for dinner. Good night."

Susan stood towering over Jenny and was about to call her a party pooper. However, she refrained from teasing her. In her opinion, lawyers rarely had a sense of humor, and it appeared Jenny Price was in that cast. *And she had the gall to call the press out of the same mold.* "Good night, Jenny, until our date then. Be careful on the way home."

Jenny nodded. "Thanks, you do the same." She marched off towards the exit.

Susan grinned as Jenny silently walked away. A point of fascination was the lack of sound from the woman's heels as the floor was polished wood. There should have been an accompanying resonance. Then the bartender who winked at her caught her attention. No sense in being alone when there was someone who wanted her company. Pocketing the card Jenny had given her, she moved towards the bar.

Jenny headed for the exit and a cab home but decided it might be wise to use the bathroom first. Who knew when a taxi might be available. As she entered the room, she was surprised at the spaciousness of the restroom, in particular the contrast of décor, which was in muted colors as opposed to the more dashing style of the main interior. Several women were touching up their makeup. Jenny walked over to the stalls and heard a conversation going on between two stalls next to each other.

"Andy, I'm just reminding you that you have to get over that crush you have on the woman. Hell, it was ten years ago. I'm not one to knock love at first sight, but you need to face that it's a one-sided love. The woman doesn't even know you exist."

Jenny couldn't help it, she listened intently, waiting for the answer. When it came, the voice sounded resigned to its fate.

"She might one day, then who knows. If I start up with someone else, how is she ever going to notice me?"

Jenny nodded. It was a valid point.

"You don't have any opportunity to meet her. You're a university professor and she's…something very different. Please, Andy, for me, will you at least try to be nice to my friend? She likes you."

Jenny felt suddenly happier that there was someone else who thought as she did and wanted to find the right someone to settle down with. *Bravo to her*. She was drawn out of her fascination with the conversation when someone tapped her on the shoulder. "Hey, are you a statue or do you need to go?"

Jenny felt her cheeks flush as she quickly walked to the free stall several cubicles away, missing the rest of the conversation, which part of her wanted to hear. As quickly as nature would allow, she exited the stall. The room had suddenly become busier, and she didn't know who anyone was. All she knew was that the Andy woman was right. If you found the love of your life, you had to keep the faith that she would eventually love you back. *Otherwise, what's the point?*

With a spring in her step, Jenny left the bathroom and pulled out her cell to call for a cab. These days, you had to be careful who was behind the wheel of a cab, and this company knew her well. She looked around the bar one last time before she left and saw Stark. She was at the bar whispering to the bartender, who obviously was enjoying the attention. The action from a complete stranger made her stomach twist. Her head upheld her original observation—Stark was nothing more than an opportunistic womanizer—and she was lucky to be rid of her attentions.

Chapter 4

Lorna awoke in the night with the same nightmare she had since she was thirteen. Her body was soaked with the cotton sheets wrapped around her like a mummy. Her heartbeat was so fast, it sounded like a drumroll in her ears. As she extricated herself from the sheets, she wondered if the restraint of the covers was her subconscious trying to hide her from the fear or if her fear was more dominant and it chose to restrain her as long as possible in the dreamscape. Either way, it never made sense. She refused to discuss the nightmare in detail with anyone, not her parents, nor the doctors at Llewellyn.

The latter were irked at her lack of detail, trying in differing degrees to get information, even to the point of force, when she had first been sent to the institution. However, she resisted and labored on with the nightmare, as she preferred to call it, which haunted her, and would, she suspected, until the end of her days.

The only thing she recalled from each time was a name. Sometimes the name was the same for numerous nightmares; other times it changed. At first, she had ignored it. However, as the years went on, the names grew louder in her head. She would research the name given to her, and it was inevitably someone who was dead.

After that, she had tried to resist the temptation to look up the names, but they grew louder in her head if she ignored them. At seventeen, she'd gone to the graveside of one of the names, and that's when she learned she was different. From then on, with each name that came, she visited the grave if they belonged to her hometown, and her life took a spiral into the unknown. She had always been a loner, but after that, she was isolated in a nightmare that was her reality. There was no one to turn to and even fewer people who would understand.

If only those boys had run like everyone else, then things would have been so different...if only.

A knock on her bedroom door heralded the end of her memories, and her mother looked inside.

"Are you okay, dear? We thought we heard you scream out. Do you still get those nightmares?"

Lorna gazed at her mother unseeingly for a few seconds. It was like a surreal dream that, instead of an orderly, it was her mother asking the question. She didn't know if it was real or yet another figment of her fevered mind.

The rotund woman with a gentle smile moved into the room and once more hugged her daughter. "You're home now, Lorna. No one is going to hurt you, I promise you that."

Then Lorna knew it was real. Her mom was embracing her, and for that, she was thankful. "Thanks, Mom. Go back to sleep. I'm fine. It must be all the excitement of coming home."

Her mother kissed her forehead before she left. Lorna sank back into the sheets. She closed her eyes, and a name began to resonate, quietly at first. It would lull her to sleep, but eventually it would grow louder—it always did. Sleep claimed her as the name Craig Henderson Jr. rolled around in her head.

Charles Price peered around the newspaper he was holding and smiled as he saw his eldest daughter's BMW pull into the long driveway to the colonial four-story building they called home. It had been in the family for two hundred years, passed to the eldest child, which used to be the eldest son back then. Two generations previously, the family had only daughters and his grandmother had inherited the property after some intricate legal wrangling. His blue gaze drifted to the open doorway of the dining room where he picked up the sounds of his wife. "Marina, Jen's arrived."

Marina Price shot through the doorway and peered over her husband's thin shoulders. Where she was willowy and amply built, her husband was the opposite. He was five-foot-seven, at least three inches shorter than she was, and in his wife's eyes, he was dangerously thin. He knew he had a particularly grotesque nose—he'd been ribbed about it growing up—and probably could give Cyrano de Bergerac a run for his money. However, he loved his family and made sure they knew it. They often called him a softy. Professionally, he had a steel rod running through his personality, which was evident in the legal community locally and nationally. Currently, he was sitting as a Superior Court judge.

Swishing back the curtain, Marina frowned. "I'd hoped that she would have brought Sheila with her. We said she could bring a friend. Why doesn't she ever bring anyone to meet us properly?"

Charles shook his head and gazed at his beautiful wife. Not for the first time, he wondered how he'd managed to snare her when she was the belle of every ball and the toast of the social circuit forty years ago, not to mention from the wealthy Margolis family. Her skin was pale but not sallow, and her green-hazel eyes seemed to smile at him whenever he saw her. Not that eyes smiled, of course, but they did to him. He'd fallen hook, line, and sinker for her when he'd met her at a charity ball, shortly after becoming a junior partner in the family law firm.

Although he'd tried to court her, she had thought him feckless and unsuitable. He'd persevered because deep down he knew she was the only one for him, and no amount of caustic words or actions changed his mind. He loved her from that moment, and if the fates were kind, he'd eventually win the day. He had and the rest had been magic ever since. With a swift movement of his hands, he dropped the newspaper and placed them around her waist, pulling her onto his knee. Her laughter completely enthralled him once more.

"When she finds the right one, she will, trust me."

Jenny heard her mother's laughter as she entered the house. She placed her overnight bag on the hall floor and walked in the direction of the amusement. Glancing in the dining room, she stopped and allowed the love her parents had for each other wash over her. This was what she wanted, and if she had to remain an old maid waiting for it, she would.

"Hey, parents, you have a child in the room."

Charles and Marina looked at their daughter and grinned. Marina moved out of her husband's grip and walked over to hug and kiss Jenny. Then she proceeded to look Jenny up and down. "You look great, darling. Did you bring a friend?"

Frowning at the look she received from her mother, Jenny shook her head and didn't respond. Instead, she walked over to kiss her father's cheek. "Great result on the Jamieson case. Before you know it, you'll be heading for the heady heights of the Supreme Court."

Charles chuckled as he hugged his daughter. "I've no desire to be a Supreme Court judge. I'm happy at this level, thanks. Besides, in a couple of years, I think I've earned that retirement plan your mother and I have been talking about for the last ten years."

Jenny grinned. She knew her parents wanted to take a long cruise to the Galapagos and South America and visit the ancient ruins. After that, they wanted to see as many other ancient wonders of the world they could possibly visit.

"Have Peter and Judith arrived yet?" Jenny asked conversationally. She then snagged a chocolate shortbread cookie from the tray in front of her father.

Marina looked slightly annoyed. "No, not yet, and she's now his ex. That boy hasn't a hope in settling down if he doesn't keep someone around for longer than a month. Judith was a lovely girl, too. What about you, darling? Couldn't Sheila make it today? You've been dating a while now, I thought you might have brought her."

Jenny creased her eyebrows and gave her mother a long tolerant look. "Sheila isn't with me anymore. She decided a doctor was more to her liking. I promise if someone special enters my radar, I'll call and let you know. Okay, when does this party get moving?"

Marina's eyebrows rose at the off-hand comment. "In a little over two hours. I certainly hope Peter is here by then. You're very much like your brother…he can't seem to keep girlfriends, either. I do wonder about young people today." She shook her head. "Now I must be off to check on the caterers. I'm sure they'll need my supervision."

Jenny watched her mother breeze out of the dining room. "Is it going to be like last year?"

Charles grinned. "Of course. Have you known your mother not to invite everyone who is anyone to her pre-birthday party weekend? Thankfully, only your uncle Al is staying over, and tomorrow, we can do the family birthday privately."

"You indulge her too much, Dad. You always have." Jenny sat and snagged another cookie.

"And you will be putting on weight if you indulge in too many of those. I thought you were getting on well with Sheila. What happened?"

"I was passed over for someone more reliable. At least that's what she said." Jenny's jaw sagged as melancholy seeped into her heart at her lack of success in the romance department.

Charles nodded. "There's someone out there for you, darling, and when she arrives, you'll know even if you think you don't."

Jenny laughed as her mood overturned in that second. There was no one else in the world like her dad. He could make the coldest day feel like a tropical oasis. She knew deep down that he was right, but how patient did she need to be? She wasn't getting any younger. "Thanks. I knew you'd make me see that tomorrow is another day."

"Do you want to know what I think?" Jenny nodded. "Your mother is right. You and Peter are alike in many ways." He grinned. "It's true. You're both high achievers and you both do what you want and not what others might want for you. You both have successful careers but could do so much better and you don't because it's what you want, not what others think is best for you. As to the reason neither you nor Peter have settled down like your sister—she was lucky, like me. We found the love of our lives early. Sometimes, it just takes a little longer, but it will happen."

"What are you saying, Dad? Instead of finding love in the summer of my life, it might be the autumn or even winter? Thank goodness, neither of you are expecting more grandchildren." Jenny laughed. Her dad was right. He was always right—*darn him.*

"Oh, you never know. We might still be good for a few more grandchildren if we find someone for you and your brother tonight. We have the perfect evening for it," Charles quipped before he stood. "I'd better go change and make sure the belle of the ball has a presentable escort."

Jenny watched him go and her heart swelled with the love she felt for him. The comment about grandchildren wasn't unusual, but she knew, and so did he, it was targeted at her younger brother. At thirty-two, Peter, although still sowing his wild oats, as he called it, had more chance of producing further grandchildren. Her options were severely limited unless she found someone who already had kids. The sound of a car's wheels screeching to a halt outside the door had her looking through the window.

With a smile, she softly said, "Peter."

A phone rang repeatedly before George Irons picked it up and cordially said, "Hello?"

"George, I need a favor."

"Suzy, you know I will if I can. What do you want, girlfriend?"

"Are you attending the Price party tonight?"

"Of course I am. It's one of the social events of the year. Why do you ask?"

"Do you have two passes to get in?"

"Yes, which reminds me, I need to check that Stefan is ready to roll. I'll need lots of pictures this evening."

"I'll do the pictures, George…I need to get into that party."

There was hearty laughter from the other end of the phone. "Sorry, Suzy, I love you, but no way. Why do you want to go anyway? I thought the social shenanigans of society weren't your thing. Didn't you once say it was frivolous?"

"Don't quote me, George. Besides, it's to do with an article I'm preparing. I need to be there tonight. Will you do this for me? I promise to take lots of photos. You know you can trust me on that."

There was a silence at the other end of the phone. "So help me, if you mess up, it will hurt both of us big-time."

"I love ya, too, George. Gotta go and find my best party frock. I'll meet you there in an hour?"

"You got it, Cinderella."

Chapter 5

"I don't believe what I'm seeing." Jenny gasped. The glass of wine in her hand lurched dangerously, and she narrowly avoided dropping it down the front of her brother's pristine white shirt.

"What don't you believe?" Peter asked.

Jenny cast her eyes to the woman walking beside a short stocky man who wore the gaudiest bow tie she'd ever seen outside of the *Sgt. Pepper* Beatles movie. "It's her! I can't believe she'd have the audacity. Wait here, Pete, I'll be back." Jenny strode off towards the couple who were conversing with the richest woman in Merit, Elisa Craig.

Peter walked with her. "Who pissed you off, sis?"

Jenny scrunched up her face as she glanced irritably at her brother. "It isn't like that."

"Looks like that to me. Can't wait for the fireworks."

Jenny stopped in front of Elisa Craig and the two interlopers as she furiously jabbed a finger into the ribs of Susan Stark.

Susan turned abruptly at the pain, and when she saw who it was, she grinned. "Hey there, Jenny, how are you doing? It's a great birthday bash."

"What the hell are you doing here? I thought I told you that I was busy tonight."

The explosive words had everyone in listening distance stopping whatever they were doing to stare in their direction.

Jenny gazed disparagingly at first at Susan, then at the little man who sniggered and was fiddling with something in his jacket pocket.

"I know tonight wasn't convenient for you," Susan said with a slight nod. "As it turns out, the job calls. Isn't that right, George?" Susan gave the man at her side a conspiring wink.

"Yes, yes, of course, the job. Ms. Price, you're looking lovely tonight. Is it an Ellis creation you're wearing or another equally wonderful designer?"

Jenny hitched the sea green flimsy dress an inch higher over her breasts at his scrutiny. She scrunched her face for a few seconds, then narrowed her eyes. "No way, Stark! From all the information I've gleaned about you, you're the star reporter at the *Post*. They wouldn't have you doing the social column. Isn't that left to some guy who gets called the cross between a pit bull terrier and a poodle?"

Susan's lips pursed tightly together. "Well, technically, we call him George Irons. I'm sure he'll trade insult for insult if you want, Jenny. Isn't that right, George?"

"That's beside the point," Jenny said, ignoring the comment. "What are you doing here? I told you I'd have dinner with you at another time, but not tonight." Jenny glared at Stark until she realized what Stark had said. Then she closed her eyes for a second, wishing she were a hundred miles away.

Oh, my god, he's George Irons. Mother's going to kill me. Finally, she attempted to breathe deeply in an effort to calm her temper so she could become objective once more. She needed to apologize to George, who now looked downcast, and his lower lip trembled at her remarks. He had every right to feel insulted and hurt. As a lawyer, she knew better. However, Stark irked her, and for some reason, she found it difficult to overcome the emotions that raged whenever she was close to the woman.

"Mrs. Craig here was actually in the middle of an interview when you interrupted. Do you want to see my press pass? Or will you allow us to continue with what we were doing? We did receive an official invite. Why not ask your mother if you don't believe me?"

Peter Price intervened at that moment, placing a hand on Jenny's shoulder. "Come on, sis, apologize, and let's go get something to eat. Mother will be looking for us since it's almost time for the birthday cake to be cut."

Elisa Craig jumped up from her chair. "We'll have to do this later. I always get the second piece of cake. Jenny, you can walk with me." She took hold of Jenny's arm and led her away before anyone could say more.

"Come on, George, let's go take the pictures." Susan tugged at George's jacket.

"I'm sorry about all that. Can I get you both a drink? I'll ensure you get the best photos in the house tonight. We have Clayton Simpson, the photographer, here this evening, and I'll have him download any shots you want, no fee attached," Peter Price said.

George's eyes widened with interest. "Shots by Clayton Simpson you say. My editor will be over the moon with an offer like that. How can we refuse? Well, I'm up for a drink."

Susan wasn't listening to the man as her gaze was following the two women who had left.

"What about you…Susan, wasn't it?" Peter asked.

Susan, in her best professional mode, tuned in when someone said her name. Realizing it was Jenny's brother, she asked, "Your sister, is she usually so highly strung?"

"Jenny? Hardly. You could generally call her the best poker face in town nine times out of ten. Lawyers rarely show emotion in public."

Susan persisted with her questions. "And the time that she isn't?"

Peter laughed. "I have to admit you've got me stumped. I've only ever seen her go ballistic with someone she loves—you know, like family. That is, unless she's holding something back from us that you might know. Being a journalist with all that juicy gossip for general fodder, do you know if she's seeing someone special?"

"Oh, no, you got it right. She isn't seeing anyone that I know of." Susan felt a bubble of laughter wanting to escape and wasn't sure why as she whispered under her breath, "Not yet anyway."

They walked off towards the bar. Susan cast the odd glance back to the retreating women, who had now reached the outer canvas of the marquee. *Interesting.*

The evening dragged on interminably as far as Jenny was concerned. It was almost midnight and she was tired and embarrassed to boot. Mortified might be the better description as she recalled in glorious Technicolor her cruel words towards the *Post* society columnist. *Damn, he could sue me and he has plenty of witnesses. Or worse, he can trash me in the newspaper tomorrow.* Whatever had she been thinking to go off into such an irrational tirade? Bottom line, she hadn't thought at all, just acted—it was all Stark's fault.

The wall she was sitting on led to the patio beside the dining area with her feet dangling. As a girl, she'd often sit there looking at the stars. She looked down at her feet. Even now as an adult, she still couldn't manage to touch the bricked walkway. From her vantage point, she could see the caterers clearing the food away. Turning her head to the left, she saw the marquee still brimming with people enjoying themselves as the music filled the surrounding area. She closed her eyes and allowed the soothing strains of a waltz to calm her frazzled emotions.

"Penny for your thoughts?"

Jenny would have closed her eyes if they weren't already. She wished the familiar irritating voice would go away. Instead, she opened them and stared at Stark. "Sorry they're not for sale."

"Are you playing Humpty Dumpty?"

Dumbfounded, Jenny exclaimed, "Exactly what do you mean by that?"

"Only that good old Humpty sat on a wall, Humpty had a great fall, and all the kings' horses and all the kings' men and so on."

Jenny wondered what gave this woman the right to harass her personal space constantly. "I'm not going to fall."

"I'm glad about that because I'm no king's man. Look, about this evening—" Susan began to apologize.

Jenny interrupted her. "I'm sorry that I insulted your colleague. If he requires a formal apology, I'll gladly present one." Jenny sighed as her gaze shifted downwards to her feet.

"Oh, don't worry about old George...he's used to that portrayal. Between you and me, I think he likes the description. Besides, your brother's handsome, and George forgets everything in the presence of a gorgeous man. Peter invited us for a drink as an apology and it worked. Plus, he had Clayton Simpson download awesome shots of the party for his feature. He won't be bringing a lawsuit against you if that's what you're worried about." Susan gestured at the wall. "Do you mind if I sit?"

"Go ahead." Jenny watched Stark sit with her legs outstretched and cross them at the ankles. From the look of her body, if she'd pulled up her legs, they would have touched her chin. Strangely enough, Jenny noticed that Stark had a dimple in her chin, something Jenny hadn't recalled seeing until now.

"I've heard about this kind of party but never experienced one before. It's very grand."

Jenny wondered if there was sarcasm in the voice but refrained from jumping to any conclusion this time. "Where's Mr. Irons?" She needed to apologize at the very least.

"Gone home. He has all his material and I've downloaded the photos to the office. Our job is done here for tonight."

Jenny glanced sharply in Stark's direction. She was looking around the patio area with lemon and lime trees in ornate pots scattered around.

"Why didn't you go with him?"

Susan smiled. "Not my type."

The teasing reply had Jenny smiling reluctantly and in an upbeat tone replied, "That's true. You prefer the petite delicate female type, right?"

"You call yourself delicate? After your tirade this evening, no one could call you that." Susan winked.

"I wasn't talking about me, but the bartender last night. I'm sure she was more than willing to succumb to your charm."

"Do I sense a hint of jealousy?"

"You do not!"

There was a chasm of silence for a short time, then Susan stood. "Good night, Jenny, sweet dreams. Oh, and if you drop by the office, I'll introduce you to the person that wrote the

Gravekeeper story. I'll even let you off the hook for dinner."

Jenny was surprised, grateful, and a tiny bit disappointed. Sparring with Stark was strangely exciting, and she'd never experienced that with anyone else before. "I'll be there Monday morning. Night, Stark."

Susan nodded before creating a distance between them with her long legs.

Jenny wasn't sure if she was relieved at the woman leaving or mildly upset. The grandfather clock in the hall chimed midnight, and a thought struck her that made her chuckle. "I'd never figure Stark for Cinderella." She jumped down from the wall and headed back to the marquee and the festivities still in progress.

The sound of her cell phone buzzing had Jenny reaching for it groggily as she searched for the offending object with her eyes closed. She glanced at the clock on the bedside table and groaned at the time. It was barely eight am. "Hi."

"Jenny, I need your help."

Blinking back the sleep, Jenny instantly recognized the tearful voice and sat up in a regimented fashion. "Lorna, what is it? Where are you?"

"You said I could call you if I needed help. Please help me."

Okay, okay, this isn't good. "Lorna, are you at home or someplace else?"

There was a heavy silence. "Lorna?"

"I'm not at home." The voice got louder and louder. "I had to check it out. I'm so sorry if I've disappointed you."

"You haven't disappointed me. Please, tell me where you are and I'll come and get you." Jenny was pulling on sweats and a T-shirt as she spoke.

"I'm in jail."

All Jenny's movements ceased at that point. If anyone had been watching, she'd have looked like she was taking part in a Pilates routine with her left leg held motionless in the air. The moment collapsed as soon as her leg hit the floor. "I'm coming to get you out. I'll be there before you know it. Don't worry, Lorna, everything will be all right, I promise."

A tearful “thanks” was all she received as the call disconnected.

“How the hell have you managed in the space of forty-eight hours to end up in jail?” When Jenny realized where she was, she shook her head and muttered, “Mother’s going to have a fit if I’m not back for birthday brunch.” Haphazardly collecting her keys and wallet, she shot out of her old bedroom door and within minutes was heading towards the central police station in her car.

Chapter 6

Jenny arrived at the police station and swiftly moved to the reception desk. When she saw the man behind the desk was someone she knew, she was inwardly thankful. "Hi, Daniel, how's things?"

A sandy head shot up from working on notes. Sergeant Daniel Smith's brown eyes widened in appreciation, then he grinned at Jenny. "Great, Jenny. In fact, it's getting better by the minute now that you've arrived. What about yourself?"

"Good, although my day hasn't started off so well. You have a client of mine in lockup from last night." Jenny smiled. She'd known Daniel for ten years and knew him to be a fair cop.

"Now who would that be?" He glanced at the computer screen to locate the people who stayed in the holding cells overnight. "The mystery woman…right?"

Jenny's brow furrowed. "The mystery woman? Surely, she wasn't the only one brought in last night."

Daniel chuckled. "She wasn't, but the other guys wouldn't even know how to ask for a lawyer."

Jenny nodded. "What's the charge?"

Perusing the details, Daniel frowned. "No charge, seems we found her wandering in the Centenary Cemetery after one this morning. She refused to give the officer her name or a reason for why she was there. We've had a few desecrations there recently, and the officer thought it wise to bring her in. We just need her name and address and you can take her home."

Jenny was shocked that Lorna chose to stay the night in a cell rather than give her information.

"Her name is Lorna Hirste and she lives at 34 Shannon Street."

Daniel smiled reassuringly. "That's all we needed to know."

Ten minutes later after signing a release form, Jenny was escorting Lorna out to her car. "Thanks, Daniel. I'll see you around."

"Good to see you, Jenny. Take care now."

Daniel Smith watched the two women leave the precinct, then entered the release log. Out of curiosity, he typed Lorna Hirste's name in his databank. When the file came up, he whistled. "Hmm, now we know why she was there. Her nickname back then was right—the Gravekeeper. Let's hope she isn't up to her old tricks." He flagged the file as a precautionary watch and resumed his notes.

Jenny hadn't started the car. Patiently, she watched as the almost morose figure next to her stared straight ahead. "Are you going to tell me what happened last night?"

The silence stretched between them and Jenny glanced at the dashboard clock. "Darn, I'm going to be late," she whispered.

"I'm sorry." The quiet apology seemed to rest uneasily in the car.

Jenny shook her head. "You have nothing to be sorry for. Today's my mother's birthday, and I'm due to attend a family brunch. If I'm late, she'll be upset. How about I take you home and you can enjoy Sunday with your folks and tomorrow we can talk about this?"

"What if I don't want to talk about it?" Lorna asked sharply.

To set Lorna's mind at ease, Jenny gave her a sincere smile. "Then it's just another mystery. Okay?"

Just as Jenny was about to set the car in motion, Lorna quietly said, "The voice tells me I have to go there."

Puzzled and a little perturbed by the short explanation, Jenny turned her gaze from the windshield to the woman at her side. Lorna's face held a blank expression—resignation. *What the hell is this voice?* Sucking in a breath, Jenny scratched her ear.

"You've experienced this before?"

Lorna dropped her head. "Yes, since I was a teenager. It began as nightmares before I realized what it was the voice needed me to do."

In anticipation, Jenny felt her lips go dry, and she moistened them with her tongue. "What did they need you to do?"

This time, Lorna's head shot up and her grey eyes appeared luminous in the darker interior of the car. "Not voices, Jenny, just one voice, it's always just one voice."

Out of her depth, Jenny asked, "What does the voice say?"

"Protect."

Jenny knitted her eyebrows. The conversation was becoming surreal. "Protect whom?"

Lorna's thin lips curve into a tiny smile. "The name…I have to protect the name."

Perhaps Dr. Gerardo at Llewellyn was right. Maybe Lorna needs more help. Although, indefinite institutionalization wasn't necessary as far as she was concerned. It was barbaric. They'd done the right thing in getting her out—hadn't they? "Can you tell me the name?"

There was a pregnant pause before Lorna nodded. "Craig Henderson Jr."

Jenny pondered the name. It didn't sound familiar, but the jumbled thoughts she was having regarding the conversation had her moving on. "Did you protect this man?"

Lorna nodded. "In a way."

Jenny's gaze flicked to the time and realized that she needed to get Lorna home or she'd be in major trouble with her mother. She fled the house in a hurry and hadn't left any message or had the time to stop to make a phone call, annoyingly leaving her cell phone in her valise by the bed. However, at the same time, she was fascinated as to how this woman, barely out of an institution, had managed to protect a stranger. "Did you know this man?"

"I never know the names. I only know that they need my help. That's why I was there last night…it usually happens after dusk." Lorna's tone was low and conspiratorial.

Jenny used the information she knew to try to decipher what was going on. “So you met this man at the graveyard?”

Lorna shook her head, and to Jenny, her grey eyes seemed to pity her. “I never meet them. I just protect what is left of them in this world.”

With a smile, Jenny nodded. She didn’t understand what Lorna was getting at. She preferred a more logical explanation, and there was probably one if she concentrated on the problem enough. “Okay, Lorna. Let’s go home to breakfast. I’m sure we both can use it. Drop by my office around lunch tomorrow and we’ll discuss this in detail, okay? Lunch will be my treat.”

Lorna’s face suddenly brightened. “I’d love that. Thank you, Jenny.”

Half an hour later, Jenny had dropped Lorna off at her home and was heading as fast as she could to her parents’ home. Her thoughts were chaotic. She now felt it was essential that she continue to help Lorna integrate back into society. To make it happen, she needed to research as much as possible about the background to the Gravekeeper story. Although the thought irked her, the one person who could do that was Stark. “I guess I’ll have to hope you’re free this evening, Stark. I need that information now. It can’t wait.” Revving the car and rounding the bend with a slight squeal, Jenny heaved a sigh of relief. She arrived on time.

Susan Stark listened to one of her vinyl records that she treasured. They mostly belonged to her parents, but she’d taken over the collection and the passion for collecting them when she moved to a permanent home. Being the only daughter of an Army officer had meant that stability on the homefront had been people, not bricks and mortar. Her parents, now stationed in D.C., lived a hectic life. Her father, a decorated lieutenant general, worked in the Pentagon. She wasn’t exactly sure what he did; it was classified. Next month, she was due to visit them for Thanksgiving. For a long time, the family holiday get-together depended on where her father was stationed. Now things were more settled, and they could plan the holiday ahead of time. She couldn’t wait to see her mom and taste some good old-fashioned home cooking, a talent totally lost on her.

The stereo pitched an almost hollow sound around her apartment as Don McLean's voice somberly reached out with the rendition of "Vincent" from the album *American Pie*. It was one of her favorites. Striding over to the rich red leather sofa, she reclined with her bare feet up on the arm. As the music invaded her senses, she felt herself gradually relaxing. When the shrill sound of the phone invaded her peace, she tried to ignore it. After the ringing ceased, it began again, so she got up and grabbed her cell phone. "Stark," she said sharply.

"Look, I know this is out of the blue, but I need that information on the Gravekeeper story today."

Susan's eyes rolled at the voice. *No polite hello, I'm so and so or any form or greeting at all.* "Why, Ms. Price, this is a surprise."

Jenny groaned. "I'm sorry. How are you, Stark?"

"I'm good and you can call me Susan. After all, we aren't exactly strangers, are we?" Susan moved to sit back down on the sofa.

"I need to know the Gravekeeper story today. Can you help me?"

Susan bit her lip, pondering the request. She could help with the old articles since she'd already spoken with Henry Mather. He had initially coined the nickname, which took on a life of its own during the case. Fifteen years later, Henry was a bit hazy about the facts but told her what he knew. "Can't it wait until tomorrow? That way, you can talk to the guy who wrote the story."

"It can't wait," Jenny said raggedly.

Initially, the sound of Jenny's voice had Susan wondering if something was wrong, now she was certain there was. "Okay, shall we meet for coffee in say an hour at Delia's on Fourth?"

"I can do that. I'll see you there. Oh, and thanks."

Susan didn't have time to answer as the line went dead. "It's my pleasure, Ms. Price." Standing, she replaced the phone back on its charger before going into her bedroom to change from her sweats and T-shirt. "I wonder what's spooked you, Jenny. I'm just the one to find out, and who knows, there just might be a juicy story in it for me."

Delia's Café/Bar was a relatively new business for it had only been on the block for a little over thirty years. The other shops in the area had been there for almost a century. Fourth Street was the second-oldest street in Merit. Only Main Street could compete for longevity—it received its name at the start of the city in 1895. The owner of the building was Elsie May Copthorne, whose father had been the mayor of Merit in the fifties. Since she was an only child, her father left her the family mercantile business when he died.

During the seventies, she recognized the warning signs when larger companies began to muscle in on her type of trade. In an inspired move, she closed the business and within three months, had set up as Delia's Café, which catered to the businesses in the area. With the various other café outlets across the sprawling city, Delia's was still a great place with something for almost everyone. Elsie May continued to invest in furnishings and equipment to stay ahead of the competition, and at seventy-two, she only came to the café to *work* on a Sunday.

Susan strode through the entrance with a wide grin on her face when she saw the owner behind the counter. "Hey there, Elsie May. How's business?"

Elsie May glanced in Susan's direction from her seated position, which enabled her to overlook almost every movement in the café. Her watery gaze crinkled at the sides as her full lips turned up at the edges into a smile of recognition. The wrinkles across her face were more pronounced as her pastel blue gaze directed at Susan. "It could be better…been slow today…but we have the Merit basketball team due for supper later."

Susan glanced around the thirty-seat dining area and saw that it was virtually empty. The bar side of the operation looked steady with at least ten people around but not Jenny Price. "The team has been doing well recently and should be in the top five if things work out at the game today."

"They'll win." Elsie May ruffled a pennant from behind the

counter and both women laughed. "What can I get you, Susan?"

Susan took a quick look at the stainless steel clock behind Elsie May. "Turkish for me today. I'm waiting for someone and she's late."

Elsie May nodded. "Is it someone I might be seeing more of in the future?"

The wink that accompanied the words made Susan chuckle. "Oh, I don't think so." With a wave towards a table in direct line of sight of the door, Susan moved in that direction. She picked up the weekend news from the stand of a rival newspaper before she sat down.

Sue read the headlines and was just about to turn the page to world news when she heard the bell of the door opening and saw Jenny walking in. All eyes diverted to the well-formed body with a blond halo effect for hair. Susan wasn't sure if Jenny knew that when she walked into a room everything stopped.

Susan had read up on Jenny, but what she found was scant on a personal level. The family tree was extensive, indicating Jenny came from the crème de la crème of Merit.

However, Jenny had once trained to be a ballerina until an injury put an end to that career choice, although there were no pertinent details of the injury. From all she found out about the woman, she was a good lawyer but apt to be fiery at times. She knew that firsthand.

It was evident from what she read that in the case of incompetence or injustice, Jenny pulled no punches. In a strange kind of way, Susan felt they were alike. They were both crusading in their own way for honesty and justice. She was certain that Jenny didn't consider journalists in that light. *She thinks I'm pretty trashy.*

"Hey, sorry I'm late. I stayed with my parents last night. I had to go home first and change clothes." As the words gushed out, Susan had the distinct feeling that Jenny was nervous.

"No problem." Susan held up the newspaper from the *Bugle*. "I was catching up on the opposition."

Taking a seat opposite Susan, Jenny appeared to relax slightly. "I'm sorry to spoil your Sunday afternoon, but I really do need any light you can shed on why your colleague called Lorna the Gravekeeper."

No small talk or butt-kissing with this one. And she's the one that doesn't think lawyers have a tarnished image. Susan smiled. "Let's order coffee…or do you need something stronger?"

"Coffee is fine." Jenny's eyes closed in on Susan's empty cup. "I'm really sorry I was late."

Susan shrugged away the apology and caught the eye of a server for their order.

A few minutes later, with the coffee ordered, Jenny twisted her fingers together tightly. The strain on them was evident as her skin began to go pale.

Susan reached across the small bistro table and placed her hand over Jenny's, causing Jenny to pull them away immediately. With a wry smile, she said, "You'll cut off the circulation."

Jenny pierced Susan with a veiled gaze, then looked back to her hands. "I doubt I have the strength to do that. Why do they call Lorna the Gravekeeper?"

"Okay, to the point…I can go with that. Do I receive anything in return for my information?"

Jenny shifted her gaze from her fingers to Susan once more. "Do you require some form of payment?"

Susan pursed her lips slightly and began to rub the side of her jaw absently. "No, but it's in the rule book they give us from journalism school to ask. You just never know what might be on offer."

"I see," Jenny said suspiciously.

Susan wanted to tease Jenny but decided to take a more professional approach. It might make the meeting easier for Jenny, and she wanted that, though she didn't know why. Jenny didn't appear to like her very much.

"The Gravekeeper tag was given to Lorna because it was found that she frequented several cemeteries in the city during the night. Apparently, after an interview given by her parents, which they regretted later for obvious reasons, Lorna had been doing this for numerous years before the incident occurred."

Jenny exclaimed, "She was one of those graffiti goons?"

"Nope, it was nothing like that. If she had, I doubt she would have done what she did. It was the young man that died who had been doing the graffiti art along with a couple of friends."

"That still doesn't warrant the nickname. Your newspaper made her out as some kind of fiendish ghoul."

Susan twisted her lips at the last word before glancing towards the server bringing their drinks. "Hi, Jane, how are things?"

The brunette grinned at Susan. Her green, frog-like eyes, which looked as if they could pop out at any moment, only focused on Susan. "Good to see you, Sue. You haven't been around on Tuesdays for a while."

"I'm afraid work has kept me away, Jane. You tell Janice that I'll be back soon to take her on again." Susan smiled at Jane. "Thanks for bringing us our coffee."

As the woman left, Jenny bluntly asked, "Another notch on your bedpost?"

Susan gazed at Jenny in astonishment, momentarily lost for words as Jenny continued.

"If she isn't, she wants to be."

Susan scratched her left eyebrow, responding in a low, quiet, menacing pitch. "She's a friend and my private life has nothing to do with you."

Jenny drew in a shallow breath. "You're right. I'm sorry."

There was silence between them for a few minutes as each sipped their coffee in contemplation.

"Her parents said one other thing," Susan said.

Jenny looked up, her gaze latching onto Susan's face in an almost hypnotic state. "And that was?"

Susan took another sip of the rich Turkish coffee and grimaced slightly as the taste exploded in her mouth. "They said Lorna had told them she was a protector of what was left of the dead when they left this world." She almost choked on her coffee at Jenny's incredulous expression.

"Why didn't I read this in the back issues?"

"Because it was gained without permission and the editor at the time felt that the family was in enough trouble. He didn't quash the nickname, though. He figured it was too good for business and the facts fit for the most part. Lorna had killed someone when he and a couple of others tried to graffiti a gravestone. I guess that's pretty close to a description of a gravekeeper, wouldn't you say?" Susan gazed into the tiny coffee cup where the dark flecks of the residue of her coffee lay.

"My father likes your work."

Glancing up at the surprising compliment, not to mention the change in subject, Susan nodded. "Thank your father for me."

"I will. He said you're one of the honest ones out there." Jenny dropped her head, mumbling, "I apologize for calling you names."

"Apology accepted, though not necessary. You're no different from the majority of people out there who think the same way—that we get our stories in less-than-honest ways and sometimes make them up. I'm a qualified journalist who went to Stanford. I have a master's degree from the Columbia School of Journalism. I've done my time in the trenches to get where I am. The paparazzi-type journalism isn't my scene," Susan said matter-of-factly. She noted the subtle change in Jenny's demeanor. She didn't seem as arrogant and bullish in her attitude. *I wonder what changed her mind about me, her father's opinion possibly.*

"This could be the worse decision I've ever made regarding a client. I had to collect Lorna from jail today. Apparently, she was found wandering in the Centenary Cemetery at one this morning. She refused to give her name and address, and the desk sergeant said there had been recent desecrations there." Jenny blew out a heavy breath as she finished talking.

Stunned at the words, Susan frowned. "Why are you telling me this? Does your client know that you're giving out private information? You could be disbarred."

Jenny nodded. "Technically, I could be in a lot of hot water. However, the detention of Lorna is part of the public record for anyone to look up. I need to understand what's going on. I don't want Lorna to end up back at Llewellyn or worse…she kills someone else. If she's capable, and we both know she is, then I have to get all the facts to help her."

Susan digested the information. It was pretty explosive from a news point of view, and in the wrong hands, well…. "Is that because you'll look bad in the press if it happens? After all, your legal firm was instrumental in her release."

Jenny chewed on her bottom lip and Susan moved one of her fingers across the table to touch her lips gently.

Susan almost chuckled at the startled reaction. "Don't do that. You'll end up with a cut and lip cuts are the devil."

Croaking a reply, Jenny said, "I…okay."

"You never answered my question. Is it because your firm will look terrible?" Susan's voice was insistent.

"No, it's because I might have made a bad judgment call and I don't want her to hurt someone else. She deserves more, and if more is to be treated for a psychiatric disorder, I'll arrange that."

"Do you think she's psychotic?"

"No, but I don't understand about the voice or voices."

Susan leaned back in her chair. "Okay, I've heard enough on an empty stomach. I can vouch for the food here. Will you join me for an early dinner and you can tell me everything you know?"

The anguish in Jenny's features eased as she answered. "Thanks, I'd like that. Would you believe sharing this with you has made me ravenous?"

Susan grinned as devilment screamed at her to reply saucily to the last comment. She refrained and stood. "Excellent, I'll arrange a table for us and be right back."

Jenny watched Stark leave the table. Her long legs ate up the distance between their table and the counter, and she watched the happy banter Stark appeared to have with the elderly woman seated there.

Inside, Jenny felt lighter for unburdening her doubts and tossed away the niggling uncertainty that she could have wrecked not only Lorna's life, but also her own, if Stark turned out to be a wolf in sheep's clothing.

She gazed at the profile of Stark, who she insulted, probably annoyed, and generally abused since the moment they met. She'd been amazed and frankly unsettled that Stark hadn't retaliated in any way other than to be polite and helpful. True, Stark had been a little free with her hands during the dances at the club, but otherwise, she was a perfect gentlewoman.

During brunch, she'd spoken to her father about Stark, asking his opinion of her from a professional point of view. He'd been complimentary about her style and articles generally.

"I think I've made the right call," she whispered. She picked up her cup and grimaced at the taste. "I hate iced coffee."

Chapter 7

Jenny smiled warmly as the firm's legal secretary, Faith Ramsey, escorted Lorna into her office. The leggy, dusky-skinned assistant returned the smile. "I'll buzz you when that file arrives." Jenny nodded and Faith left the office.

"Hi, Lorna, how are you today?"

Lorna moved awkwardly to the chair that Jenny indicated and sat with a heavy sigh. "My parents are upset."

Stroking her chin, Jenny recalled her own parents' reaction to her lack of communication about leaving the house. Her mother summed it up in one word—courtesy. Finally, Jenny murmured, "It's understandable. Did you tell them what you told me?"

"Kind of. My mom figured it out when I wasn't there for breakfast. They eat early in my house." Lorna looked like a lost child. Her chin trembled, and her eyes shimmered with tears that were about to fall.

Standing, Jenny pushed back her professional persona, went around her desk, and placed a comforting hand on Lorna's shoulder. "It's going to be all right. Remember, I promised."

Lorna blinked back the tears and gave Jenny a puppy dog look of trust. "Can you really promise that? Can you stop the voice?"

Swallowing hard, Jenny didn't want to lie. She had no definitive plan to solve Lorna's problem because she wasn't sure what the problem was. "We can try together." Jenny walked back to her chair behind her desk and steepled her fingers. "Do you remember I gave you a card from a journalist when you were released?"

Lorna frowned. "Yes, why?"

How can I say this and not look like it's a foregone conclusion? "She's due to arrive shortly and I'd like you to talk with her and have your side of the story presented."

Agitated, Lorna stood with her fists clenched. "I can't talk to her. I just can't. I trusted you. Did you tell her about last night?"

There it was—the accusation. Did she lie or evade the question, knowing that the truth was going to come out eventually? "In your best interest, I told her that you'd been picked up by the police and that there were no charges made against you. It will only be a matter of time before the *Bugle* and the less reputable newshounds find out. Then you'll be back in the limelight again at their mercy. Trust me, the reporting these days hasn't improved with some of them. This way, you can tell your side and not get it blown out of proportion."

"You think it will help me?"

Jenny nodded. "It can't hurt you. Besides, I'm going to be here the whole time. Just know that the choice is yours." The phone buzzed, and that meant the *file* Faith was talking about had arrived—Stark.

"I can say no and you'll still help me?"

"Yes."

Lorna hung her head, and there was a charged silence in the office before she said, "I'll do it."

Jenny smiled reassuringly. "The journalist is in the outer office. It's better to get it over with now, don't you think?" She picked up the phone to ask Faith to show Stark in but waited a second for Lorna to agree.

A minute later, the door opened and Jenny held her breath as Stark moved stealthily into the office as the door shut behind her. Her long body was clothed in beige tailored slacks and a brown leather jacket. Stark had a strong face, solid jaw, high cheekbones, and long dark curling lashes over large eyes. The more you looked, the more it compelled you to look. Jenny moved her head to another position, thereby ripping her gaze away. She glanced down at some papers not relevant to the case and said politely, "Good morning, Ms. Stark," before looking up to see Stark's reaction.

Susan inclined her head. "Good to see you again, Ms. Price."

Jenny almost laughed at the politeness. It wasn't like Stark to be so…formal. She barely knew the woman as they'd only met three days before. Yet she felt it could have been several years. The woman had that effect on her. With an incline of her head, she said, "Ms. Stark, this is my client Lorna Hirste. You mentioned you wanted an interview and Lorna has agreed."

Jenny watched as Stark turned to Lorna and beamed a warm smile. "Hi, Lorna, thanks for doing this. I think it's long overdue, don't you? Your side of the story, that is."

Jenny saw Lorna tilt her head a fraction and give Stark an appraising look. Lorna seemed to relax. Stark appeared to weave a net of trust around her, pulling Lorna inside its orbit. It had happened to her the night before.

Lorna shyly said, "Pleased to meet you, too. What do you want to know?"

"Please call me Susan. This will be painless, I promise. It will be nothing like going to the dentist and having your teeth pulled." Susan winked at Lorna, who allowed a ghost of a smile to relax her even more. "I want your version of events, the actual events as you remember them that night fifteen years ago. First, can you tell me what made you go to the cemetery?" Susan moved to sit on the edge of Jenny's desk. She smiled and winked at Jenny, who gave her a frown of disapproval.

Incredibly, Lorna responded. "I hear a voice. It asks me to protect the resting places of the dead. That's what I was doing there that night. I'd never been in any trouble before. People I've turned away have usually been frightened when I appear from behind the headstones and just run away. Those boys wouldn't stop and just laughed at me and called me terrible names. When he…the boy who…." Lorna hung her head.

Susan leaned her tall frame over and lifted Lorna's chin with a smile tugging at her lips.

Jenny watched and wondered at the technique for Stark had done the same thing to her the previous night.

"Take your time, it's okay."

Haltingly, Lorna continued, "He came over to the stone I was protecting, and I asked him again to stop, but he ignored me. I had to stop him…I had to…the voice hurt so much, it was the only way. I picked up a branch that was lying at my feet. It wasn't my intention to hurt him. I just needed him to stop. When I hit him with the branch, he stumbled and fell against the stone and hit his head before slumping to the ground. The others with him rushed to help, and when they saw the blood, they tried to revive him. It was too late, I'd killed him. They ran off and came back a little later with the police."

Susan frowned. "Why didn't you run? You had the opportunity, and I bet it would have been hard to track you down if it was dark."

Lorna shook her head violently. "I couldn't run. It wouldn't have been right for the boy would have been all alone. I needed to face what I'd done. To run would have been a coward's way out."

Jenny almost fell out of her chair at the admission. A part of her was pleased now that she'd helped Lorna, but a greater part wished she'd been around fifteen years ago. She knew Lorna had meant no evil intent with what happened. Inside, she vowed to continue to help Lorna until they could solve this voice dilemma.

Susan looked at Lorna. "This voice, did you hear it all the time you were at Llewellyn?"

Lorna nodded and stood. "I think it knew I couldn't help because it wasn't insistent. Now that I'm back, it is adamant about my helping. I kept a notebook of all the names. I have it at home."

"On Saturday night, was the voice insistent again and who did you have to protect?" Susan watched Lorna carefully, produced a spiral pad, and began scribbling.

Jenny peered at her action as discreetly as possible, feeling foolish as Stark tipped her notebook towards her, and she saw that Stark had written in hieroglyphics on the notepad. Susan hadn't turned a hair at Lorna's words, making her wonder if Stark had heard of this kind of thing before. *If she had, she didn't say so during dinner last night.*

Lorna spoke the name with a slight tremble to her lips. "Craig Henderson Jr."

Susan nodded and continued to write before she spoke again. "Did you know this person?"

Lorna shook her head.

"Can you recall who you were protecting that night fifteen years ago?" Susan turned her hazel gaze to Lorna.

Jenny saw Lorna begin to shake before she replied in a reedy voice filled with fear.

"It's etched into my memory forever. I lost my life because of it. Savannah Lucas." Lorna, who had been quietly pacing the small office, sat heavily in the chair, causing the leather to protest with a sudden rush of air from the seat.

"That's enough for now, Stark." Jenny glanced at Lorna, who looked drained.

Susan looked down at her notes. "For now, I agree. Lorna, would you talk to me again?"

"I've told you everything."

"I'm sure you think you have. Perhaps we could have one more interview. I'll treat you to lunch or dinner, whichever you prefer."

At the invitation, Lorna's face brightened significantly. "I've never been out to a proper dinner."

"Then dinner it shall be. Do you have a preference for food?" Susan asked.

"Any food is good after the stuff we had at Llewellyn."

Susan chuckled. "Any food it is then." She winked at Lorna, and for the first time since she'd arrived in the office, a glimmer of a smile remained on her face.

Jenny watched the exchange and yet again, Stark seemed to have a way of putting people at ease. Taking a woman out to dinner who had spent the last fifteen years incarcerated certainly gave her the edge. It was like giving a kid candy before dinner. "Lorna, I need to speak with Ms. Stark alone for a couple of minutes, then we'll have lunch."

Lorna gave Jenny a thread of a smile at the request and duly left the room.

"What do you make of that?"

Susan didn't answer immediately, then replied, "You think she's crazy, don't you?"

Initially, Jenny wanted to reply in the negative but stopped herself. "And you don't?"

Susan stood and flexed her shoulders as she picked up her jacket lying on a chair. Jenny saw the muscles on the woman's arms bulge slightly through the short-sleeved shirt. The attire Stark wore—plain pink shirt and body-hugging beige slacks—had that casual air, which was exactly what Lorna had needed. Not someone dressed up in an expensive power suit as she was.

"Some things in the universe have yet to be explained. I take it you're familiar with mediums and ghost hunters and the like."

"Are you trying to tell me that this is spiritual? Give me a break. I have yet to see any report of anyone killing someone because of a direction from a spirit. Are you placing me on the crazy train, too, Stark?" Jenny stood from behind her desk.

Jenny felt Stark's gaze on her, and it appeared to see right through her.

"I wouldn't dare do that, Ms. Price." Stark's voice had an exaggerated pitch as she continued. "I have other deadlines to keep. Want me to keep you in the loop on this or are you hoping for a miracle and the voice will go away now that she's spoken about it and made it public?"

Under her breath, Jenny said, "I'm hoping for a miracle." A little louder, she said, "I'd like to be kept informed, particularly on what you decide to print."

"Oh, don't worry, I'll not paint her as a psychotic murderer. Although, I have the feeling there's more to this than meets the eye. See you later, Jenny." Susan winked and walked towards the door.

"Don't come on to her, Stark, she's too vulnerable right now," Jenny warned.

With a chuckle, Susan shook her head, then turned to face Jenny. "She's not my type. I'm the one who likes small blondes that are easy, remember?" Then she opened the door and left Jenny's office.

"Damn you, Stark!" Jenny rapped her fist on her desk so hard that pain shot through her knuckles.

The week had been long and hard for Jenny, and now at nine on a Friday evening, she was ready for bed rather than a night on the town. As she thought of that, she recalled this time the week before and her unexpected assignation with Stark. She shivered slightly as she remembered the feel of Stark's hands on her body. At the time, she had been repulsed, but now, she wasn't sure that had been the reason. Perhaps, it had been fear—fear of the unknown. As sure as apples were apples, she felt an attraction to Stark and couldn't seem to shake the feeling.

All she knew of Stark's activities since the meeting in her office had been from a conversation with Lorna. Stark had taken Lorna to a beautiful restaurant by the harbor, and she'd had lobster for the first time in her life. The report had been glowing, and Jenny had to admit Stark knew how to charm people. That had been Wednesday morning, and since then, she'd expected to see a preliminary article from the *Daily Post* regarding Stark's interview with Lorna, but there hadn't been any.

She rested a hand on her forehead and looked towards the window and the sound of rain hitting the glass. The weather forecast for the weekend wasn't good with rain and an icy wind about to hit the city. Well, it would give her a great excuse to relax for that was exactly what she needed. She picked up her briefcase and stuffed several files inside. With a swift look around her office, she shut off the light and locked the door. Her thoughts traveled to Stark. "Why didn't she at least call me with an update?"

Susan paused in her research when she heard the sound of rain pelting the windows. Then she looked at the small clock on her desk, noting that it was nine. Her musings roamed to Jenny, and she whispered, "I wonder if you think about me at all." Immediately shaking those insane thoughts aside, she looked at the case files unopened in front of her. She knew she had at least another three hours to go. Standing and flexing her shoulders, she walked over to the coffee machine and made a selection.

"Johnson working you hard, Starky?" a balding stocky man

asked as he walked up beside her. Once Susan had her coffee, the man made his selection, then waited while it drained into a cup.

Susan hated the nickname but was too tired to give the man a hard time. "When doesn't he work everyone around here hard, Jimmy?" Susan grinned at the man. He was one of the old school journalists, having been in the business for over thirty-five years. Although some of his methods didn't agree with hers on how you achieved a story, he had created some marvelous articles. Suddenly, one of them triggered in her memory. "Do you recall that article you did some time ago about spiritualism?"

The man chuckled and his face became ruddy. "How could I forget? That gypsy sent her burly son after me with an ax. Why do you ask? That was a long time ago."

"Have you time for a chat…like now?" Susan eyed their steaming coffee cups.

Jimmy gave her a long hard stare. "You're up to something, Starky, and if it comes off and you use my stuff, will you credit me?" He didn't need to ask for she always did; she was an honest journalist who others trusted. That work ethic was a rarity nowadays.

Susan grinned. "It's a deal. Come on, I want to show you something."

Chapter 8

Jenny had her head crammed in the kitchen cupboard and decided that since the weekend was so unpleasant, she'd clean out the cupboards. It had been a while since she'd done any major spring cleaning in her house since work usually took a priority. This weekend, she was going to make an exception and had determinedly shut the briefcase with the work files in her study and closed the door. Everyone needed downtime, and this was hers. Even though most would think cleaning was hardly a relaxing pastime, Jenny found it cathartic.

The sound of her phone ringing had her jumping up and colliding with the underside of the kitchen sink. Groaning in pain and rubbing the bruise that was sure to surface, she reached for the phone on the countertop. She barked, "Yes."

"Wow, who got out of bed in a grouchy mood this morning? Did you have a bad night on the town?"

"No," Jenny complained as she rubbed her throbbing painful head again. "What can I do for you, Stark?"

"I'm flattered…at least you didn't have to ask who was calling. Is there any chance we can meet up today or tomorrow? I want to run something by you on Lorna."

Intrigued by the request, Jenny considered how to answer while massaging the receding pain in her head. She cautiously said, "I noticed you haven't filed your article on Lorna."

"True, I haven't. Will you meet with me?" Susan asked again.

"I'm in the middle of something right now," she said, pursing her lips. "However, I can meet with you after lunch, say around two this afternoon."

"Great, can you meet me at the *Daily Post* building?"

Jenny was surprised at the venue. "Sure."

"Thanks, I'll see you at one," Stark said before ending the call.

Jenny held the phone to her ear as she mulled over the short conversation. *Damn, I said two. God, that woman irritates the hell out of me.* She rubbed her head with her thumb. "I wonder what she's found out that she needs me to see." Curiosity began to take hold. Jenny looked at the kitchen appliances scattered all over the floor and countertops and sighed. She replaced everything back where it came from. Spring cleaning would have to wait for another time.

Arriving at the *Daily Post* at a quarter to one, Jenny drew in a deep breath as she mounted the white steps and pushed at the revolving door, but it didn't move. Then she spied a sign that read *press for attention*, which she did. She cursed as rivulets of rain dripped down her umbrella and onto the back of her neck. She should have pulled up her hat. A young man appeared at the side door and opened it, asking her what she wanted. Jenny mentioned Stark's name, and he nodded and allowed her inside, indicating he'd contact Stark immediately.

Jenny glanced around and made for the part of the floor that wasn't covered in carpet as she felt the water trickle from her raincoat. Close to the wall, she looked around to the stories displayed beside her. There was a montage of old and new photographs and headlines from major events. As she moved closer to the counter, she looked them over, wondering if any of Stark's stories were on display. Her gaze caught one about a fire that happened twenty years ago, and she vaguely recalled her parents talking about it since she was away at Harvard at the time. The pictures took in the horror and the glory that fire often portrays to the naked eye.

"Ms. Stark, Ms. Price is here."

"Thank you," Susan said before she hung up and made for the elevator. Once she arrived in the reception area, her gaze rapidly surveyed the room before it rested on Jenny. Susan didn't approach Jenny at once, opting instead to watch the expressions crossing Jenny's delicate features as she read the material on display. Finally, taking a deep breath, she walked over to Jenny and stood a couple of feet away. Jenny, engrossed in the wall hangings, hadn't seen or heard Susan's approach.

Clearing her throat that had gone dry, Susan waited for Jenny to look her way. "Hi, thanks for being prompt. I'm sorry I had to bring you out in the rain."

Obviously caught off-guard, Jenny blinked up at Susan, who was within a couple of feet of her. "I prefer to be on time for appointments. Besides, a little rain never hurt anyone. These are good and intriguing…you almost think the stories are fiction." Jenny pointed to the display, then stood and was almost toe to toe with Stark.

"Ah, and I thought the fascination in your expression would have been because of my phone call," Susan said casually.

Jenny shot her a swift glance. "Initially, it was. However, it's amazing how much has gone on that you forget about until you read about it again. What do they say…life is stranger than fiction?"

Susan nodded. "So very true. I told you once before that as soon as the ink is dry, it's forgotten and something new takes its place." She shrugged. "It's the fickle society we're in, I guess."

Jenny paused before nodding in agreement.

"Here, take this." She handed Jenny a visitor's badge. "I've signed you in, so you're good to go."

"Any chance I can stow away my rain gear until I leave?"

Susan nodded. "Sure thing." Then she shouted across to the young man who had spoken to Jenny earlier. "Jerry, take care of Ms. Price's belongings until she leaves, will you?"

"I can do that." He grinned.

Jenny quickly removed her raincoat and handed it the young man with her umbrella and a short thanks. Then she pinned the badge to the cashmere sweater she wore.

Susan gestured with a wave of her hand. "Shall we?"

"Of course," Jenny said, walking pace for pace next to Susan to keep up.

Susan allowed a smirk to curve her lips at the heavy breathing of the woman next to her. *She needs a workout.* Another thought filtered through, but she buried it for it was not a good time to dwell in the sensual realm.

A few minutes later, they were on the fifth floor and walking down a quiet corridor before entering a swinging door into a large open office space. Several desks were mostly empty, and she only saw three or four other people there. No one noticed their entry. Eventually, Stark stopped beside a small office and opened the door. Inside were a projector and computer along with numerous documents strewn on the glass table.

"Here we go." Susan pointed to the mess on the table. "As you can see, I've been doing research."

Jenny walked towards the items and picked up one of the documents. With a quizzical expression, Jenny turned. "Spiritualism?"

Susan laughed at the incredulity on Jenny's face. "Please, sit. Do you want coffee, tea, or something else before we start?"

"I'm good, thanks. I've just finished lunch. I'd like to know what you're thinking. Also, what does this have to do with Lorna?" Jenny sat in the chair nearest to her.

Susan nodded and felt her stomach rumble. "Lucky you, I haven't had the chance for lunch yet." She scanned Jenny's face for any reaction—there wasn't any. Susan sighed. "Sure, we'll get started. I'll try not to waste too much of your weekend. I'm sure you have a lot to do." She sat opposite Jenny and opened the computer, switching it back to life.

Jenny bit on her lip and nodded in agreement.

Susan then concentrated on the computer and pressed a few keys, causing a Web site to shoot onto the previously blank screen. "I'm going to project this so we don't have to squint to see it."

Both women looked ahead, and the image increased to fit the hundred-inch screen.

"I found several sites dedicated to EVPs, otherwise known as electronic voice paranormal, and EMFs, which are electromagnetic forces. Not that it's what I think Lorna hears, however, it could be a connection to another path we haven't considered."

"But if you've done this research, you must have considered it," Jenny pointed out as she read the blurb on the subject.

Susan grinned. "I have an open mind, which is why they think I'm worth my salary around here. Lorna was the one who actually said she could be possessed."

Jenny frowned.

"Hey, before you say anything, let me tell you what she told me, okay? And before you say it was a private conversation and I need permission, I asked if I could share the information with you. Besides, it's going to be public soon enough." Susan diverted her attention to the notebook to her side.

"I'm all ears, Stark."

Susan looked at the body part. *She has lovely ears.* "Basically, she thinks that the voice, which has been the same since her teens, might be a spirit. She's never really discussed this with anyone, not even her shrink at Llewellyn. Although I think her parents have an idea from what she told me. I personally have never heard voices inside my head except my own berating myself for overindulgence at parties and that kinda thing." Susan smiled as a particular party came to mind when she was twenty-one.

Jenny glibly retorted, "Haven't we all? However, surely this voice thing is mental. Have you considered schizophrenia? It's probably why the judge sent her to Llewellyn in the first place. In fact, I know that's the reason." Jenny reflected for a moment, then said, "This isn't a journalistic trick to spice up an otherwise normal story, is it?"

"I'll forget I heard that last part, and yes, I have considered all the angles." Susan brought up another Web site and several articles and points of view on the subject. "Look at this."

An hour later, having read articles and listened to Lorna's interview, Jenny had a bemused expression on her face as she stared at Susan. "That notebook she mentioned, did she show it to you?"

"She did more than show me." Susan moved some of the papers on the table and placed the hard-backed, well-worn notebook in front of Jenny. "Take a look." Susan stood. "I need to find a sandwich before I collapse on you. Can I get you anything?"

Jenny shook her head.

"Okay, I'll be back before you know it. Don't do anything I wouldn't."

Jenny gazed long and hard at the door as Stark left the room, recalling the woman saying she might collapse without food. The thought of Stark collapsing brought the image of a falling tree to mind. Then she turned her attention to the notebook. Carefully picking it up, she noticed that the dog-eared pages looked ready to fall apart. The front cover once had sketches emblazoned on it. She could still make out some of them and raised her eyebrows—they were very good. Inside were dates and names. As Jenny thumbed through the book, she was amazed to find hundreds of names with some repeated.

Sitting back farther in the chair, Jenny touched a finger to her bottom lip and pulled it down in concentration. She considered all the possibilities that Stark had researched. Stark had been diligent, to the point of not hiding any of her research material, and some were crazier than spiritualism. Stark had provided all this information. However, a personal opinion had been less forthcoming about Lorna's true state of mind.

After what seemed like an age, Stark walked back in the room with a sandwich and two cups of coffee on a tray. "Thought you might like a caffeine fix. I remembered what you had at Delia's." Susan placed the steaming cup in front of Jenny and sat down.

Indicating the object in her hand, Stark ripped open the wrapper of the sandwich saying, "Hope you don't mind," as she took a bite.

Jenny looked down at Lorna's notebook, then across at the numerous other references Stark had provided.

"You look pensive," Susan said between bites.

"I guess you've given me a lot to think about. Have you shared any of this with Lorna?" Jenny finally looked up and felt a tender emotion flood her as she watched Stark eat. She clearly was relishing the sandwich.

Their gazes caught as Susan swallowed before replying. "No," she said with a shrug. "I frankly don't know what I'd tell her…that she's either possessed or crazy? Can you imagine what that might do to her fragile existence?"

Jenny sipped the coffee. "After your meetings with her, what do you think she is?"

"Oh, no, I'm not going first. You tell me." Susan chuckled, sipping her coffee.

Jenny pondered the question for a moment. "Troubled comes to mind."

Susan nodded. "Good way of looking at it. I think that, too. However, in addition, I have an assistant who has been working on something for me and she's almost done. I told her to come by as soon as she can. In fact, here she is now."

A woman of average height with very short auburn hair and horn-rimmed glasses giving her an owlish impression at odds with her cheerful fresh face, knocked on the door and entered at Susan's request.

"All done, Suzy. Do you want me to do anything else before I go home?"

Jenny watched the interchange between the two women. Stark was warmly engaging the newcomer in conversation, and a nervous reaction hit the pit of her stomach.

"Not today, Deirdre. Has the boss gone yet?" Susan asked with a wink.

Deirdre shook her head and made a face. "Not yet. I think he's waiting for the update you promised him last night. Don't leave it too long or he'll come thundering in. Between you and me, his condition is acting up again. See you Monday if you're in the office. And don't forget the drink at Charley's this evening if you're free." Deirdre casually included Jenny in the latter remark with eye contact before she left.

Jenny watched Stark's face change from passive to contemplative as Deirdre left the room.

"Don't you get on with your boss?"

"Mostly. Look, I don't want to take up any more of your time right now. I think it might be good if someone sat down with Lorna and asked her if she'll see a psychologist and let them determine what's going on."

"I'm not sure she'll accept that kind of professional option. Fifteen years of seven days a week wouldn't have me rushing back for more of the same. What about the information your assistant gave you?"

Susan looked at the pen drive Deirdre had given her and closed her fingers around it. "I'm sure it can wait. It was an analysis of Lorna's notebook from a theory of mine." Susan's gaze shot to the voice that she could hear through the glass of the office.

Jenny heard a gruff voicing calling for Stark, and she had a good idea from the bellowing that it was her boss. "Looks like you're needed elsewhere. I can see myself out." Standing, Jenny looked around for the source of the noise.

"Thanks. I'll be back in touch when I've written the article unless something else crops up for me to consider." Susan frowned as a man approached the office window. "Safe journey home, Jenny, and thanks again for indulging my theories and for coming out in the rain."

Jenny nodded and walked ahead of Stark out of the office. She was grateful for Stark's reminder that she had a raincoat and umbrella to collect on the way out.

"Ah, there you are, Stark. I want you in my office now!" the blustering voice roared. Jenny wondered if the glass would break in the door window.

"Duty calls. Talk to you soon, Jenny. Bye." Susan headed off in the direction of the short man, and Jenny could only hear snippets as she headed for the elevator.

"Look, boss, I can't create a fabrication. You know it isn't my style."

Contemplating that statement, Jenny wondered in what context it was and if it had anything to do with the article on Lorna. As she entered the elevator, she muttered, "Spiritualism. Next thing I know, Stark will be researching Harry Potter." That name made her smile as she recalled seeing the movies with flying cars, dragons, and wizards. *What a mix.*

Chapter 9

"Why do I get the distinct impression you're avoiding making a lasting commitment, Susan? That other situation has been over for years. Surely, you've gotten past that."

Susan listened with only half an ear to the conversation. Each time they hit that particular subject, it ended up the same. Her mom blamed her for lack of commitment in relationships, and as a dutiful daughter, she listened, if only halfheartedly. Finally, her mother gave a heavy sigh as she always did when Susan's response was lacking.

"Your father thinks you've abandoned us. You haven't been to see us in over eight months. Please don't give me that old excuse of work again."

"Mom, it really has been hectic, and right now, I'm in the middle of what could be a very interesting article. Besides, Brian is being difficult and wants everything yesterday." Susan hoped for sympathy about her boss's attitude, as her parents knew him well.

"He's a good man, now don't you go giving him a hard time. His ulcer doesn't need a helping hand. Besides, Dad's birthday is next weekend, and I know he'd be over the moon if you turned up, even if it's only for an overnight stay."

Susan rolled her eyes. She considered her options carefully before replying. "You have a deal. I'll call you when I know the flight. Now I have to go as my lack of commitment awaits me."

Her mother muttered something that Susan couldn't make out, then with an "I love you," she was gone in a flurry of goodbyes.

She gazed around her apartment and scratched the back of her neck. "Options, options, and even more options." She could go back to Crescendo and maybe hook up with that delicious willing bartender and make it more meaningful. Or she could call Kaylin and ask her out. The woman had been angling for a date ever since they met two months before at the gym. Kaylin had a great body, and she looked wonderful for her age, which was at least twenty years Susan's senior. She began to chuckle as she wondered what her mother's reaction would be if she turned up with Kaylin on her arm. The term "sisters" came to mind since they were about the same age.

Her final option, and one that she already decided to do on a rainy Saturday evening, was to examine the file Deirdre had completed for her. It was seven thirty, and she was waiting for the pizza she ordered forty-five minutes earlier. Walking over to the fridge, she pulled out a bottle of cold beer, removed the cap, and took a long pull as she contemplated the previous week. Her thoughts barely began to form when the doorbell rang. Putting the beer down and grabbing money from her wallet, she headed for the door and her dinner.

Susan munched on a slice of pepperoni pizza and recalled various events. The one thing that stood out the most was watching the unguarded expression on Jenny Price's face earlier in the day. It stopped her in her tracks and took her breath away. It wasn't good to ponder over something that was impossible. Perhaps one day, Jenny would at least be friendly to her. She chuckled, wondering if she could hold her breath that long. Wiping away the moisture from the beer on her upper lip, she put two slices on a plate and headed for her study where she could pore over the information.

Jenny groaned as she lost another life in her quest for the jewel board. It was her favorite online game and she'd decided with the lousy weather that that night was the night to kick back and chill. Besides, she'd had her fill of rain after her outing that afternoon. Her car had decided to stop working for no apparent reason. Monday, she'd call the BMW dealer and have it fixed. The car was top of the line, and she didn't want just any mechanic looking it over. It was lunchtime when she started calling around for a taxi, but none was available. She then walked to the end of the street and waited for a bus to take her to the rail station where it was so busy that she had to stand on the outer edges of the platform getting soaked. When she turned the key in her modest suburban home, she was grateful to be there.

She'd bought the house soon after passing the bar. It was her opinion that it was better to invest in property than rent and watch all her hard-earned cash disappear into someone else's pocket. The house, after several good bonuses in her first five years, was now mortgage-free.

Her parents had broached the subject of her moving to a more palatial residence in a more upscale neighborhood, but she dismissed the idea. She loved her house and had over the years gotten to know the neighbors and them her. She felt safe and she couldn't say that about many places, especially these days. A couple of years earlier, several of the local elementary school's PTA officers asked that she join and lend her legal expertise to the organization. At that time, they were embroiled in a dispute over what they considered dangerous playground equipment. She took that responsibility seriously, attending most meetings, and was roped into several school functions. She was also the coach for the neighborhood Little League team, and she loved every minute of it.

Unexpectedly, the doorbell rang and she looked at the clock on the wall. It was a couple of minutes after nine. She wasn't expecting anyone, and it was too late for a visit from any of her friends or family. The bell rang again, and she tentatively picked up her cell. If she felt threatened, she'd call one of the neighbors, an ex-police officer who lived two doors away.

"Who is it?"

"It's me, Susan Stark. I need to speak with you, Jenny."

Jenny felt her eyes bulge. *What the hell is Stark doing calling on me at this hour? How does she know where I live?* Unlocking the door, she dragged it open and couldn't prevent the laugh that echoed down the hallway as she saw the tall Stark looking like a drowned rat. "What are you doing here?"

Susan gave a shrug. "If you offer me some coffee and let me dry out for a while, I'll explain."

Jenny opened the door wider and allowed Stark to step into the hall where she shook herself like a dog.

"Hey, watch that…I have to clean up after you," Jenny reprimanded. Inwardly, she smiled at the repentant expression she received in return. "Here, give me your coat and I'll put it on the towel rack to dry. You can take those boots off, too. I don't want a trail of water all over the house."

"Thanks." Susan handed her the coat as she untied her boots and slid them off, leaving them on a cork mat by the front door.

Several minutes later, Jenny sat down after making coffee. She gave Stark a speculative look. "Why are you here?"

"As always, Jenny, you're straight to the point. You remember that file my assistant gave me?"

"Yes."

"Well, you just have to see what she found. I've brought it with me. Can I show you?" Susan's voice seemed to rise in excitement.

Jenny groaned. "Do you have a life? Or do you spend all your time figuring out how to annoy me?"

Susan cheerfully replied, "Oh, I don't know, I think you like it and you're just too chicken to admit it. Please, you'll see what my assistant correlated is pretty interesting."

Jenny rolled her eyes and nodded to the computer.

"You play online games?" Susan asked casually as she walked towards the machine.

Jenny ran to the console and disconnected from the Internet as she inwardly cursed the fact that she'd lose a life. "Not really."

Susan's lips twitched in reaction. "Pity, we could have had something in common. I prefer the game Bejeweled. Have you ever tried it?" Susan placed the pen drive in the computer's USB port and pulled up the file.

Jenny remained silent, not wanting to admit she and Stark had anything in common. "Exactly what am I looking for?"

"You'll see." Susan crossed her arms as she watched the data flood the small screen.

An hour later, Jenny asked, "What are we saying here?"

"With every single one of those names, something happened to the grave or gravestone. By graffiti, desecration, or the cemetery closing down and the graves being built over. Don't you think that's too much of a coincidence? I think our friend Lorna might be possessed by a spirit or have a gift."

Jenny had pondered her visit with Stark earlier that day when she got home, but the only conclusion she could derive from it was that Lorna needed further psychiatric help. Perhaps the doctor she'd written off as less than capable wasn't. "I tried to call Dr. Gerardo to discuss this with her. At the moment, she's out of town, so I won't be able to get back to you with her opinion until she returns."

Susan bit her lip. "Is this a shrink?"

"You haven't done as much homework as I expected. She's the psychiatrist who was in charge of Lorna at Llewellyn." Jenny felt that for once she had Susan on the back foot.

"She can't go back there!"

Perplexed at Stark's explosive retort, Jenny didn't answer immediately. Finally, she said, "The only way she goes back there is if she does something wrong or…"

"Or?"

"Or she voluntarily seeks professional help."

Susan shook her head. "I was wrong to come here." She pulled the pen drive out of the machine and marched towards the front door.

For a second, Jenny was confused as to what she said to cause such a reaction from Stark. She followed the woman and watched her drag on her boots. "I guess I'll get your coat, but it won't be dry yet."

"Who the hell cares?" Susan stood from her crouched position with one boot on and one off. "I figured as you were supposed to care about Lorna, you'd want to check this out. Hell, here I was thinking a lawyer could be open-minded. I think I'm the crazy one."

Jenny resented the inference. "I do care about Lorna. Just where were you when the very paper you represent was persecuting her?

Who called her the Gravekeeper and probably helped to convict her? What did you expect me to say?"

Susan traded glance for angry glance.

"For the record, I was a senior in high school when Lorna was convicted. Right now, I think the Gravekeeper name is apt, and as to what I expected of you—too much," Susan ground out, placing the remaining boot on her multicolored-socked foot.

Jenny swallowed hard, watching the boot slide onto Stark's foot. The socks were a bit garish and she hadn't expected something so trivial to dissipate her anger, but it did. "If my reaction is so wrong, then what did you want me to say?"

Susan breathed heavily, giving Jenny a harsh look. "I expected you to visit every avenue before deciding she's a mental case. Seems I was dead wrong on that one. My coat, please?"

Jenny didn't move. Mulling over Stark's behavior, she wondered why it mattered so much to her to delve deeper. Stark could probably make a juicy story out of the innuendoes that she already had. Jenny calmly ignored the request for the coat. "What do you think Lorna will make of your new leap on her condition?"

"That's the first thing you've said that makes any sense. Why don't we ask her? After all, it's her future we're dealing with here." Susan gave Jenny a stony gaze.

The sound of rain splattering against the windows had Jenny moving her hair away from her face. She shook her head at the unpleasant noise.

"Is that a no?"

"What? No, no, it isn't. How are you getting home?" Jenny asked in exasperation.

"The same way I came, why?"

"The weather report is for severe storms. You should have come in a car. Cabs will be hard to find tonight."

Susan looked out onto the porch where the rain was driving heavily onto the wooden floor. "Then ask me to stay."

Flustered, Jenny said, "No, you can make your way back the same as you came." She felt panic rising rapidly because the idea was so tempting.

"Okay, will you at least think about other options for Lorna? She's spent too many years behind bars—figuratively speaking, that is. Right now, she needs a champion who will do the right thing," Susan said.

The tone was Jenny's undoing. Somehow, Stark had that ability, and it made Jenny scowl as she reached for the wet coat. "I've tried to do that from the moment I met her. Besides, it looks like you've taken up the mantle yourself."

Susan frowned slightly as she collected her coat. "I hope we can still work on this together. With us both involved, we'll solve this mystery, of that I'm sure."

"I think that's fairly obvious as you've asked me to consider other options. The only question I have is where do I start?"

Susan zipped up her jacket. "I'd talk to your brother. He has contacts at the university. Maybe he'll be able to set you in the direction of someone in this kind of field. "

Jenny frowned. "My brother? What made you think of him? I didn't know you could study this kind of thing for a degree."

Susan hesitated, her cynicism replaced by a reflective tone. "I knew someone who studied that once."

"Okay. I guess I could call him tomorrow." Jenny wondered why Stark looked sad. She had to prevent her hand from reaching out to stroke away the worry lines.

"Sounds like a plan to me. Hey, I'm sorry you lost a life because of me." Susan opened the door and grimaced at the rain, which was heavier than before.

Jenny moved forward. "Here, take an umbrella, you'll need it."

Susan gave Jenny a long look, then spontaneously dropped her head and planted a kiss on unwilling lips that quickly turned pliant.

When Stark had gone, Jenny contemplated the kiss they shared for a few long moments before dragging open the door to call Stark back. The wind and the rain whipped around her. She walked to the edge of her porch but saw no sign of Stark. "Oh, my god, I don't think it's Lorna who has mental problems. I think it might be me." She wandered back inside thinking about what options Stark might be thinking of. She also wondered exactly what she would say to her brother.

Susan climbed into her vehicle a street away from Jenny's house. It had been a gamble, and in this instance, it hadn't paid off. She had hoped to stay the night, even if her information hadn't incited Jenny to think outside the box.

"You're stubborn, Jenny, but I'll get through to you yet." She turned the ignition and set off for her apartment. The more she considered this scenario with Lorna Hirste, the more Jenny popped into her head and clouded her judgment. That had never happened to her before. The kiss she stole only increased her bewilderment. Although she'd never admit it, her heart had pounded heavily during the kiss, and she had only felt that once before.

The loud sound of a horn behind her had her thoughts coming back to earth as she shifted away from the light, cursing herself at her lack of concentration. Hopefully, she'd receive a call from Jenny with news, but once again, she wouldn't hold her breath. Jenny was a tough cookie. The only question was how tough.

Chapter 10

Lorna felt the tension in the SUV as she climbed into the vehicle. She was initially surprised that Susan had picked her up, until she saw Jenny sitting in the passenger seat. Jenny's features were unmoving, and even a pleasant hello had barely touched the surface. Jenny gave her a small smile, albeit a genuine one.

Jenny had called her that morning to ask if she could make an appointment at two that afternoon. She said there was someone she wanted Lorna to meet. Hopefully, the person could shed light on what she was going through—she bit off the chance. What had been unexpected was the arrival of Susan Stark, but it was a welcome one. Susan was someone she felt she'd like to be friends with. Every time Lorna saw Susan, her stomach reacted with a ripple of nerves.

When they'd begun their journey to Merit University, the conversation had been minimal. She did, however, note that Jenny gave Susan a frosty look after anything Susan said. Something had happened, although it was hard to speculate what that was. Jenny in her opinion didn't give much away, but then she was a lawyer.

"Almost there, Lorna. How you feeling?" Susan negotiated a bend, and the complex of academic buildings came into view.

"I'm kind of nervous. Who are we meeting again?" Lorna switched her view from the back of Susan's head to Jenny.

Jenny apparently didn't hear her at first, and she repeated the question that Jenny answered. "Oh, right, sorry, I was miles away. Dr. Campbell, who, according to my brother, is the resident guru in this field, and this was the only time the doctor could fit in an appointment."

Jenny recalled the phone conversation with her brother, Peter, that morning. She had him laughing his socks off at her initially…

"Are you serious, Jen?"

"Absolutely. Otherwise why would I have disturbed your Sunday morning?"

There was a chuckle down the line. "You know me, I'm up at the crack of dawn to go running or rowing. However, today you're in luck, I was otherwise engaged and decided to sleep in."

Jenny shook her head. She didn't want to know about his new conquest. It reminded her of Stark. Right now, she just wanted to forget that Stark had kissed her and her reaction to it and the woman generally. "Do you know anyone on campus, a shrink maybe?"

"From the facts you've given me, it isn't a shrink you need. That poor woman has been in the hands of that profession for the last fifteen years, and nothing has been determined. It sounds like you need to look outside the norm, and I know just the person. You met once, but then you'd never remember, but I digress. Dr. Andy Campbell works in that particular field, usually debunking all the hokum about paranormal sightings and such stuff. Andy is a brilliant academic. Therefore, don't be surprised if the conversation gets beyond you. It does most of the students around here and some of the academics, too, but they love the aspect of the unexplained these days."

Amazed, Jenny asked, "Are you telling me that there really is a syllabus about this and you can get a degree? God, what is the world coming to?"

"Hey, don't knock what you don't understand. You need an open mind, particularly if you want to help a client of yours. Although, I'd say you're going out on a limb for her."

"You sound like Stark." Jenny could have bitten off her tongue at the words.

"Oh, so the beautiful Susan Stark is still around. Now I

understand perfectly. It would make a great story for the *Daily Post*. Of course, she might be sticking around for something else or maybe *someone* else."

Jenny scowled. "Stark is doing a story on Lorna, and we want it to be truthful, that's all."

"Okay, whatever you say. I'll call Andy and set up a meeting, the rest is up to you."

Here they were, and the more she thought about Stark in this equation, the more it riled her. Initially, she delayed calling Stark after setting up the meeting but decided it was unfair to leave her out. Then Stark had taken over by picking her and Lorna up in the Jeep. Stark had disregarded Jenny's protestations that she was perfectly capable of picking up Lorna and arriving at the university without her help. She still bristled with anger. In fact, she was so angry that she had only spoken to Stark when necessary since the woman picked her up. Now they were on the cusp of finding out what was happening to Lorna. With that done, she could finally say a heartfelt goodbye to the annoying Stark.

"Where do we go?" Susan asked in a tight voice.

Jenny looked at the campus board indicating various departments on the large map. "Peter said the doctor would be in the science block, building three, room seven."

"Science block it is then." Susan negotiated the small winding roads around numerous buildings. Initially, they only saw a smattering of students until they neared the recreation building—everyone seemed to be there. "Universities never change," Susan said with a slight chuckle. "Like ants, there are always people milling around."

Jenny didn't reply and knew Lorna couldn't, never having the opportunity of attending such an establishment. She continually scanned each building's name until she saw the one they wanted. "It's over there." She pointed.

The sound of Lorna sucking in a deep breath made Jenny realize how selfish she had been during the journey. What they were doing wasn't about her or Stark, it was about the lonely woman who had spent her youth and early adulthood in an institution. "Lorna, don't worry, we'll be with you all the way... won't we, Stark?"

Susan had a small smile tugging at her lips. "Yes, we will. The whole idea fascinates me. I've done a little research on Andy Campbell and..."

"Not now, Stark," Jenny bit out. "Let's go...the sooner we get there, the sooner Lorna will have answers."

Duly reprimanded, Susan parked the vehicle opposite the building, and everyone got out and headed towards the building and room seven.

The main door was open, and once inside, everything was eerily quiet—no students, security, or anyone else.

Jenny looked at the phone on the wall that had a notice to call for assistance. "Do you think we should wait here?"

Stark was already gone, her long strides taking her down the corridor. "Room seven is this way." Her voice echoed in the emptiness of their surroundings.

Jenny shrugged. "Looks like the intrepid reporter is used to this kind of thing."

Lorna giggled. "Probably. This person can help me, can't they, Jenny?"

Unsure how to answer, Jenny gave Lorna a squeeze on the shoulder. "Let's go see, shall we?"

As they approached where Stark had stopped, Jenny was surprised to see a woman stick her head out of a door before her body followed. From the distance of the corridor, Jenny saw casual clothes, jeans, and checked shirt over a slim frame. The woman was looking at Stark, but Jenny couldn't see her face. When the woman turned to face Jenny and Lorna, Jenny saw that she was a little taller than she was. That made her about the same height as Lorna but no match for Stark's towering presence. Shining brown hair was in a neat, almost shapeless, style topping a round face with pinched-in cheeks. Grey eyes peered at them through heavy-framed lenses.

"Jenny Price, Lorna Hirste, meet Dr. Andrea Campbell," Susan said. Lorna went forward first and shook the offered hand, but Jenny held back. Peter had said she had met Andy before, but she had no recollection. She hadn't even known it was a woman. If they'd met, she surely would have recalled that salient point at least.

"Hello, thanks for seeing us on a Sunday." Jenny politely shook hands with Andy, finding her palm sweaty. *Not a good start.* Still, she reminded herself that this wasn't about her but Lorna.

Andrea Campbell grinned broadly, stammering, "Wonderful to see you again, Ms. Price. You, of course, wouldn't remember me, but I know your brother very well."

Jenny smiled and wondered when she'd get her hand back. "My brother spoke well of you, Doctor. Sorry I can't recall the exact moment we met before, but perhaps later we can reminisce."

When Andy seemed to be mute and glued to the floor, Susan said, "Shall we go inside?" Susan gave Lorna a smile and a wink as they moved towards the open door.

"Yes…yes, of course." Andy almost fell over her own feet as she stumbled into the room.

Jenny tried desperately not to wipe her hand on her skirt once she'd been released from Andy's sweaty grasp. She glanced at Lorna, whose eyes appeared like saucers as she gazed around the laboratory. The room was full of equipment attached mostly to monitors or computers. In the far corner was a piece of equipment that looked at first like a broom cupboard, except that wires came out of the top and sides of the *beast*. She fervently hoped that particular piece didn't come into the equation.

"Peter told me a little about your problem. I'd like to ask questions before I recommend a course of action," Andrea muttered absently as her gaze drifted to Jenny.

Jenny shrugged at the expectation that she'd reply and turned to Lorna. "Okay with you, Lorna?"

Lorna continued to look around the room at monitors. "Sure, what do you want to know?"

Andy selected a clipboard from a desk strewn with other papers and nodded to a chair opposite her. "Right, when did this all start…?"

Feeling like a spare wheel as the questions began, Jenny moved around the room investigating several of the monitors as Lorna had moments before. At one monitor, she tentatively touched the screen only to pull back when Stark whispered in her ear. "It won't reach out and grab you."

The low chuckle from Stark had Jenny curling her upper lip in distaste. "How would you know? I thought you were open-minded. With that mind-set, it just might."

Susan shook her head. "Touché, my legal friend. It looks all technical and quite scary in here, don't you think? Scientific geniuses always frighten me. I remember the first time I saw a blown-up picture of Einstein, freaky-looking guy."

Jenny looked at Stark. There was no way that Stark could possibly be afraid of anything. "I can't imagine much scaring you. In fact, I'd go so far as to say on a dark night you'd be pretty scary if someone didn't know you and saw you coming."

Susan raised her eyebrows. "Ouch, how cutting. Has anyone ever told you that you don't have a good bedside manner?"

"I'm not a doctor, therefore it doesn't apply."

"I figure a good bedside manner is necessary for everyone and particularly important to whomever you share your bed with."

"Well, I don't share my bed," Jenny spat out.

"I can see why." Susan turned away and felt the grip of a small hand on her arm. "Yes?"

"You don't know me or who might want to share my bed. For the record, you never will."

Susan smiled. "Is that a challenge?"

Jenny was about to answer when Andy said, "Jenny, will you join us? Ms. Stark, you of course, too?"

Both women walked the short distance to where the other two women were.

Susan quipped in amusement, "What's up, Doc?" and grinned teasingly.

Andrea scowled. "I have all the questions answered, and I've persuaded Lorna to allow me to measure her brainwave pattern. It's a harmless process."

Half an hour later, the equipment measuring Lorna's brain pattern had Andy eyeing the screen and muttering incoherently.

Jenny decided that she and Stark should stay as far away from each other as possible. She chose to be on the other side of the desk where Lorna was sitting with some evil-looking contraption on her head. Discreetly, she peered at Stark, who was watching the process with a fascinated expression on her face.

"How long will this take?" Jenny glanced at her watch.

A disappointed expression crossed Andy's face, making her bottom lip drop at the question. "Another hour or so…if you're bored, you could always go to the student union. It's only a five-minute walk from here…you passed it on the way in."

"I remember seeing it. I think I'll do that because this is more technical than I can understand. I'll leave it to the expert," Jenny said with a friendly smile and saw Andy beam a smile in her direction.

Susan entered the conversation. "You could bring back some coffee for the rest of us."

"Good idea," Andrea piped in. "Here, take my pass, and you'll get my discount." Andrea passed Jenny the object and at the touch of their hands fumbled with the card before dropping it. "Sorry." She retrieved it from the pile of papers on her desk.

Jenny didn't say anything more but gave Andy a smile. Passing Stark, she whispered, "You can pay me back," and left the office before Stark could comment.

Susan chuckled as she watched Jenny leave the room. *She's certainly not the friendliest person in the world...Andy is welcome to her.* That thought twisted her stomach in knots. It reminded her of when Andy had seen Jenny earlier. Andrea seemed to be ogling Jenny. It irritated her and she'd had to prevent herself from standing in front of Jenny and blocking the woman's view. Initially, when Andy opened the door, Susan explained who she was and was about to indicate Jenny and Lorna when Andy looked at them and gasped as her gaze cast around Jenny like a net. Susan heard Andy's strangled whispered words. *Oh, my god, at last...please, please, don't let me blow it.* Then Susan had stood back in quiet speculation. There had apparently been no reaction from Jenny, but she could be faking it. Lawyers had that kind of reputation, just as journalists had the reputation of having a paparazzi mentality. This whole situation was weird—the story, Jenny, and now this …supernatural stuff. *What next?*

Half an hour later, Jenny hadn't come back, and Susan decided to go check that she hadn't forgotten them. Besides, a break would do her good, and she needed that caffeine fix. Five minutes later, Susan opened the cafeteria door and glanced around. Students huddled in corners and milling around the counter made it impossible to see where Jenny was. Finally, she spied her sitting idly looking at the fountain in the courtyard adjacent to the building.

As usual, Susan stopped to gaze at the woman. It wasn't until someone jostled her to move out of the way that the preoccupation with Jenny was broken. She went to the counter and ordered two coffees. Susan noted that Jenny didn't move an inch, maintaining her solitary watch over the water fountain, and assumed that Jenny hadn't noticed her. Once she had the coffee, Susan moved towards the table.

"Do you mind if I join you?" Jenny absently looked up and her unshielded eyes gave Stark a different view of her. Her stomach did a triple flip. "I figured that you might need a refill."

Jenny shrugged. "I was going to bring the coffee to you shortly."

"I never thought anything else," Susan said. "However, I needed a break and thought you might need a hand. I promise I had no other ulterior motive than that." Susan looked down at her black strong coffee and took a sip.

"Nothing I do or say makes any difference to you, does it, Stark? You still keep trying. I'm not interested. Is that black and white enough for you?" Jenny moved her cold coffee away and took a sip from the hot one. Absently, she said, "Thanks."

Susan considered her words carefully before replying. "A girl has to try, and I didn't think you disliked my kiss last night. In fact, I'd say…"

Jenny held up her hand. "Don't…don't say it, Stark. You'd be wrong."

"Okay, you've hit me over the head enough. I promise the rest of the time we spend together will be purely professional. How does that sound?"

Jenny narrowed her eyes. "It sounds too good to be true. How's Lorna doing?"

"Good, I think. Once you left the room, Andy became quite chatty, and that put Lorna at ease. You must have a tongue-tying effect on her." Susan looked at Jenny in question and casually asked, "Have you met her before?"

"My brother says I have. However, I never allowed him to say where or when it was. I'll have to rectify that when I get home." Jenny took a sip of her coffee. "Why do you ask?"

"Oh, purely an observation from when you just met. I think the doctor is smitten with you. If you play your cards right, I'd say she might well be interested in sharing your bed."

"Oh, for goodness sake, give it a rest. Not everyone thinks about sex as soon as they meet someone of interest."

Susan grinned. "Ah, she may be of interest then."

Jenny closed her eyes. "This conversation is absurd. If she was, I certainly wouldn't discuss it with you."

Susan gazed into Jenny's eyes intently and opened her mouth, then closed it and remained silent. When she did speak, she changed the subject. "Did your brother say what might be in store for Lorna?"

"Not really, only that they would probably do a barrel of tests and that was it."

"I wonder if we're going to go on a ghost hunting trip."

Jenny laughed. It disconcerted Susan slightly, especially as the table next to them turned to look. Susan held up her hands in a *what did I say* gesture.

The lines around Susan's eyes crinkled as she focused her attention on Jenny. "Wow, I made you laugh. I must try it again sometime."

"I'm sorry, but you have to admit that it's so preposterous. Does anyone really do that? I thought it was only fiction on TV, or worse, I've always thought people who take part in those kinds of scenarios were nothing more than attention seekers or nerdy sci-fi buffs." Jenny sat back in her chair, still chuckling and wiping away the laughter tears.

"Andy does. Apparently, she's an experienced ghost hunter.

Although, mainly to debunk what most people think are ghost or paranormal activity. She is well known and trusted in this field. Even wrote a book about it," Susan said seriously, allowing a smile to grace her lips.

Jenny narrowed her eyes. "Would you go on a ghost hunting trip?"

Susan leaned back in the chair and winked. "Of course I would. You know me…I'll do anything for a story."

"At last you admit it. But coming on to me last night wasn't necessary, was it? I'd already brought you into the loop."

Susan caught the disbelief in Jenny's expression. "You're a very beautiful woman. I'd be a fool not to at least try."

"We'd better go and take the others their coffee. Did the doctor say what she preferred?"

Susan equably allowed the change in subject. "No, but I think they'll probably know behind the counter. If they don't, I'm sure as long as it's you that gives it to her, she'll accept it even if she hates it."

Three hours after arriving at Andy's office, each woman knew a little bit more about the work Andrea Campbell was involved in. Particularly, her main research program called Spirit Dimension Theory.

While they drank their coffee, Andrea had explained the theory to them...

"Spirit worlds co-exist with the conjunctive *real* world that most people believe in. When a person truly believes in every aspect of fate, the dimension theory is defined in its entirety. If one is fated, they cannot change what is to happen. Therefore, it is not unreasonable to assume that if the universe works in a pattern that the human mind generally cannot conceive, it's not within the realms of possibility that some can tune into the dimension that holds the *spirit* of a person who had once trodden that same path. Like a merry-go-round that you can't get off. Does that make sense?"

"Not to me," Jenny said. "However, does any of what you're saying have a bearing on Lorna?"

All eyes turned to Lorna, who looked strange with the head cap full of wires.

Andrea looked disappointed. "Well, not exactly unless she's fated to be attached to the spirit that sends her these messages."

Susan pulled at her firm chin. "I thought you debunked theories like that, Doctor…at least that's how it's written in all the journals."

Andrea shifted her gaze to Susan. "I've read some of your work, too, Ms. Stark. Has the fact that you've debunked material in stories ever stopped you from believing in a particular subject close to you? I recall some feisty reporting on the Johns Air Force Base last year. That had the government upset with you, didn't it?"

Susan's expression remained bland. "Touché. What do you think we should consider next for Lorna?"

"You brought a file. Allow me to consider the contents tonight. Right now, I'd like to run a few more simple tests. Then I'd like Lorna to think about being a guinea pig in a trial when she hears the voice and the name. Perhaps next Saturday evening would be good?" Andrea smiled at everyone, and when her gaze traveled to Jenny, she left it there.

Jenny glanced at Lorna, whose eyes had lit up at the news. "If that's what Lorna wants, then I'm game."

Susan remained stoically silent, eventually saying, "I'll have to pass. Maybe you can update me with the pertinent details when you've come to a conclusion."

Disbelief crossed Jenny's face. "I thought this would be right up your alley, Stark. What's wrong? Have you gone all weak in the knees suddenly?"

Susan's nostrils flared at the taunt. "It's almost four, and I'm sure we could all do with going home for some relaxation before our workweek begins again tomorrow."

Andrea nodded as she began to fiddle with the controls on her equipment and transferring her attention to the task at hand. "Okay, Lorna, this won't hurt, I promise."

Jenny stood and walked over to Stark. Her stance was

imposing, giving the impression she was much taller than she was. “I meant what I said. You’re the one with the open mind, remember?”

“As if I could forget with you around, Jenny. I’m out of town next weekend and I can’t break the appointment.”

“Can’t or won’t?”

Susan growled, her face taking on an angry expression. “That’s enough! It’s my father’s birthday, and I made a promise to be there. Will that satisfy your cutting tongue and enquiring mind?”

Jenny looked down in discomfort. It wasn’t any of her business, and once more, she’d gone over the top. God, she was becoming more of a shrew around Stark than an intelligent, tolerant lawyer. “I’m sorry.”

Susan blew out a sarcastic laugh. “Good grief. At last, the woman actually understands that everything isn’t about her.”

“That’s not what I think at all.”

“Well, hell, you could have fooled me.”

Silence invaded the space. Enough had already been said. Jenny moved back to the chair she’d earlier vacated, and both women remained silent until the end of the tests.

Chapter 11

Where did the week go? I can't believe it's Friday. Jenny glanced up when her partner walked into her office. "Hi, Sam. Anything wrong?"

Sam hesitated before pulling up a chair. "I thought you had completed the case on Lorna Hirste."

Jenny bit the bottom of her lip. "I have, technically speaking."

"And this technicality is?"

"Oh, helping her to get settled in the real world again. Is that a problem?"

Sam shook his head. "There are people out there to help her, Jenny, her parents, for instance."

Jenny's eyebrows rose. "Have they complained about my involvement? Is that it?" That's all she needed, a complaint, as well as looking forward to spending her Saturday in a cemetery after midnight.

"There are numerous cases we have to become embroiled in without getting personally involved." Sam stood and went to the door, grasped the knob, then turned back around. "Take it from an old-timer in this game…the more you become involved, the less objective you become."

"I promise you this will be a one off."

"That's a promise I'm not going to hold you to because that's one of the reasons I accepted you here. You do actually care." He opened the door slightly. "For the record, no one complained. I was just worried when I saw that requisition for a rental for the weekend." He left the room.

Heaving a sigh of relief, Jenny groaned. She'd totally forgotten she'd requested a rental for the expedition. When they were about to leave Andy's office, she had thrown into the conversation that she didn't have a personal vehicle and that the van assigned to her department was in repair and probably wouldn't to be ready when they needed it. Jenny had said she'd organize things.

Now on reflection, she should have done so privately. The BMW was in the shop and not due back until next week. They were waiting for a part from overseas, although it wouldn't have been suitable. "Oh, well, Sam didn't seem upset. He was more concerned than anything else…if only he knew where it was taking me."

Faith Ramsey, their legal secretary, walked in moments after Sam left, her face wreathed in apologies. "Sorry, Jenny, he was browsing on my desk like he does when he's at a loose end. He saw what I was going to do next."

Jenny smiled. "No foul, Faith. Did I mention that it isn't a car I need but a van or something larger than a car?" Her thoughts traveled as they seemed to these days to Stark—*her vehicle would have been perfect.*

"Well, actually…" She dangled a set of keys in her hand. At Jenny's puzzlement, she added, "A courier has just handed me the keys along with a note for you. He said a black Jeep is parked in your spot. How did he know that your car is in the shop?"

"Beats me." Jenny took the offered note and tore the envelope open. Bold confident strokes stood out on the paper.

J,

I figured that you might need something larger than your car for the jaunt this weekend. As I'm out of town and not taking the vehicle, I thought it would better to be of use than in a garage. Take care of my beast, she's special to me. Happy ghost hunting!

S

Speechless, Jenny held the note before realizing Faith was still standing in her office, presumably waiting for an explanation. "It's okay, Faith. Someone I know has allowed me to borrow her vehicle for the weekend."

"Wow, she must be a good friend. I had a peek at the Jeep, and it's the top of the line. Lucky woman, she must think a lot of you. I hope she knows that you drive like a maniac." Faith chuckled and left the room.

Jenny allowed a tinge of doubt to cross her face at Faith's flippant words. It was true, she did drive fast, although not generally to work. What was the point since the subway was fast and efficient? She saw no reason to drive around town with all the traffic congestion, and riding the subway gave her time to think. What could be better in her job? For once, her thoughts about Stark were entirely positive, and the way it made feel inside had her smiling. Shaking away the thought, she picked up her next case file and digested its contents.

Susan had arranged for Friday off and arrived at her parents' home late Thursday. Now having spent the day together enjoying a birthday lunch, Susan had decided to ask the question that hadn't exactly haunted her but had her wondering, particularly after Andy had mentioned it the previous weekend.

"Dad, you never commented about that story regarding Johns Air Force Base. I hope I didn't disappoint you."

David Stark caught his daughter's gaze, his hazel eyes focusing so hard that they became hypnotic. His lips curved into a smile, the upper one covered by a moustache the color of his salt and pepper hair. The smile had a relaxing effect on the atmosphere in the room. "You did your job and I commend you for that."

Susan shrugged. "That doesn't answer the question, does it?"

"When did you need my approval for your professional life? Don't you remember that we agreed to disagree a long time ago?" He moved to look out over the lawn, and Susan followed him. They stood side by side. Her father was of basketball proportions, and she only came up to his chin. They both watched Sheryl, Susan's mother, chatting with the next door neighbor as she collected a package from the car.

"Never, I guess, but even so, I'd like to know your thoughts."

David chuckled, and it reverberated through his rangy frame.

"You gave some people the odd palpitation, but otherwise it was necessary. We've placed a few changes in our protocol since that event."

Susan couldn't help but smile. In fact, the grin she had almost split her face in two. His comment said it all. She'd done a good job and he was proud of her. "Have you ever come across people who think they might be possessed during your career?"

"Possessed? What do you mean? Possession of drugs?"

Susan shook her head. "No spirit possession…ghosts and all that jazz."

"Oh, my god, don't tell me you're going down the loony trail. Trust me, I wouldn't approve." David gave her a sharp glance.

Susan shook her head. "Not exactly, have you?"

"No, I'm a practical man. It's all mumbo jumbo. If you want to have someone to talk to on that subject, you should ask your mother."

"You sound just like Jenny," Susan mumbled.

"Ask me what?" Sheryl Stark walked into the room holding a brown paper package.

"Your daughter wants to ask you about possession and ghosts. If only your Aunt Dorothy was alive, she'd have a story or two," David said lightheartedly.

Sheryl tut-tutted and dropped her package on the sofa. Walking towards the two by the window, the three of them together would have made quite an impression. "Don't be mean, David, Aunt Dotty was lovely."

Rolling his eyes, David whispered to Susan, "Yeah, Dotty is right. Why don't you two talk about this and I'll make a couple of phone calls, then we can have dinner?"

Susan laughed. Her dad had a habit of starting a conversation, then leaving her and her mother to finish it.

"So, dear, what do you need to know about Aunt Dotty?" Sheryl asked as her sea-green gaze tenderly settled on Susan.

"Why don't you show me what you've brought first?" Susan winked at her mom.

Sheryl picked up the package. "I made this for you at my craft class." She handed the package to Susan.

Susan didn't open it immediately. She hugged her mom and kissed her cheek. "Thanks, Mom." Loving surprises, she tore open the package. When she did, out spilled the most amazing embroidered blanket she'd ever seen. It was a multitude of colors and patterns, reflecting more a painting than a fabric. A wonderful rainbow was the central theme with a figure on either side of it, hands outstretched. "Wow, this must have taken you ages! It's wonderful, Mom, I love it."

Sheryl sucked in a proud breath. "I'm glad you do, but you're not just saying that, are you? Because if you are…"

Susan stopped the doubt in mid-sentence by hugging her mom close. "I love it and I love you. I'll cherish it forever…it's absolutely beautiful."

"I love you, too, Susan. Now what do you want to know? Possession, your dad said."

"Oh, it doesn't matter. Tell me about Aunt Dotty. Did I ever meet her?"

"I'll tell you about Aunt Dotty if you spill the beans on Jenny." Sheryl held her daughter's gaze. "Deal?"

Both women looked at each other and smiled.

"I thought I'd gotten away with that slip. I should have known better." Susan shook her head.

Sheryl chuckled. "You can't get away with anything, darling. I'm your mother, remember? Besides, I'm glad that I can finally forget all about Leigh…she was never good enough for you."

Susan chuckled. "Now that's a mother's love talking. Leigh just felt she wanted someone else, that's all."

"Yeah, your best friend and you'd spent what, two years living together. I swear if you hadn't come out of it so well, I'd have tracked that bitch down and given her a piece of my mind. Now spill, this Jenny, what's she like?"

Susan burst out laughing. "Jenny isn't interested in me in that way. She thinks I'm a womanizer."

Sheryl smiled. "Well, I like her already. I've been telling you the same thing since that Leigh Chambers played dirty on you, you've became a womanizer."

Andrea Campbell stared into space or the empty void that stood between her and the next experiment, her mind engrossed in Jenny Price. She had been surprised a week earlier when Peter Price called asking for her help. It hadn't been convenient, but when he'd mentioned casually it was a favor for his sister, she'd dropped everything. Jenny had captured her heart when she had first set eyes on the woman at Peter's twenty-first birthday party.

She and Peter had been students together during their college days, and the friendship continued through the years. Although she hadn't seen Jenny again, it hadn't changed the way she felt. Deep in her gut, she felt that one day they were destined to meet again, and now it seemed she had been right. Jenny was as beautiful, if not more so, in the years since they'd met.

Although the initial meeting hadn't been that conducive, at least not all had been lost. They were going to see each other again that night, and that had to be her second chance at making a mark on Jenny. She'd make an effort with her attire and hair, allowing Jenny to see more than the scientist. She'd convey, she hoped, that she was a woman of interest, too.

A sudden tap on her shoulder had her startled out of her reverie.

"Doctor, are you okay? You've been staring at a blank screen for the last ten minutes."

Andrea glanced up quickly and smiled at Leigh Chambers, one of her associates who taught classes on the occult and ancient rituals of the dead. "Sorry, Leigh, did you need something?"

Leigh shook her head as her black fashionably styled hair moved perfectly back and forth. Then she shrugged. "Not really. I've finished the assessment on the information you gave me, and I think it makes for interesting reading. I would very much like to meet this Lorna."

An idea came to Andrea. "What are you doing tomorrow evening? Would you be up for a field trip?"

"Sure, I wasn't doing anything in particular."

"Excellent, be here around eleven, and you'll meet Lorna. I have a feeling it might prove interesting."

"Dare I ask where we're going?"

Andrea chuckled. "I don't know yet, but all will be revealed tomorrow." Collecting her papers, Andrea nodded at Leigh and left the room.

Leigh watched Andrea leave, sitting in contemplation as the door shut behind her. Her thoughts traversed to why she was here in Merit—Susan Stark. Since arriving in Merit and tracking down her ex, she'd followed her as much as possible when she went out socially. It wasn't as if she was a stalker or anything nefarious like that. No, she hoped against hope that she had the courage to approach the woman she had once professed to love.

She had dumped Susan for a few months of exciting passion. Eventually, the infatuation fizzled and left her wondering how she could have been such a fool. By then, it was too late and Susan had left town. It wasn't until she made national headlines with a story she'd written about an Air Force base close by that she finally tracked her down to Merit.

With a shake of her head, she pondered the logic behind her compulsion to see Susan. If she hadn't been so engrossed in Susan and needing to see her again, she'd have tried to flirt with Andy. She daren't make that kind of complication. Not if there was any way she could make it up to Susan and perhaps have a second chance.

Chapter 12

Wind swirled gently around Centenary Cemetery, causing the leaves that had fallen to glide over the ground like a floating carpet. Several trees punctuated the oldest cemetery in Merit, looming in the darkness like sentries on guard. Strained light permeated the darkness in several places as overhead street lights allowed a diminutive glow to illuminate a proportion of the area. Darkness swallowed it up in the distance. Four figures approached from the south that might appear to a casual passer-by as potential phantoms cloaked in the shadowy recesses of the night.

Jenny pulled the heavy jacket she wore farther up her body where the collar rested under her chin. "This is one gloomy place. Are you sure it's necessary, Doctor?" Right now, her bed, or anyone else's for that matter, was far more welcoming than this place—even Stark's bed.

"Yes, I believe it is, Jenny. This is the core of Lorna's problem, and we need to see what she does and why." Andy laid a hand on Jenny's arm. "You can call me Andrea or Andy…it's a lot less formal."

Jenny halfheartedly nodded. "Thanks, Doc…Andrea. Lorna, are we close yet?"

Lorna looked almost ghost-like herself in a beige jacket and light-colored slacks. "Yes, but we need to go farther." Her finger pointed to the darkness.

"Great, is it okay for me to use my flashlight now?" Jenny groaned. She didn't want to sound as if she had the jitters, but she did—big-time.

Leigh, laden with an EMF detector, digital camera, and around her neck a low light video camera, grinned at Jenny. "Is this your first ghost-buster field trial?"

"My first, and let me tell you, I'm hoping my last." She scrunched her nose as the cold wind hit her face. "Do you do this often?" She'd been introduced to Andy's associate briefly when they arrived at the campus earlier.

Leigh gave a soft chuckle. Her almond-shaped brown eyes were barely discernible in the dim light. "Oh, I've been on three since I arrived here and conducted several more for my thesis back home. I was delighted to find that Andy was still at the university. She's excellent in her field." Leigh waved some of the equipment around, attentively checking levels. "If at any time you feel threatened, Andy will call it a night. Negative influences are not good for our research."

Jenny rolled her eyes. "Thank goodness for that. Not that I intend to be scared, of course, as I don't believe. It's all mumbo jumbo to me."

"Really, so why are you here? Are you a close friend of Lorna's?" Leigh kept checking the readings on her meter.

Cautiously, Jenny responded. "I'm a friend, yes. Lorna needs answers, and we're trying to find them for her." Jenny was about to mention Stark and decided against it. Why bother? She wasn't here. Leigh was hardly likely to meet her if they found what they were looking for.

"You and Andy, how cool. Although I doubt you thought you'd be involved in this kind of operation when you agreed to help your friend. It's a fascinating subject matter, don't you think? Andy believes in different dimensions, of course, but others believe it's a part of the soul left behind. I personally believe the latter, which is why it's always interesting to go on these hunts with Andy. I live for this thrill, and there's always something in the air, even if you can't tangibly see it."

Jenny wasn't sure what to make of the cheerful way Leigh described this expedition. "Exactly how successful in seeing the paranormal have you been, Leigh?"

"Leigh, did you bring your infrared glasses?" Andrea asked

as she approached them, already sporting a pair of the glasses herself. "Lorna is waiting by the gravestone."

"I have them, Andy."

Jenny pulled at her bottom lip as a chill ran down her back when she spied Lorna sitting behind the headstone. Jenny pointed to Lorna where she sat alone. "Is that wise?"

Andy whispered, "One of three things will happen tonight. Absolutely nothing, or someone will arrive to desecrate the grave. Failing those scenarios, the third is open to speculation...what you ultimately believe determines what you see. Let's take our places. This could be a long night."

Leigh and Andy moved to flank Lorna behind headstones several feet away. Jenny, unsure what to do, was grateful when Andy smiled and waved her over.

An hour went by and nothing happened. Lorna looked serenely happy sitting behind Samantha Grey's last resting place. Then her head jerked up at the faint sounds of voices in the distance.

Jenny held her breath, and the two academics stared into the dark void in front of them. Slowly, two figures emerged. They were possibly teenagers, two boys, and one held what looked like a pistol. Everyone held her breath waiting for what might happen next. Jenny heard Andy mutter an oath under her breath. "What is it?"

"The EMF is going crazy," Andy said, her attention focused on the counter with swift glances in Leigh and Lorna's direction.

All Jenny knew about an EMF was that it meant electromagnetic field, and that it was permanently part of our lives as the earth was one giant ball of the phenomenon. Feeling uncomfortable with nothing to do, she watched as she grew fearful for Lorna's safety sitting in a vulnerable position. However, as she surveyed the area in question, Lorna didn't look the slightest bit worried. In fact, her face in the dark, although difficult to see properly, seemed to have a glow about it. Jenny nudged Andy. "Is that normal?"

She didn't get an answer as the two strangers walked closer to where Lorna sat, their voices clearly audible.

"Your turn this time. There's a good one big enough for you to hit." The pistol passed to the other boy.

"I can beat you at target practice anytime, dork. I'm going for that one." He pointed to Samantha Grey's headstone and took aim.

Then like a specter from the crypt, Lorna moved slowly and stood behind the headstone before she raised her hand in a halting action. A crackle of what looked like electricity seemed to spark from behind her, and she spoke in a hollow voice. "Leave now."

The two boys, wildly looking for an escape, dropped the pistol and fled with a deafening scream of fear.

Jenny, who had watched in morbid fascination, though worried about Lorna, was motionless to do anything other than watch the scene. Finally, she ran across to Lorna. "Are you okay?"

Lorna didn't answer, but Andy and Leigh began asking the darkness if there was anyone there.

Leigh began to chant, "Did a spirit want to talk to us if they did show themselves? We mean you no harm."

For ten minutes, this went on and Jenny glanced down at her watch, flashing her mini flashlight on the glass to see the time. It was a quarter after two. As she followed the others, milling around Lorna and the gravestone, she heard snippets of the conversation between Andy and Lorna—the forces were getting stronger.

Jenny, not wanting to interfere with the process, chose to remain out of the way. At night in a graveyard wasn't for her. Footsteps sounded behind her. She turned quickly but didn't see anyone. She tried as she could to peer into the murky depths of the abyss in front of her, but it was useless.

Motionless, unsure if that was because she didn't want to move or was plain scared, Jenny listened intently. There it was again, but this time it was a rustling. Then Jenny felt what seemed like a breath in her left ear. She moved her head with half-closed eyes, wondering what was going on. The gentle breeze that had been here when they arrived now seemed to take on a vortex-like feel around her. She looked down at her feet, and the leaves that covered her boots seemed to be a creeping vine moving up her legs.

"Oh, crap." From deep inside, all she could do was scream and run like hell. Instead of heading towards the others, her sense of direction took on a whole new meaning of scatterbrained as Jenny headed the opposite way. All she knew was that leaving the area was paramount. The experience had freaked her out. Then she cannoned into a tree, or it seemed that way as her fevered mind took in the limbs of branches that settled around her, and she let out a bloodcurdling scream.

"Hey, hey, Jenny, it's okay. I have you. You're safe. It's me, Susan."

The voice permeated Jenny's brain. She welcomed the familiarity, allowing that to be her focus. Slowly opening first one eye, then the other, she realized that the malevolent tree was the tall body of Stark. The branch limbs were Stark's arms that held her tightly. With the rapid beat of her heart finally slowing to a steadier pace, her body instinctively identified a safe haven. "Thank God it's you, Stark."

Susan smiled. "It's good to see you, too."

Finally, Jenny's logic kicked in. "What are you doing here? I thought you were at your father's birthday party."

Susan laughed softly. "I had a premonition that there might be a damsel in distress, and lo and behold, I was right."

Jenny stared up into the muted features of Stark's face, and no matter how many acid retorts went through her head at the teasing, she refrained from using any other than a sardonic, "A premonition, huh?"

Footsteps heralded the arrival of the cavalry as three figures charged into view. "Are you okay, Jenny?" Andy asked. "What did you see?"

Then Jenny felt the warm emotion Stark had brought to her suddenly doused with icy water. Stark's arms dropped away like lead. Frowning, Jenny looked up and saw Stark's attention on the others in front of them. Confused, she turned to see what had upset Stark. It wasn't Andy or Lorna. She was looking directly at Leigh Chambers.

Leigh spoke softly, her smile tentative. "Hi, Susan."

Jenny, so close to Stark's body, felt it go rigid as Stark clenched and unclenched her fists.

Her face a blank mask, Susan coldly replied, "Leigh, what are you doing here?"

Andy chose that moment to answer for Leigh. "Leigh is helping me conduct the trial. She's very experienced in the field. Do you know each other?"

Stark snarled. "I didn't ask you, Doctor. I was speaking to her."

Jenny cringed at the tone. For the first time since meeting Stark, she saw unmitigated anger manifest. Attempting to warm up the icy atmosphere that had developed, she answered Andy's original enquiry. "I didn't find any spooks, only a Stark." There was a distinct giggle from Lorna, but the others remained silent.

Leigh stepped forward. "Perhaps you and I can go somewhere and talk, Susan."

Susan drew in a ragged breath, and with her jaw set, she said, "Not a chance. Are you done for the night, Doctor?"

Andy gulped. "We can be."

Susan nodded briefly and turned her attention to Lorna. "How about you, Lorna, are you okay? Did you receive any personal answers from the expedition tonight?"

Lorna gave a bright smile. "I'm good, thanks, Susan. I know something happened. I'm hoping that the professor can inform me of what exactly. I know I wasn't wrong…Samantha Grey's headstone was in danger."

"No, she damn well wasn't. This is the oddest thing I've ever seen in my life," Jenny muttered, attempting to look anywhere but at Stark and Leigh, which was almost impossible. In her humble opinion, the two could be trading pistols at dawn if their body language was anything to go by.

"I think we have enough data to explain some of what went on this evening, Lorna. Anyone up for a preliminary go-through around three tomorrow?" Andy asked, looking at Jenny.

"I promised to spend the day with my family. I don't want to upset my parents." Lorna's face seemed to fall at the prospect of not being at the meeting.

Jenny felt the tension in the air increase. "I can spare a couple of hours, but then I have to go. I'm due in court Monday, bright and early, and I'll need to do my last-minute preparation."

Andrea beamed at Jenny's acceptance.

"I'll be there. I need the background notes for my article," Susan said unemotionally, her disapproving stare still cast on Leigh.

"I'll have to let you know," Leigh said with her eyes focused on the equipment she carried.

"Excellent, right. Do we have everything?" Andrea looked around. "Let's all go home to bed then."

Three-quarters of an hour later, Stark stopped the vehicle outside Jenny's house, her fingers drumming on the wheel as the engine idled.

Jenny had grown irritated by Stark's manner and glowering expression during the quiet journey from the cemetery. "Hey, look, I didn't ask you to take me home. I could have called a cab from the university and you could have talked with Leigh."

Stark didn't appear to register the words, and with a heavy sigh, Jenny opened the door of the vehicle, slamming it for good measure.

Jenny cast an angry glance backwards and saw Stark swinging her long legs out of the car. She then caught up to her as she fumbled with the door lock.

"Hey, I'm sorry."

Jenny shook her head. "We agreed it was business not personal between us, end of story." Jenny blew out a breath, then her temper got the upper hand. "All I ask is common courtesy."

"Is this polite enough for you?" Susan turned Jenny in her arms and kissed her.

Jenny found herself resisting for all of two seconds, then her lips became yielding under Stark's, allowing them both to explore each other's mouths intimately. With her back to the door, Jenny couldn't help herself as she gave in to the craving of her body for Stark's attentions. At this moment, she allowed the vulnerability of tiredness to ignore her mind's warning that this could be all wrong. Instead of pushing Stark away, Jenny's hands encircled her broad back, instinctively running her fingers up and down the taut body. Moments later, she reached between the trousers and shirt Stark wore, dragging the material away so that her hands could feel burning flesh. Except it wasn't burning, it was cool to the touch, and a shiver ran from her belly to the apex between her legs. Right now, all she knew in her fevered mind was that she wanted Stark.

Stark eased her body over Jenny's as they wedged themselves against the door, then Stark's booted foot connected with the door and it swung open. In a swift move, Stark picked Jenny up and carried her into the hallway, their lips never disconnecting.

Seconds later, Stark pulled away. "Do you want this, Jenny? Do you want me?"

A strangled cry broke through Jenny's lips. "Yes."

Stark moved farther with Jenny in her arms into the hall towards the lounge, and seconds later, she laid her on the wide sofa, placing her body over the much smaller one. "Then you shall have me."

Lips claimed their prize as hands began to unbutton jackets and shirts, and feverish minutes later, they were naked and staring into each other's eyes.

"Last chance to turn back."

Jenny, her eyes glazed with passion, knew that she couldn't. Her body scorched with lust. Even if she was just another notch on Stark's bedpost, she didn't care. After all that she'd gone through, she needed to feel someone beside her and know she wasn't alone. Her left hand curled around Stark's dark head and pulled willing lips to hers. Her hand deftly placed between them began to incite Stark's moans as fingertips pulled at a turgid nipple.

Stark groaned and pressed her body closer as her hands began their own trip of exploration, starting south.

Chapter 13

Jenny awoke when she rolled off the sofa and landed with a soft thud on the floor. "What the hell!" For a crazy moment, she'd thought she'd fallen out of bed. Blinking rapidly, she looked around her. *I'm pretty sure this is my house.* Everything was as she remembered—the furniture, the ornaments, the photographs. Then her face contorted as she realized her nakedness was complemented by the marks on her breasts and the general feeling of lethargy in her limbs. Her memory tripped in, pushing her in the right direction. "Stark!"

There was no answer. In fact, except for the ticking clock on the wall, the house was quiet. Scrambling up, she saw her clothes scattered where she and Stark presumably had thrown them. After she dragged on her shirt and took the time to go to the bathroom, she checked every room. Stark wasn't there. If she hadn't the marks on her breasts to prove the lovemaking, she'd have figured it was a dream. Except it wasn't a dream. The more she thought of those long fingers trailing, enticing, and drawing her to the heights of passion, the more she knew it was the real thing. "Where is she?"

In a daze, she showered, changed, then headed to the kitchen to make breakfast. When she moved towards the coffeepot, she saw a note that had slipped onto its side. A part of her didn't want to open it, but she sucked in a deep breath and did.

J,

Sorry I had to leave before you woke. Perhaps after the meeting with the professor, you and I can talk about what happened—or not, I'll leave it up to you.

S

"It's all up to me! What a cop-out." Jenny scrunched up the note and threw it across the room. "She could have woken me."

Sitting at a red light on her way to the office, Susan smiled as she recalled the night before, or should she say early morning. She summed it up in one word—unforgettable. Fortunately for her, Andy had told one of her senior students where they were going. Like most people that age, Saturday night didn't end at midnight, and Stark tracked one down at the coffee house. Bone weary from taking a late flight to arrive and participate in the graveyard quest, she hoped that her actions would appease Jenny's intolerable impression of her. In retrospect, Jenny's opinion shouldn't make a difference, but it did, and that was scary. However, seeing Leigh again had been like a bullet to the chest.

Her irritation increased at seeing Leigh Chambers after five years. It grew even more when her cell buzzed as she held Jenny close to her while the woman slept like the dead. Brian Johnson, her editor, sent a text message saying he wanted her in the office immediately. There was no excuse for not being there for it was all part of the job—leaving everything at the drop of a hat if a story emerged. Then she gazed dreamily at the relaxed expression on Jenny's features.

There was no doubt in her mind that she'd just spent the best four hours of her life in the arms of someone who she now realized was very important to her. All she had to do was convince Jenny of that. Their night together was a start—unexpected, wonderful. There had been no doubt that they were compatible in bed. She smiled. The couch too.

For a second, she debated ignoring Johnson's request. Jenny's warm soft body like a second skin next to hers spun a web around her as she kissed the top of the blond head. She found it difficult to extricate from Jenny. If she was lucky, she might get back before Jenny woke. A conundrum faced her as Jenny moved slightly to allow her the choice of staying or leaving.

The cell buzzed again, and Johnson left another message. *Now means now.* With a tender smile, she whispered into Jenny's ear and moved to retrieve her clothes. Leaving a short note propped up against the coffee maker, Stark locked the door behind her and headed for the office.

Half an hour later, she was in Johnson's office.

"You look like you haven't been home."

Susan almost said, "I got lucky," but let it pass. She didn't want to tarnish what she'd had with Jenny with some smart remark to her boss.

"Whatever. You said you wanted me here now, so here I am. What's the story?"

Brian gave her a sharp glance, then settled his heavy frame in a chair. "This came by special courier to me, and I thought you'd want to know immediately."

He pushed an official-looking letter across the desk to Susan, and she glanced down at it. Her heart did a double somersault as she read the contents.

"I thought you'd be hanging from the rafters after reading that," Brian said as he gave Susan a curious look. "I suppose you figured they'd pass you over after that exposé last year."

Susan was digesting the information in the letter. It was a chance she couldn't refuse, and she wouldn't, but the timing sucked. "I'm astonished, I guess."

Brian's eyebrows met in the middle at her remark. "You deserve the break, and I know you'll do us proud. You need to be at the Air Force base by midnight."

Susan shook her head. "Damn, they don't give much notice, do they?"

Brian frowned. "What do you expect from the armed forces? You should know better."

Susan shrugged. *Thank god I decided to go through the security clearance formalities when I put my name forward last year.*

Brian didn't wait for Susan to answer. "Have you finished the Hirste story?"

"No," she blurted out harshly.

The explosive tone of Susan's voice had both of them surprised.

"Right then. Well, you can pass it over to your assistant. I'm sure Deidre will do it justice," he said matter-of-factly.

Susan frowned. She didn't want to pass it over. If she did, her tenuous link with Jenny might be lost forever. "There's more to the original story, and I'd like the chance to complete it when I get back."

Brian gave her a hard look. "That's three months down the line, and you might never come back."

Susan eyed the man and let a devilish grin curve her lips. "You can't get rid of me that easily. Are you expecting someone will shoot me down so you can have a humdinger of a headline story?"

Brian pushed his chair from the desk and stood, considering her words. "That's a darn fool thing to say and you know it. Okay, I'll hold you to the story. After all, it would be good for business if you suddenly become famous, and I still owned your ass." He grinned in satisfaction and held out his hand.

Startled at the gesture, Susan shook it. "What's that for?"

Brian gave a rare smile. "It's not often the *Daily Post* in Merit has a reporter chosen to do a series of articles in Afghanistan embedded with the troops. I'm proud of you."

"Thanks, but I'm coming back, therefore I can't see how that will change anything. There are a lot of good reporters there already."

"I'm sure there are, but you're a very talented young woman." Brian gave her a long hard look. "We'll see who's right." Brian sat back down. "On your way now, Stark…I'm sure you have plenty to do before you leave tonight."

Susan walked out of the building in a daze. For years, she'd dreamed of a plum assignment, particularly in current affairs. When she lived in D.C. and Leigh was part of her life, she had been close to joining a national newspaper. But Leigh and her best friend's betrayal had spun her out of control, and with that, her aspiring career.

Her father had contacted Brian and made her see that leaving town and picking up the pieces was good for her. He told her that when the time was right, she'd get the break she needed to be a nationally known reporter.

Right now, it looked like she was heading for the one place that would make or break her provincial dreams of going national—Afghanistan. The timing, however, couldn't have been worse. "Crap, Jenny is going to think I used her for a one-night stand."

As she climbed into her vehicle to head home to shower and change, she sighed. "How am I going to convince Jenny that I don't have a love-them-and-leave-them policy?"

Chapter 14

Andrea carefully combed her hair, applied a thin layer of ruby red gloss to her lips, and made an effort to look presentable. Her goal was twofold. First, the team needed to go over the details of their early morning hours at the cemetery, and she had some interesting aspects to tell them about. Secondly, she hoped to secure a date with Jenny. The only fly in the ointment she saw to her second objective was Susan Stark. Stark appeared to have a knack of always being part of every conversation she'd had with Jenny. Although, with luck, she hoped that Leigh, whom she'd persuaded to join them, would whisk Stark away for a friendly get-together since they appeared to have known each other in the past.

She glanced at the clock and saw it was two. That meant another hour to kill, and she knew how to do that. Her finger pressed the switch to turn on her computer so she could assess the strange results from earlier that morning once more.

Seeing Susan in the cemetery the night before had shocked Leigh Chambers. She closed her eyes and saw the look of surprise, then distaste on her ex-lover's face. A part of her understood the reason while another wished it hadn't happened. Staring into the bathroom cabinet mirror, she assessed her assets or at least those that were visible that had once been a source of attraction for Susan. Susan had always told her that she loved the way her face would glow whenever they made love and her smile would lighten any bad day she had. However, that was in the past, and she'd been the perpetrator of their relationship ending.

Even after five years, she wondered why she'd been such a fool. One always assumes the grass is greener on the other side and she'd sampled the offerings. They hadn't lived up to expectations. When she'd realized that fact three months after leaving Susan for Van, it was too late. Susan had gone. Since then, she'd worked hard to attain a credible reputation in her own field. The lucky break that brought her to Merit University had a bonus—Susan. Andrea persuaded her to attend the meeting that afternoon, which was her chance to talk to Susan. She'd do her level best to achieve that.

Lorna was solicitous to the family that had arrived for the barbecue that her parents had arranged. With little money to spare, inviting the vast numbers of the family in the area had been a sacrifice for them. However, they wanted her to feel that she was home and the years of her incarceration were over. As far as she was concerned, they were in the past. Now she had people—no, friends—willing to give up time and energy to solve the dilemma that she had fought alone for over twenty years.

Looking over their small lawn strewn with people, she barely recognized who they were. She wondered what Andy had deduced from the events of the early hours of the morning. One thing she knew for sure—sparks were going to fly, and it had nothing to do with the electromagnetic field or her.

It had everything to do with the unexpected meeting between Susan and Leigh. If looks could kill, Susan would have ended up with a jail term. Jenny had even broken that poker face of hers and looked confused. Then there was Andy, who obviously had a crush on Jenny, making the whole situation mind-boggling. *I must be the only one who isn't having any chemistry with anyone but ghosts.* Lorna chuckled at the thought, then dwelt on the relationship between Jenny and Susan, both of whom she liked. From the first time she'd been in the presence of Jenny and Susan together, she'd seen the embers ignite between them, and Leigh arriving on the scene could mean only one thing in her mind—trouble.

The fountain in the university courtyard called Jenny's name. In the recesses of her mind, she'd hoped that Stark would call and offer to give her a lift, but there had been no contact at all. Not even a phone apology for leaving as she had. In a way, that told its own story and the basic note that Stark had left that morning had been the foundation. Stark didn't want a relationship. Stark just accepted what had been offered on a plate—a one-night stand.

Jenny was mortified that she'd been the person who did much of the seducing. She blamed it on the adrenaline rush of fear and a perverse annoyance that the Asian beauty Leigh Chambers had meant something important to Stark at one time. However, there was no point in dwelling on that. It happened and it had nothing to do with her. After all, her liaison with Stark had only been lust—*right*? She hadn't quite convinced herself on that front.

The bus stop where she'd disembarked was only a stone's throw from the cafeteria where she ordered a coffee. A few minutes later, she sat at a table that faced the fountain. Sunday, as she found out the last time she was here, was a popular day on campus as numerous students of all ages milled around the area. Stirring the sugar into her coffee, she looked up in surprise as she heard someone say her name.

"Nice to see you again, Leigh." Inside she wasn't so sure that was the truth.

Leigh smiled. "Hi, Jenny, do you mind if I join you?" Not waiting for a response, she sat down.

"Go for it."

Leigh sat staring directly at Jenny and looked slightly embarrassed when Jenny caught her gaze. "Have you known Susan long?"

Jenny felt her stomach clench at the question. "Not that long…a few weeks. She's working on a story about Lorna. How long have you known her?"

Leigh had a faraway look in her eyes. "Sometimes I feel it's forever. We met eight years ago. She was covering a beauty pageant for a local newspaper."

"You were in the pageant?" Jenny knew the answer for the woman was strikingly beautiful. Then her bitchy inner persona spoke. *Her looks are superficial and unappealing except from an aesthetic point of view.* However, the hardest pill to swallow was that, in the beauty stakes, she was no match for Leigh.

The pretty smile beamed across the table as Leigh breathlessly said, "Yes, I came in second, but not according to Susan."

"Oh, I see. That's when you became friends, right?" Jenny knew she was only inviting pain in knowing more about Leigh and Stark. However, she couldn't help herself. Her mind was taunting her that the more she knew about Stark and her womanizing ways, the better she'd feel about what happened between them.

"Yeah, that was the beginning. Susan doesn't take no for an answer, and I was glad of that." Once more, Leigh seemed to drift off into her memories.

Summoning her inner calm, Jenny retorted, "Yeah, she does have an insistent streak. Look at the time. I think we should go and see Andy, don't you? I assume you're coming."

Leigh grinned. "Oh, yeah. I got a royal summons from Andy who, if you didn't already know, has the hots for you. Andy is lovely. She has kind of old-fashioned values about love and all that stuff. If she makes a play for you, please be gentle with her feelings."

Jenny wasn't a fool. She knew Andy was sweet on her. The only problem with that was that Andy wasn't her type. No, she was damn fool enough to like them irritating and entirely opposite to her own personality—Stark. *And look where that went—absolutely nowhere.* "I've never been intentionally cruel to anyone in my life, what about you?"

The scraping back of the chairs and a few people moving towards them to take the table ended the conversation. They walked in silence towards the building and Andy's office.

Susan had driven like a bat out of hell across town to surprise Jenny and pick her up. She hoped they could have a chat before the meeting, but Jenny had already left. Now she sat alone in her Jeep next to the building where they were to meet with her thoughts in disarray. She wondered if what was happening to her now was how it felt to fall into fate. Maybe she'd been duped by Andy's theories. Her dreams of a relationship with Jenny and the old nightmare of Leigh colliding head-on in the same twenty-four hours must have had the fates laughing big-time. The question for her to answer was what to do next. Whatever she did, it wasn't going to be easy. Her relationship with Jenny at best teetered on primitive attraction and needed work. Leigh was someone she hadn't wanted to see again in her lifetime, yet here she was.

Leigh hadn't changed much; she was still as beautiful as the day they'd met. The only thing she knew was going to happen was that in a few hours she'd be on a carrier taking her to a classified location for briefing prior to moving to the war zone.

The call to her parents when she'd arrived home after seeing Brian had been bittersweet. Her dad was over the moon, but her mom had reservations. Her mom would never say outright she thought it a bad idea. She'd spent the best part of thirty-five years with a man who had lived in the frontline most of his career. When she arrived back in the States, the first place she'd go would be to her parents' home to ensure her mother she was in one piece. The second would be to Jenny, even if her heart would be stomping all over her mind to change that around.

Looking up, she saw two figures making their way towards the door of the building and sighed heavily. *Jenny and Leigh together...how ironic is that.* She closed her eyes and shook her head. *I can only imagine what Leigh has told Jenny about our relationship and me.* Contemplating her next move, she waited until they'd gone inside, then climbed out of the vehicle and marched inside with determination.

Jenny shook her head, then looked at Andrea with an incredulous look in her eyes. "What exactly are you saying?"

Andrea smiled warmly. "Let me show you." She clicked on the mouse, and moments later, the video footage from the night before came on the screen.

Jenny watched but didn't see anything out of the ordinary, at least not to her.

As the young men approached, the EMF counter went awry. "Watch carefully, Jenny, watch."

Jenny scratched her head. She didn't see anything. What she saw was what she suspected was the diffused light from street lights. Then her mind wandered completely off track as Stark reached over her shoulder and pointed to various glowing lights. Stark's light perfume and the touch of her skin on her arm sent a thrill through her body. Since Stark's arrival, she didn't dare look Stark fully in the eyes. She was such an emotional coward.

"There, Jenny," Susan said.

Muttering, "Thanks," Jenny concentrated on the screen. "Surely, that's just a filtering of the lamp light from the trees."

When what she considered a light show was over, Jenny shook her head. "Is that it?"

"No," Leigh interrupted. "Listen carefully until it ends with your scream."

Embarrassed at that reminder, Jenny cast a hard stare in Leigh's direction. In the background, there was a tune with a bell-like quality. Jenny frowned. *Is that a voice?* "I don't remember any of us having a radio."

Andrea nodded. "Quite right. No one did, and as far as we know, those boys didn't, either."

"Ah, but you can't be certain, can you?" Susan asked.

"No, we can't, Susan, but these results are really interesting. I'm going to ask Lorna to come back and do more trials and tests." Andrea looked at the image of Lorna as she stood with an aura of orbs over her head. Andy's voice filled with awe as her eyes widened. "Doesn't she look just wonderful?"

Reasoning that Lorna had been through enough tests in her life, Jenny wasn't sure it was a good idea to involve the woman again. "I think you should ask her, but please don't push her. She's had a tough couple of decades."

Andrea smiled understandingly. "I'm aware of her past… Lorna told me. I promise to be gentle with her sensibilities."

"I guess that's it then," Susan said. "Good to see you, Doctor. I hope when you do all your tests and have the results, you'll give me first option on any breaking story."

She held out her hand and Andy shook it.

"Oh, I could show you more footage, and I thought maybe we could all get together over coffee and have a discussion." Andrea looked directly at Jenny rather than Susan.

"I'm afraid I can't make it. I need to be on another story early this evening." Susan glanced at her large wristwatch.

Andrea beamed at the news. "Right, I understand, but you should know that it could be quite some time before I have anything concrete."

"That's okay…I'll wait." Susan nodded briefly to Leigh and Jenny, who had finally looked in her direction when they heard she was leaving.

Susan moved towards the door, and Jenny moved to leave, as well.

"Jenny, would you kindly stay a few minutes? I have something I want to discuss with you," Andrea asked hesitantly.

Leigh rapidly collected her belongings and headed for the door. "I'll see you later, Andy. Jenny, good to see you again." Leigh rushed out of the room.

Jenny blew out a breath, and the hair on her forehead moved slightly. She wanted to speak with Stark even if it was to do what she seemed to do well—spar. However, she said, "Yes, what can I do for you?"

"Susan, please for old time's sake? Won't you at least let me explain? Can we go have dinner?" Leigh pleaded as she held on to Susan's arm.

A cold expression consumed Susan's face. "What can you possibly say to me that hasn't been said already? Didn't the fact that you left me for my best friend spell it out to me? Incidentally, how long did it last with Van? A week, a month or two maybe?"

Leigh paused before answering. "You knew it wouldn't last? Why didn't you try and stop me?"

"Are you blaming me for your infidelity?" Susan looked at the tiny hand attempting to stop her from leaving. It had happened with Jenny once, but this time, the touch couldn't stop her. With Jenny, she hadn't wanted to move away. She craved the warm contact. However, with Leigh, she violently shook it off.

"It's her, isn't it? No, don't say it 'cause I already know by the way you look at her. You once looked at me that way. I accept that I broke your heart and…" Leigh's voice rose with emotion.

Susan held up her hand. "Hold it. For the record, you didn't break my heart. If you had, I wouldn't have been capable of falling in love as I have. You dented my pride, that was all." Susan realized what she'd said and a happy jolt coursed through her veins.

Leigh's expression changed several times from shock, surprise, and finally resignation. "Okay, I'm sorry. I guess that's all I really wanted to say to you in person."

Susan felt the glow of her feelings for Jenny resonate in every part of her body, and she felt pity for Leigh. She realized that part of her life was over forever, and she'd come up from the dark into a world that held the promise of something better—Jenny.

The door to Andy's office opened and Jenny walked out. She rushed by with a "sorry for interrupting."

Leigh glanced at Susan's crestfallen expression. "You'd better go after her, Susan. Misunderstandings can be the devil to sort out later."

For once, Leigh said something Susan could agree with. "You and I will have that talk one day. Maybe we'll get together when we're both old and grey with nothing but the better memories to share." Susan nodded and walked quickly towards the still swinging outside door.

Jenny felt tears forming and dashed a hand across her eyes to wipe them off. "I will not cry for you, Stark. I will not." Her legs moved rapidly towards the café where she knew there would be a bus stop.

Footsteps seemed to be getting louder behind her and Jenny was sure someone was running, but there was no way she'd turn around. The chat with Andy, who professed her feelings for Jenny, had been hard. The poor woman was besotted with her, and letting her down easy was difficult. However, in a nice and caring way, she'd made it clear that there could never be anything between them. She explained that she was already in a relationship. In part, she was right. Stark had taken over her inwardly. It was only outwardly that they didn't quite have balance.

The closeness she saw between Stark and Leigh closed the lid on that possibility. She knew that old loves had a habit of sneaking up and shredding the tender progression of a new one. *Who the hell am I kidding? I'm not the love of Stark's life. I'm just another notch on her bedpost. End of story.*

"Jenny, wait up."

Jenny closed her eyes and breathed deeply but kept going until a hand dropped onto her shoulder and Stark stopped her in her tracks. "Jenny, didn't you hear me? I asked you to wait."

With a determined jut of her chin, Jenny looked at Stark with an expression devoid of emotion. "What do you want?"

"I wondered if you and I could have a coffee now and talk about what happened between us."

Jenny's nostrils flared. "Why bother? I can see you've been smitten again by Leigh. She is rather beautiful in an exotic way. I'm sure she'll willingly go to bed with you if you ask."

"Is that what you think of me? You really think that I'm that shallow? Do you think that I can go from your bed to Leigh's or anyone else?" Susan frowned.

"Yeah, as a matter of fact, I do. For the record, it wasn't a bed but a couch. Is that it?" Jenny said dryly. She folded her arms to calm her nerves and stop her base instinct to impulsively put her hands around Stark's neck and kiss her. She looked directly at Stark. When she saw the devastated look on Stark's face, she wondered if she'd made another dire assumption.

Susan ran her tongue briefly over her dry lips and nodded before moving away, allowing Jenny space. "I'll say goodbye then."

With her arms still folded across her chest, Jenny glared at Stark. "That's it?"

Blinking in confusion, Susan drew a breath. "I thought that was what you wanted."

"What kind of journalist are you, to give up at the first hurdle?"

"Obviously not a very good one. Will you allow me to explain?"

Jenny frowned. "I'll take you up on that offer of coffee."

There was a distinct lightening of Stark's features as she smiled. To Jenny, the tiny twist of Stark's lips was a very private smile that was easily missed if you weren't looking.

"Thank you."

"Hey, don't thank me yet. You're not off the hook until you explain exactly why you left, leaving me only with that horrible note." Jenny glanced around, sure Stark's Jeep would be parked somewhere close.

"Do you want to go to the coffee shop here or…?"

Jenny shook her head. "Nope, not here. Let's go somewhere neutral. I know a place, Kincaid's on Fifth Street. We'll have to go in your car."

Susan nodded eagerly. "Kincaid's it is. The car is over there." She pointed to the Jeep parked a hundred feet away.

Kincaid's wasn't a café as such but more a bar with a continental feel about it.

Susan elected to draw up a chair beside one of the tables outside the establishment and waited for Jenny to sit, which she duly did.

"Thanks, they don't wait outside."

Susan grinned. "I know. Believe it or not, I live two blocks away, and I come here often." At Jenny's raised eyebrows, she qualified her statement. "When I have any free time, that is. My work doesn't allow that very often."

Jenny chuckled as her lips curled into a smile.

"I'm rambling, aren't I?"

"Yes, but that's okay."

Susan shook her head and gave Jenny an apologetic expression. "What can I get you?"

Jenny glanced at her watch. "Will you give me a lift home?"

"Absolutely," Susan said immediately. Then she chastised herself internally. *What if Jenny wants to stay until it closes? I'll cross that bridge if it happens*. "What can I get you?"

"It's Sunday, a beautiful late afternoon and, if you don't think it too decadent of me, I'll have wine."

"Pierpont Shiraz, right?" Susan interjected.

Jenny gave Susan an all-encompassing stare, then shook her head. "No, I think a chardonnay suits my mood right now."

"Okay, any particular winery?" Susan gave the menu a cursory glance. "It's almost five and I don't know about you, but I haven't had much to eat. Want to join me in an early supper?"

Jenny glanced at the menu, then to Susan. "The snacks do look appetizing…sure, I'll leave it up to you to order, and that goes for the drink, too."

Susan felt her heart do a double flip as she gazed into Jenny's face. In her last few hours of being in a safe environment rather than a potentially lethal location like Afghanistan, she couldn't have asked for anything better than this moment. "I'll be right back."

Five minutes later, Susan placed the glass of wine on the table along with her light beer and drew up a chair opposite Jenny. With a bright smile, she said, "I've ordered the seafood platter for two, then followed it up with a hamburger and fries."

Jenny's eyes bulged. "I thought you just wanted a snack, not dinner. I can't remember the last time I had a hamburger."

Susan grinned as she drank the cold beverage. "Then you'll remember this time was with me."

"That's true." Jenny sipped her wine and her eyes flew open incredulously. "This is my favorite…how did you know?"

Susan tapped her nose. "Good guess. No, actually, the bartender seems to know you."

Jenny blushed and peered towards the large window that gave her a view of the bar. "Marco, yeah, he would remember."

"So do you come here often? I've never seen you here," Susan asked, speculating that there was more to the blush than the bartender knowing her preference for wine.

Jenny snorted. "Not often…at least not now…I suppose on reflection I did once."

Susan took another sip of her beer and narrowed her eyes. "Would that once have anything to do with the reason you had more than one VIP pass to the nightclub?"

There was silence for a few moments, then Jenny nodded. "Could be. Sheila, my ex, loved the nightlife. However, this isn't about my past, is it? This is about you and me. Didn't you mention something about an explanation?"

Suitably warned that the topic was off-limits, Susan flexed her fingers, then threaded them together. "I had a call from my boss about a story."

Jenny double blinked. "A story! Oh, don't tell me last night was all about a story including me as the icing on the cake, to titillate your readers."

Susan saw Jenny moving her chair about to get up and placed the full weight of her hand on Jenny's before she could leave. "No, no, it wasn't about a story or you! Jenny, I have an obligation to the newspaper that sends me at the drop of a hat to a story. I can't control it or when it happens, but I have to go."

Jenny stopped moving and stared hard at Susan.

"I'm sorry, if you thought, think, I could do a thing like that. I wouldn't."

"You're sorry, so that makes it all right. Look, my first reaction was to cut and leave earlier. I was an idiot to think that you and I could ever..."

Susan clung onto the fact that Jenny didn't complete the sentence. Her hand that still held Jenny's began to move in a caressing motion. "You are not an idiot," Susan said with a quirky smile. "Hell, you could probably wipe the floor with me intellectually."

Jenny shook her head with her lips pursed in what looked like irritation.

Before either of them could say any more, the seafood platter arrived.

A few minutes later, the food sitting between them looked delectable.

"Let's eat this, and if we can't hit a happy medium after we've finished, I'll take you home. No more questions. How does that sound?"

Jenny didn't say anything, but her actions answered for her as she picked up her fork and speared a battered prawn. She pointed her fork threateningly. "The story you left my bed…couch…for better be good."

Susan swallowed hard. She knew that where she was going was on a need-to-know basis, and that only included her immediate family. She crossed her fingers that she could come up with a creative way of telling Jenny where she was going without actually saying it.

"Let's eat and talk afterwards, deal?"

"Deal."

Susan regaled Jenny with some amusing anecdotes about her early days as a *journalist*. She was skeptical about that term for the first year of her professional career. She was mostly sent on assignment for absurd stories regarding UFO sightings, animals that could do exceptional tricks, and kids' pageants.

"Leigh told me you met her at a pageant." Jenny eyed Stark. "You must have progressed from kids to the next generation."

Susan felt her anger begin again at the mention of Leigh but managed to keep a lid on it. In a clipped fashion, she said, "Leigh isn't on the subject list."

Jenny's left eyebrow shot up as she chewed on the last prawn smothered with sauce. Susan reached out instinctively with her napkin and removed the trail of pink fluid from Jenny's chin. "Thanks."

"You're welcome." Susan looked at the empty plate with satisfaction. She was certain that she wouldn't have this kind of food on her next assignment.

"Leigh is part of the subject, though, isn't she? Wasn't that the real reason you fled my house so early? Leaving that note was cruel. You could have woken me if it was as simple as a call from work." Jenny's voice had dropped to an accusing level.

Closing her eyes briefly, Susan summoned her inner karma. "No, she wasn't the reason. Leigh and I were finished the day she walked out on me for my best friend. I don't do those kinds of second chances. You briefly saw my boss in the office when you were there. He has the temperament of a bull at full charge if he's in that frame of mind." Dragging out her cell from her pocket, she deftly retrieved the text message screen and passed the phone over to Jenny. "Check the times and the messages. I've never lied to you."

Jenny held the phone but didn't look at the messages. Instead, she gave the instrument back to Susan. "I believe you."

Those three words had Susan's body give one of the biggest sighs of relief she'd ever felt in her life. "Thank you, that means a lot to me."

"I might believe you, but what happens now? Exactly what was last night…this morning…whatever…all about?"

Susan mulled that question over. She knew how she wanted to answer it, but as she'd earlier realized, the timing sucked. She cleared her throat while mentally attempting to come up with a way not to make Jenny regret her last words and shot a look at their respective drinks. "How about I order us a refill first?"

Jenny nodded, her face like a taut mask as her fingers ran a tempo over her almost empty glass. "I'll have the same again."

Susan left and returned almost immediately. "Marco said he'd send out the drinks." With a wry smile, she flippantly said, "You must have come here often."

"I told you I did once. It seems like a lifetime ago now and yet…about us."

Susan allowed a tender expression to cross her face for a second, then she gave Jenny an intense stare. "I'm going out of town for three months. I will not be able to communicate very often if at all. It's an opportunity that doesn't arise for a journalist on a provincial newspaper usually, and I can't turn it down." Susan took the opportunity to watch every facet of Jenny's expression and wished she hadn't. Jenny's words confirmed her worse fears.

"Three months! Oh, why did I even think you could handle a relationship? I must be crazy. Leigh is welcome to you. I, for the record, don't want to see you again, and if I do, it better not be in speaking distance." Jenny stood, and the chair made a scraping noise on the mosaic-tiled floor.

Susan stood, too, and shot out her hand, which latched on Jenny's arm. "Please don't go, Jenny, not like this."

"Why not? I'm obviously exactly what I thought I was this morning—another notch on your bedpost."

Jenny's angry expression and explosive words seemed to reverberate around them. Thankfully, no one else was outside to hear.

"You asked me what last night was all about. It was about finding someone that might mean something very important in my life, and I want to explore that relationship properly when I get back." Susan drew in a breath and waited. If Jenny were adamant on leaving, she would have to respect that. Hate it but she'd respect it.

Jenny shrugged off Susan's hand and glared at her. "Exactly where could you possibly go on the planet that doesn't have communication? Outer space? The moon?"

Susan felt a smile begin to form as she looked down at the table they were standing over and made a decision. "There is one other place, actually a few of them, unfortunately."

Jenny gave Susan an astonished shake of the head. "Okay, educate me. Where?"

"Afghanistan." *One security rule broken and I haven't even left yet.*

Susan didn't expect the next reaction. It was almost as if she'd thrown a heavy body blow at Jenny. Jenny's petite frame doubled in two, and she held on to the back of her chair. A few seconds later, she drew it out and sat down.

"Are you okay? You look pale." Susan took her cue from Jenny and resumed her seat.

Neither women spoke as their drinks arrived.

"I need that drink," Jenny announced and in seconds had consumed almost half of the contents.

"Drinking like that will make you drunk, but if you want to drink like that, it's fine with me," Susan qualified, not wanting to irritate Jenny any more than she had.

"Afghanistan…you're really going there. Why?"

Susan chuckled. "I'm a journalist. It's what I do—report the news from around the globe."

Jenny's expression looked unsure. "Yeah, that's true, but usually the national reporters do that sort of thing. A local paper like the *Daily Post* doesn't exactly cover those criteria."

Unsure what to say next, Susan sipped her light beer. "They must think I'm good at what I do. I was asked to do a series of articles on the troops there."

Jenny gazed into Susan's eyes. "When you say *they,* you mean the government, not your bosses?"

Embarrassed, Susan shrugged. "Something along those lines." Then she felt a small hand clasp hers on the table.

"Do you have to go? It's dangerous."

It was an earnest question from Jenny, which bordered on being a plea, and that made Susan sigh inwardly. "If the tables were turned and you had to do something that was equally difficult, wouldn't you go?"

There was silence for a few moments, then Jenny said, "I'd like to say I'd consider a less dangerous path, but no, right now as our relationship stands, I'd go, too."

Susan nodded. "When I come back, do you think there's a chance that you might go on a proper date with me?"

Jenny cast her gaze away from her drink to look directly at Susan. "When you come back, I'll be waiting."

Susan beamed, then their hamburgers arrived.

"Unless I die of cholesterol indulgence after this," Jenny said drolly.

"Never going to happen. Thank you for waiting." Susan poured ketchup on her burger.

Jenny's stare never wavered. "Come back in one piece, Stark, that's all I ask. Oh, I'll expect a decent meal at a swanky restaurant on our first official date."

Susan was delighted at the way the day was turning out. She winked and said, "Deal," just before she took a giant bite of her hamburger.

Chapter 15

Susan lay in the hammock-style bed in a canvas tent that she shared with three other people. There were the basics of life in the tent. They each had a bed, one table, folding chair, portable canvas locker, and the odd picture of home. She'd spent the last twelve weeks there in the outer regions of the mostly desert base camp. Soldiers were around 24/7, and she'd seen her fair share of pretty much everything. The laughter of camaraderie, the tears of pain, anguish of loss, desperation of fear, and the most significant emotions—pride and strength inwardly and outwardly of those who served. This wasn't a walk in the park for the soldiers who were thousands of miles from home. It was a place where the men and women exposed their lives to assassins and suicide bombers for the sake of their country and fellow man.

Susan understood to a greater degree the reasoning behind some wars and knew that in the end, it came down to one thing—politics. Nevertheless, that didn't take away from the courage of people who fought for what they believed in and for what their uniforms represented. True, some called soldiers sheep that followed orders without thought to what might happen or to whom, but these men and women didn't start the wars. They were merely pieces in a chess game that moved to strategic positions and did what they had to do in the name of their country. Her goal in what she wrote hadn't been political. It was factual about the men and women who had lived and died there while serving their country.

A stocky figure loomed in the tent doorway, covered from head to toe in military gear with barely an inch of skin exposed.

"Stark, time to go. Don't forget the body armor. I'll see you at the bus in five." Then the figure was gone.

Susan shook her head, smiled, then stood, giving a belated salute. "Yes, ma'am." She collected her digital voice recorder and slipped it into the pocket of her jacket. With a rueful smile, she looked at the body armor in the corner of her personal space in the tent and recalled arriving at the camp for the first time…

"Well, as I live and breathe, the general's daughter."

A familiar sarcastic voice seemed to echo around Susan as she hopped off the helicopter that transported her to the remote troop site. Her gaze glued to the stocky woman who stood before her. "It's good to see you, too, Cathy."

Major Cathy James gave Susan an assessing look, then beamed a smile. Seconds later, she hugged her tight. "Good to see you, Stark, it's been a while."

Susan hugged the much smaller woman back, feeling the hard muscles in her back. Cathy had always been built like a war horse. "Yeah, it has. Let me see…it's been five years since you worked for my dad."

They pulled apart and gave each other a look.

"Hmm, I think that's close. Orders came down and they dispatched me to the war zone shortly after you left D.C. How is the old goat?"

"He's the same as always. He can't understand why they don't give him a posting here or in Iraq. You know Dad, he gets itchy feet when he's in an office." Not long after that, Susan collected her belongings, and ten minutes later, Cathy escorted her to the tent she was to share.

Cathy pointed to a spot. "We have a couple of photographers here and someone from the BBC. I'm sure you'll all get acquainted at some point. That's your bed over there and a locker for your stuff."

Susan felt that reality was taking hold as she looked at the meager amount of personal space she had. *This is going to be interesting.* "When do I go out for the story?"

Cathy shook her head. "Patience never was a strong point

with you, was it? Take today and check things out around here first. I'll have one of my men assigned to you, and he'll show you what you need to know for your safety while you're here. Then tomorrow, I'll personally take you on your first tour. Now I have to go. See you tomorrow and remember one thing— always wear the body armor when you go out."

Susan frowned at the heavy jacket and peripherals. "I'll roast with all that on."

Cathy grinned. "Better to roast a little and live than to be cold on a slab. Good to see you again, Stark. It's nice to have a familiar face around. Sorry, but I gotta run."

Susan sat on the allocated bed, groaning at the slight swing. She hated hammocks. As she placed her bag on the end of the bed, she smiled. "At least I don't feel so alone. Dad must have known Cathy was here. I wonder why he didn't tell me. I'll have to write him and ask."

She opened her bag, and the first thing that came out was the blanket her mother had made for her. Hugging it to her, she smiled. It was a link with home. At some stage, she was going to need it, having heard that the nights could be cold in the desert. Then her thoughts traveled to whom she left behind in Merit. "I wonder what you're doing right now, Jenny. Do you miss me as much as I do you already?"

Susan brought her thoughts back to the present and the body armor she began to strap on. As she picked up her pack, she collected a letter she needed to mail. She ran to the tent that housed the postal and communications personnel and handed them the envelope. Above the roar of three helicopters hovering nearby, she asked, "When will it go out?"

"Tomorrow, ma'am," a young soldier said.

Moments later, she was running as fast as her long legs would take to a waiting armored transport.

The normal banter around her slid in and out of Susan's mind as she sat in the armored vehicle that was ferrying them to their destination. She enjoyed the mild ribbing and laughter that each sortie brought with it until the harsh reality of where they were going and what would happen next came upon them. Then her gaze caught Cathy's, and she smiled slightly.

Cathy moved to sit alongside her, shifting her weapons to get more comfortable. "This is it, isn't it…your last foray into a battle zone. I bet you'll be glad to go home to that nice bed and no flying objects."

Susan smiled warmly at her. When they first met, Cathy had been her father's aide, a lowly first lieutenant working through the system. Now she was a major in command of her own platoon. She was the epitome of a disciplined warrior. "Oh, I don't know, there are plenty of flying objects back home. They're just not so deadly all the time."

Cathy, ever watchful of what was happening around them, nodded in understanding. "You'd best tell the general that I might want my job back real soon. It's time for a rest."

Susan heard an almost wishful thinking in the words, and she understood them for what they were—a tentative hold on a reality away from war. "He'd be happy to have you back." She reached out and touched Cathy's hand. "Thank you."

"For what? From the stuff I've read, we should be thanking you." Cathy's gaze shifted to the other members of the squad and shouted barely audible over the noise of the vehicle, "Isn't that right, guys?"

They either agreed or saluted Susan before resuming their own chatter.

"I couldn't have done it without you and you know it," Susan said as she felt the transport slowing down.

"Let's table that conversation for dinner this evening. We shouldn't be stopping."

Cathy moved to the front of the vehicle to consult with the driver.

The next few minutes were a whirl of intense activity, none of it good. Susan heard rapid gunfire and Cathy shouting commands. Seconds later, she found herself flying out of the vehicle as a mortar bomb exploded on the transport. Shards of metal bounced everywhere, pinging off other metal, scorching the ground as it fell. Then she heard the sounds of more gunfire. The scene became a waking nightmare for Susan as she heard screams of pain intermingling with the weapon fire and shouts in several languages. On what had been an innocuous stretch of peaceful road moments before, all hell was breaking loose. Susan glanced around her for any sign of a safe retreat and saw a partial brick wall and crawled towards it before ducking behind it for as much security as it could offer. The gunfire receded, creating a vacuum of eerie calm. Susan shook from head to foot; she couldn't help it. No training in the world could have stopped the feeling of inadequacy and helplessness with an overriding fear of the possibility of impending death. She wasn't a soldier.

A voice she didn't recognize, which spoke English, came from a position some yards in front of her. "Incoming!"

The sky lit up as mortar bombs blasted their location, and the wall next to her shook at the impact. A split second later, she felt rather than saw something slamming against her chest. Her world went black.

"Mom?"

"Hey, baby, how are you feeling? Want me to get you a doctor? David, come quickly, she's awake."

Susan groggily heard the words her mother spoke but wasn't entirely sure what to make of them. "Where am I?"

Susan's father hovered at the bottom of her bed. "You're in the Walter Reed Medical Center. Do you recall what happened to you?" David Stark's voice sounded gruff.

Susan pondered the question. She tried to move, but a shaft of pain spread from the small of her back to her shoulders. She let out a squeal more out of surprise than actual pain. Instead, panic began to surface as she cried out, "I can't move, what's wrong with me?"

Sheryl Stark moved to sit gently on the side of the bed, mindful not to disturb any of the contraptions that supported her daughter. "It's okay, honey, you hurt your back. A wall fell on you. They've kept you sedated for the journey home until they could make you more comfortable."

"You call this comfortable?"

David threw his head back in a deep roar of laughter. "That's my spunky girl. I'll fetch the doctor."

"Mom, you'd tell me the truth, wouldn't you? This isn't permanent, is it?" Susan allowed her mind to focus on her surroundings, not the least of which were the restraints holding her in place.

Sheryl shook her head. "Darling, I promise you that it's temporary. You injured your spine, and they want to operate once you're lucid."

Susan reached out and clutched her mother's hand. "What kind of operation? How long will I be like this?" Fear began to filter through to Susan's voice as it rose in reaction.

Sheryl's eyes filled with tears as she bent and kissed Susan's sweat-soaked hair. "A few months. They say if everything goes well with surgery, you'll be up and running around as if nothing happened in six months, tops."

"You make me sound like a baby," Susan said before she tremulously asked, "And if it doesn't work?"

"What kind of question is that?" David asked as he stood in the doorway.

A woman in a white coat had preceded Susan's father into the room and stood at the opposite side of her mother. "Good to see you awake, Susan. I'm Dr. Carey Lewis. I'm the consultant responsible for your recovery, and we have a superb track record with your type of injury."

Susan turned her attention to the woman. The doctor was about five-six with a pale complexion and intense blue eyes that seemed to bore into Susan. Her mousy hair in a short wavy style complemented her oval face.

The doctor checked Susan's pulse, then motioned for a nurse who now hovered at the bottom of the bed. "Ruth is your case worker here. If you need anything or have any worries, she'll take care of it or let me know. I've scheduled your surgery for six thirty tomorrow morning. It should take about three hours." She turned to the nurse. "Make a notation to have Susan prepared and call hematology. I want the blood work on my desk in an hour." She looked at Susan and smiled before she patted her leg. "I'll see you soon." The doctor gave her parents a reassuring look and left the room.

Ruth, a plump woman with a ready smile, grinned at Susan and gave a meaningful look towards her parents. "I'll be back in five."

Sheryl sucked in a breath and her hand tightened on Susan's that she hadn't relinquished when the others came into the room. "I guess that's our cue to check out the cafeteria here."

David moved towards the bed and peered down at his daughter. "Told you everything was going to be just fine. We'll be back to sit with you when the nurse has done her job." He bent almost double to reach her forehead and kissed it tenderly.

Susan was in shock. Everything was happening far too fast. *Why is that?* She was about to ask but saw the unshed tears in her mother's eyes and decided against it. She'd given them a hell of a shock by being here in the first place. "I'll be just fine like Dad said, Mom." Her words sounded braver than she felt. Right now, she'd rather have her mom's arms around her and not be here at all.

Sheryl finally allowed their clasped hands to disengage and she nodded. "I know you will." She kissed the pale cheek closest to her and whispered, "You'll always be my baby. Never forget that."

Tears of emotion shimmered in Susan's eyes as she looked at her parents. "Go check out the facilities and let's get this show on the road."

"You heard our daughter, Sheryl. Come on, there must be more than plastic food on offer. I could eat a burger."

"David, you will not have a burger. They are so bad for you. See you soon, darling." They headed out the door with a wave.

Susan allowed the tears to fall, and it wasn't because of her state of health but one word that had triggered the final floodgates to open—burger.

There is no way you're going to see me like this, Jenny. I don't want your pity. I want your love, and the only way I can be sure is if I'm fully able to court you, as you deserve. I know you're going to understand...I have to believe it. Her thoughts evaporated as a hematologist arrived to draw blood.

Susan drummed her fingers on the table drawn across her bed. It held the remote for the TV, which was switched on. Idiot reality programs irked her. Her gaze traveled around the room. Several bouquets of flowers had arrived from various sources, and not surprisingly, George Irons had been the most flamboyant. She missed him, her work, and most of all, she missed not being able to see Jenny. As her thoughts traveled to Jenny, she felt melancholy take over. "I hoped you would have called me."

Her eyes flicked to the copy of the two-day-old *Daily Post* that Brian Johnson had brought with him when he came to see her. Remarkably, he'd been courteous, and from what she could discern, concerned. They'd held back on the update of her condition until the surgery was complete. Then they ran an article stating that she had been injured and that her final account would be when she recovered sufficiently enough to write it.

Surprisingly, she hadn't thought about her last day in Afghanistan until her dad had mentioned that morning that Cathy's memorial ceremony was going to take place that afternoon. He was going to deliver the eulogy. Now as she lay there alone in a hospital bed, the full horror of her situation took over, and the whole scenario came flooding back in alarming clarity. Her eyes, like laser beams, latched onto the notebook computer Brian had deposited on the locker next to the bed when he visited.

"That's what I need to do. I can't be there to give you a proper send off, Cathy, but I can do this for you." Her finger pressed the button for help, and shortly afterwards, a nurse appeared, who duly settled the computer on the bed and plugged it in and left Susan to it.

Susan booted up the computer, and her fingers flexed as she positioned the computer in such a way she wouldn't disturb her lower body movement. "This is for you, Cathy..."

Her fingers began to type.

Chapter 16

Charles Price gave his daughter a long assessing stare. For the last three months, she'd degenerated into preoccupation. Where normally she would be outgoing and bubbly whenever she was with her family, lately there was an air of melancholy. Jenny smiled, talked, and gave the impression she was happy, but he knew she wasn't. He hadn't spent the majority of his adult life watching people in trial settings not to know when someone was just going through the motions. He scratched his nose while reading the article that had attracted his attention, then placed the newspaper down.

"Do you want to talk about it?"

Jenny looked up and gave him a puzzled look. "About what?"

"About why for the past few months you've looked like you're in mourning. You don't have a cat or dog that has died recently. No one in the family is dead or sick, so that leaves only two other possibilities."

Jenny gave him a half smile. "All those facts are true. What has my father, the judge, deduced are the two other options?" She stirred the coffee in front of her absently.

Charles shook his head for his daughter was clearly preoccupied. "Hmm, now let me see…perhaps a case not working out as you'd expect?"

Jenny smiled. "Nope, it's quite the contrary. We've done pretty well over the past few months now that Sam is back. The last case we won brought us some great publicity from the press. Sam mentioned that the *Daily Post* in particular was supportive." Her features became sad.

"Great story, the reporter was very complimentary about your firm. I thought you were working with one of their journalists on another story about a client a few months ago. Didn't it pan out?" Charles asked, pretty sure that had been the case.

"Yeah, I was initially, with a reporter named Stark. It didn't work out. They obviously decided the story wasn't newsworthy enough, particularly as they haven't printed it."

"Stark you say. Hmm, now let me see…isn't she the one doing those weekly reports from Afghanistan?" Charles motioned to the newspaper on the table.

"Yes, she is," Jenny whispered tightly.

With a serious tone, Charles said, "Susan Stark. That's right. She does excellent work. That article says that next week will be her final post. The reports have been gritty, sympathetic, funny, and concise. I'm betting the woman isn't working locally when she gets back. Some national daily will snap her up. How well do you know her? Must be a tough cookie…it isn't a place I'd be right now."

Schooling her features, Jenny coolly replied, "I really didn't know her that well, Dad. It was mostly on a professional basis."

The word *mostly* had Charles wondering if there was more to the story than what she was telling him. "You haven't read her articles? Don't you read the *Daily Post*?"

"I've had my head stuck in case files for the past couple of months. The world news has had to take a backseat. All I've had time for is eating and sleeping."

Charles nodded. "Oh," he said as he cast a knowing eye in Jenny's direction. "Anyway, back to what we were talking about. The last thing that could be making you unhappy is that you've fallen in love."

"Don't be silly, Dad. I haven't had time to fall in love. Besides, if you've noticed that I'm out of sorts, I could hardly be termed loving material right now."

Charles sought Jenny's gaze, concentrating on her long and hard. "In most circumstances I'd agree, but I think I've got the drop on you this time. Call it my age or a father's intuition, but my choice for your mood would be a broken heart. How close am I?"

Jenny looked away and stood. "I'll catch up on the news, Dad, the real news, not what you appear to be fabricating."

Although Jenny's reply didn't answer his question, he was intrigued by her sudden interest in the real news, as she called it. "Yeah, read those reports from Stark. She may go up in your estimation after you have."

Jenny frowned, then nodded. "I'll let you know what I think of those articles she wrote. Are they in the study?" Jenny was halfway out the door when she heard her father's reply.

"Yes, but don't forget lunch is in an hour and your mother doesn't like waiting." Charles watched Jenny leave the room in haste. He was pleased with himself—he'd received the answer to his question in a roundabout way.

Jenny didn't need to read the *Daily Post* articles Stark had written. She knew them by heart, the ink embedded in her hands. Her dad was right; they were good, informative, dramatic, and sometimes downright sad. It was clear the more time Stark was over there, the more her writing of events and the people in them changed. She didn't compromise her objectivity, but clearly Stark had made friendships. When they faltered or died, it came out with her words painting the picture for all to share. The more she read, the less she knew who Stark really was. At least, the woman she had thought she knew and had been particularly mean to except for the odd occasion.

However, Stark's current assignment brought a new dimension to how she felt. She realized that by a twist of fate, the opportunity to give Stark a second chance had been almost lost because of her pig-headedness. "I'll be so darned glad when you get back, Stark. I think the swanky dinner date will be on me."

The intervening months since Stark left filled with work and sleep. She'd burnt the candle at both ends on the work front in the hope that the time would pass more quickly. Although the fact that the article on Lorna hadn't transpired had surprised her a little. It had Lorna, too, who had called her only the day before to ask her a question about Stark.

"Hi, Jenny, I wondered if you knew how to contact Susan Stark. We tried the newspaper, but they refused to give us any information, saying we had to wait until she returned from overseas. We have some results for her."

Jenny frowned at the word *we*. It had a familiar tone attached to it that made her speculate. "Actually, no, I don't. However, maybe she intends to write the article when she comes back. I'm sure the information can wait."

A sigh came over the phone and Jenny heard Lorna say to someone in the background, "She doesn't know, either."

"Is this information so important?" Jenny asked, now curious about who was with Lorna.

"Nope, not really. It was only Andy. She's anxious that Susan gets the correct version of events."

Jenny heard the warmth of Lorna's voice at the mention of Andy. "Ah, so you're with the doctor?"

Lorna gushed, "Oh, she's been wonderful, Jenny. She asked me to be the official guinea pig on her case study. They even pay me, and she snagged me a place at the university to study literature. How awesome is that?"

Jenny felt a smile tug at her lips. She was happy for Lorna, and it looked like things were looking up for her. "Hey, that's wonderful. Say hi to Andy for me."

"I will. If you're ever near the university, drop by…I think I owe you at least coffee for all you've done for me."

A few seconds later, they said their goodbyes and Jenny reflected on the conversation, recalling her own impression of Lorna. *I might still think she's slightly schizophrenic, but what the hell, it takes all kinds to make the world go around.* Then her thoughts turned to that night at the cemetery, which had been unexpected in lots of ways. *I know the whole damn episode was some kind of trickery with the light. However, if it makes people happy to think otherwise, who am I to judge?*

As Jenny opened the folder on her desk for a new client, she paused before reading it. "What if something happens to you, Stark? How would I know? Or worse, how would I get to see you?" As she contemplated that point, the urgency almost exploded, and she made her mind up to rectify that situation even if she never needed to use it.

Jenny tried the newspaper and debated her choice of contact. She eventually chose George Irons. From what she could glean from her mother's birthday party, he and Stark looked like friendly colleagues. He was a logical choice in finding out how to contact Stark.

"George Irons, how can I help you?"

Jenny sucked in a breath, then spoke calmly. "Hi, George, this is Jenny Price. I wondered..."

"Why, Jenny, how wonderful to hear from you. I thought that Suzy had forgotten."

Jenny's forehead puckered at his words. He was obviously expecting her call. *Why*? "Yes, it's been a while. Look, George, I don't know what you mean, but I was going to ask you if—"

"Oh, I know you probably don't do interviews, but I asked Suzy if she might persuade you. The boss was hoping for an exclusive maybe at home, then in your office."

"George, please, I didn't call about me," Jenny said tautly. Her knuckles were turning white as she gripped the phone tighter in her hand.

"Oh, well, that's a shame. We could do with a feature for the next issue under the circumstances."

Jenny heard a deflated tone, but there was an undertone of sadness, too. "We can discuss it another time...fairly soon. I was wondering if you could—" Once more, George interrupted her. Jenny felt like shouting for him to stop doing that, except she needed him, and getting on his bad side wouldn't achieve anything.

"Of course, you won't know, will you? I wanted to see her but had to be content with sending flowers."

This time, Jenny's anger flared and she shouted down the phone, "What do you mean you sent flowers? What are you talking about?"

"To Suzy, of course. She was injured quite badly. We were told in a mortar attack. She's in a hospital in D.C., and they say she'll make a full recovery eventually."

Jenny dropped the phone as her fingers went numb. She tried to put what she was thinking into words. Then, she swallowed hard and picked up the phone. "When did this happen?"

Jenny heard commotion in the background and someone speak to George.

"Sorry, Jenny, I have to go. The boss is going berserk again. Oh, you should check out the late edition…our girl can really tug at the heart strings."

Before Jenny could stop him, he disconnected, making her toss back her head in frustration. Then there was a knock on the door to her office and Faith popped her head inside.

"Your four o'clock appointment is here early. Do you want to have your coffee now or afterwards?"

Still disturbed by her disjointed conversation with George Irons, she didn't answer immediately.

"Jenny, are you okay? You look a little pale."

The anxious tone drew Jenny out of her trance. "What? No, no. I'm good. Do you think you can find me a late edition copy of the *Daily Post*?"

"Absolutely. I'll send in Mrs. Dulwich. I've downloaded the recent pictures from the police for the case."

"Jenny, lunch is ready now."

Jenny sighed heavily and cast one last look at the black and white photo of Stark next to the storyline. "I miss you, Stark." She opened the door and left to catch up with her family.

Chapter 17

The story, which caught the public's imagination, *When Do You Stop Falling*, enthralled most who read it. The concept had been simple—a day in the life and the final story from the Afghanistan frontline by Susan Stark.

As Jenny read it for the hundredth time, she wondered how Stark was. George had indicated she was going to be fine, but there had been that word attached—eventually. Although, if she'd been able to write this piece, she must be coherent and able. The article was Stark's final rational moments of a day that stripped her soul naked, leaving nothing to the imagination...

When the light came back on, the shouting had diminished and only the bewildered, injured, or worse dead had remained glued to the spot. I confess to being confused and scared.

"Can you move, ma'am?"

The simple answer was not really, but I would because Cathy had taught me well. I looked around and saw the debris of the bombing. The shards of glass, metal, and human flesh were clinging to the desert road like algae in a stagnant pond. I felt completely useless and knew that I was. This was no setup or creative font I'd imagined to boost the news ratings. This was reality at its harshest. Death was floating in the air, fouling each breath you took. I needed to feel or hear something—anything—that was familiar. A dark precipice called my name, and I was afraid to fall into it.

"Cathy."

My lips barely moved, but I heard my voice in the silence that surrounded me. There was no reply. I called again, this time louder with panic evident in that single word. I wasn't a soldier. I had no right to be there. I felt like a baby without its mother to take care of her, and I cried. I could feel the tears on my dirt-stained face. A hand settled on my elbow, dragging me away from my prone position. Looking around, I was pathetically expecting to see Cathy. I didn't.

"We need to move now, ma'am. Please, it isn't safe here and you need medical attention."

My breathing was shallow, and I knew that each movement caused severe pain in my chest and worse in my back. I was barely able to walk. My legs felt like jelly. The solider was correct, we needed to go, but my inner need took precedence. I needed to see Cathy and feel her confidence flow through me again. The soldier was pulling me along, and all I could do was gaze in fascinated horror at the carnage around me. It wasn't until they had virtually thrown me inside the helicopter that I finally saw Cathy.

There was no solace in that moment of recognition. As I clenched my fist, I rammed it into my mouth in trepidation that I'd scream the place down, and because of my action, more harm would befall us. As the medical transport whirled into the air, the sound of the blades were deafening as the sand billowed around the chopper like a storm. The distance away from Cathy became greater, and my mind finally stopped deluding itself. In a moment of lucid thought, those unseeing eyes, which had once been so alive, conceded defeat. As my mind traversed that minefield, it allowed me to accept the causality as the once vital soldier and my good friend had fallen as many before her. Along with it, I had fallen. Mine—into a freefall of fate as my arrogance of long-held beliefs and assumptions were no longer acceptable.

My day was almost done. The hospital took charge, and I was allowed to rest. My final thought as my eyelids closed from the drugs was a moment that seems so long ago now. It was back in a world that no longer existed for me. Where I once quoted a nursery rhyme about Humpty Dumpty, who had a great fall, to a friend who I thought might fall from a wall. I was wrong. It wasn't my friend in trouble, it was me. That very wall called life was tumbling down around me and I was still falling.

Jenny prevented a sob from escaping. No matter how many times she read the account, it was always the same reaction. The key thing that kept creeping into her mind was that Stark had thought of her when she was injured and hurting. At the same time, she admitted that the world of that moment was gone—presumably forever.

"I should have been kinder. God help me, I shouldn't have been such an antagonistic idiot. If I had been kinder, I might know how she is and where she is." The muttered words berated her inadequacies as she thought of their night of passion, how different things could have been if only she'd listened.

"Do you want a refill?"

Jenny glanced up and gave the server a thoughtful look. She'd seen her before but couldn't remember her name. "Sure, thanks."

Since Stark had been abroad, Jenny had taken up going to Delia's Café/Bar twice a week after work. It was a tentative link with Stark. Her heart had yearned to see Stark if only briefly. As the days drew on, she realized with every elapsed moment, that her own insecurities about relationships had potentially stolen the chance of a lifetime with someone special. Although Stark had said they were going on a date when she came back, maybe she'd changed her mind. The article clearly indicated the world she once knew was gone. *Does that include me, too?*

Moments later, the vaguely familiar woman returned with a steaming refill. "You know Stark, the journalist, right?" Jenny asked.

The woman's frog-like eyes stared at Jenny. Their color reminded the lawyer of a dirty green pond. "Well, sure, who doesn't? She has celebrity status in Merit these days…not that she's come back yet. My partner misses her at the chess club. She was a damn fine opponent."

Jenny's face turned incredulous for she never figured Stark as a chess player. But then, what did she know? She hadn't allowed a meaningful relationship to develop, and that sat squarely on her shoulders. "She was injured. Maybe she's convalescing somewhere on a tropical island."

"From what I heard through the grapevine, she went home to her folks in D.C. Can I get you anything else?"

"No, thanks." Jenny watched the woman walk away and she pondered the new information. Stark was staying with her parents. Ten minutes later, having stirred the coffee so much she was sure the spoon would go through the bottom of the cup, she got up, paid her bill, and left. Her goal was to contact Stark at her parents' home, and she knew exactly where to get the information. Then a lightbulb went off in her head, and she quietly exclaimed, "Of course!" She dragged out her cell phone, dialed Stark's number and waited for it to be answered. Disappointment flooded her body as she heard a disembodied voice request her to leave a message. "Back to plan A," she muttered.

Leigh, her head thrown back in laughter, shared coffee with four students and looked up in surprise when she heard her name. Scraping her chair along the linoleum floor, she said something to the people she was with, then moved in the direction of Jenny, who was a few feet away. "Hey, Jenny, long time, no see."

"Hi, Leigh," Jenny said, suddenly nervous at what she might learn. "I know this is out of the blue and I guess I could have gone to her boss and asked but…"

"You want Susan's number, right?" Leigh allowed a smug look to filter her expression for a second when she saw Jenny blush.

Jenny felt disconcerted. *Am I that obvious*? "Her cell seems to be switched off, or maybe she's lost it. Do you have her parents' number?"

Leigh stared intently at Jenny's drawn features and nodded. "As a matter of fact, I do. She's not the same as she was when you saw her last."

"I don't imagine she is." Jenny swallowed hard. The last thing she wanted to do was to break down and beg for the number. But if that's what it took, she would. "Will you give me the number? Please."

"Wait a minute." Leigh returned to her table, rummaged in her backpack, and pulled out a BlackBerry. She walked back to Jenny. "Do you have a pen and paper?"

Jenny pulled out a PDA and began to process the number Leigh gave her. "Thanks." About to leave, she drew in a shuddering breath. "You said she isn't the same. Have you spoken with her?"

Leigh gave Jenny a measured glance and sighed. "A couple of days ago, she called me out of the blue and we talked."

Jenny felt her heart lurch at the comment. *Why her and not me*? Swallowing slowly, she acknowledged the information with a curt nod. "I don't want to step on your toes if you and Stark are—"

Leigh chuckled. "You have got to be kidding me. Susan isn't interested in me anymore. I wish she was, but I screwed up big-time, and she doesn't forgive easily and now…well, who knows what's going on in that head of hers."

"How is she? Are her injuries bad? Is that the reason she hasn't been back here? There really wasn't much said about her injuries in the papers except for the veiled reference to her chest and back in that last article of hers." Jenny closed her eyes, attempting to calm her heart that was hammering in her chest. *Damn, this is hard.*

"Would it matter?" Leigh asked seriously.

Jenny shook her head. "No, I just want to talk with her. I want to hear her voice and know she's okay. I guess you wouldn't understand."

"Call the number and talk to her. I have a feeling that she'll welcome a call from you."

Jenny was going to ask what she meant, but Leigh's friends called her away.

"Got to go, Jenny. Good luck with Susan, and I'll expect a full report when you get back." Leigh waved and left Jenny standing in the middle of the café, still clutching the PDA.

Then Jenny turned and left the building to drive home. She had a call to make.

Sheryl Stark shook her head at her husband and daughter. They'd been playing the same chess game for almost a week. *Surely, it can't take that long to finish a game.* "Hey, you two, I'm bored. Isn't anyone going to take pity on me and talk? I'm sure the next move can wait until tomorrow."

The two looked up at Sheryl and pulled faces.

"Darn, that gives Sue here an advantage. She can mull over her move. I call that lousy timing, Sheryl." David winked at his wife as he stood. "I need a bathroom break. I'll be right back."

Susan smiled and attempted to move her pillows and stretched the muscles in her back. A grimace of pain flashed across her face.

"You know the surgeon said not to do that. How many times do you need to be told?" Sheryl gently chastised as she proceeded to punch the pillows into order.

"Oh, I was never that good at being a patient, and I'm sick of Jill, my physiotherapist, shaking her head at me." Susan wrapped her arms around her mom and hugged her tight. "What culinary delights have you ordered for us this evening?"

Sheryl chuckled. "Lasagna from Pepi's. He's sending it by special courier." She glanced at her watch. "It should be here in a little over ten minutes."

"How did you manage to get permission to bring food in? I thought it was a policy of the hospital not to do that."

"I used the ammunition at my disposal, namely your father. He's not a general just for the title, darling. Which reminds me. You had a call today. There was a message on the machine."

"Yeah, who?"

"Jenny. I've brought the number with me."

Sheryl was about to take the note with the number out of her pocket when Susan said explosively, "No, I can't talk to her now."

Sheryl frowned as she stared at Susan, who looked uncomfortable and bleak. "Okay, I think. What if she calls again? What do you want me to tell her?"

There was a pause before Susan distractedly said, "Something, anything, nothing."

"That isn't very polite, darling. Why not call her and at least explain how you are? She sounded worried about you. Is she the same Jenny you mentioned when you were last home?"

Susan drew in a deep labored breath and exhaled it almost immediately. "Yes, but it's complicated."

Sheryl nodded. "How much more complicated could it be than to not let someone you care about know that you're on the mend and not have them worry unnecessarily?"

"I'll think about it," Susan said grudgingly.

Sheryl beamed a smile, then saw David talking to a young motorcycle rider who was carrying a box. "Wonderful. Dinner's here."

The cool phone call Jenny received from Stark had at least put her mind at rest that she was recovering. The rest of the conversation had been far less convincing. Her mind then replayed the conversation.

Jenny attempted to concentrate on the screen in front of her, but once more, the timer on the game she played beat her. Usually, it helped to relieve the tension of the day playing the odd online game. They could be challenging at times, but you didn't need a degree to play them. Today it wasn't working, and she pushed back the computer chair in frustration and stood. Then the phone rang, and for a second, she stood rooted to the spot, unable to move. When her brain did engage, she reached for the phone and answered as calmly as possible. "Hello?"

"Hi, Jenny, it's me, Susan."

Jenny felt like her heart was doing a double shift as her hand shook slightly holding the receiver. "Stark, how are you?"

There was a moment of silence, then Stark's voice, which appeared disembodied somehow, answered, "Good, I'm good, Jenny, thanks for asking. What about you?"

Tears filled her eyes as she tried to calm her emotions to have a meaningful conversation. After all, they'd only been to bed together and she knew after those articles in the newspaper that she hadn't scratched the surface of whom Stark really was. She stiltedly replied, "Oh, you know me…busy as always. I hope you didn't mind me calling your parents' home. Your cell seems to be on voice mail permanently. I just needed to—"

"No, I didn't mind you calling me. My cell was damaged, and I've not had the opportunity to replace it. I've had other things on my mind. Did you trace me by nefarious means being a lawyer and all?"

Jenny should have realized it was a teasing comment, but her emotional state was too fragile to understand. Instead of laughing, she went the opposite way. "I don't break the law, Stark, I uphold it."

"Point taken."

Jenny bit her bottom lip in consternation—*this is a stupid conversation*. "Well, I just wanted to check that you were okay. I'm glad you came back. I'd better let you go now."

"Some things never change. It was good to hear from you, Jenny. I'm sure we'll catch up when I get back."

"Are you coming back to Merit or has a national paper stolen you from the *Daily Post*?" Jenny asked, unsure why she was being so damn cold. It wasn't what she was feeling or what she wanted to say.

"I've had tentative enquiries. I guess like everything right now, it's all fluid. However, I'm kind of stuck here for the next couple of months, but I will be back. I have unfinished business in Merit that only a personal appearance can rectify."

Jealously, Jenny said, "Leigh, I know you've called her."

There was a sigh followed by a hollow laugh at the other end of the phone. "Ah, right, now I understand. Did Leigh give you my parents' number?"

"Yes, she did. What I want to know is why you called her but not me. You asked me to wait for you, and I have…but I don't get a call? I have to beg your ex for a phone number! Tell me, is that fair?" Jenny blurted out agitatedly.

"No, it isn't, and I'm sorry you feel that way. Right now, for me at least, the world isn't playing ball. I need some time to work through that. Being prostrate in a hospital bed for the next few weeks, then having to take baby steps while my back heals isn't helping me, either. I'm dealing with the fact that I faced death, and right now, I don't need you or Leigh complicating that for me. Jealousy isn't what I need. I was hoping for a friend who could understand."

Jenny felt like Stark had given her a body blow. She reeled from the feeling. "I'm sorry. That's all I ever seem to say to you."

There were background noises like a stretcher wheeled along with inaudible voices—nothing from Stark. "I want to be that friend, Stark, please."

"I'm leaving the hospital in two weeks, then I'm going to stay with my parents. I'll call you and let you know when I'm there and we can have a friendly chat."

"Thank you. I'll be waiting."

"Don't give up on me. I promise to explain when I can. Okay?"

Jenny felt the hot sting of tears on her cheek as she nodded, then realized that Stark couldn't see her. "I know you will. Take care of yourself."

"I will, Jenny, you too."

Hell, she had been so juvenile and awkward, it had almost ended the tentative relationship they did have. Anyone would think she didn't know how to have a cordial conversation with someone who was injured. In truth, she didn't know how to react—not with Stark at least. There were so many variables in their relationship. The biggest one was that Stark had so many dimensions that were all good, it put her to shame. Yet deep down, she knew they had a soul deep connection.

She'd been a dreamer for so long, waiting for the knight in shining armor to sweep her off her feet. When in reality, the knight had, and she hadn't recognized it. Now, God help her, she had been bereft without Stark and hadn't the courage to admit it. She'd even bawled out people she knew who had remarked that Stark had sensationalized the reports from Afghanistan. There was no doubt in her mind that Stark had laid her emotions bare for anyone to see. She showed, as a knight would, that courage was alive and kicking even in this jaded world.

"Stark is going to call me even if it is just for a *friendly* chat. Except I want more. I don't want to be a one-off conversation as a final goodbye as you appear to have done with Leigh." The words echoed off the walls and she felt out of control. "Let it be me, Stark. Please let it be me remaining a part of your world."

Jenny sank down on the sofa and closed her eyes. The memories of making love to Stark were so real that she could virtually reach out and touch the lean body and feel Stark's nipples respond to her touch. Then she experienced the sensation of making love all over again. Stark crying out her name in the final throes of orgasm, her emotion raw and filled with primal passion continued to echo in her mind for a long time afterwards.

Chapter 18

Delia's Café was the same as always as Susan walked inside. It had been almost six months since she'd visited the establishment, and it was so damn familiar that it made her smile. Walking inside, she was astonished when Elsie May came from behind the counter—a first in her recollection. Elsie May hugged her tightly and welcomed her back.

"Good to see you, too, Elsie May." Susan grimaced as the proprietor hugged her so tight her back began to protest.

Elsie May drew back and shook her head. "You did good, kid. Whenever you come here from now on, it's free. And before you say it, don't."

Susan bemusedly shook her head. "You got it. I'm expecting someone. Can I book a table for dinner?"

"Book a table! Susan, you can do whatever you want here. Now is it a business or pleasure dinner?" Elsie winked as she saw the perplexed expression.

Susan hesitated a second, then a voice from behind her announced, "Pleasure."

Elsie May grinned, then returned to her counter.

"Hi, Susan." Those few words had bittersweet connotations as Susan turned towards the voice and frowned.

"I wasn't expecting you, Leigh. Why are you here?"

"I come here most weekends…you can ask the old woman. Besides, you mentioned it was your favorite coffee house, and I can see why you feel that way. I knew one day you'd come back." Leigh smiled sensually.

"We said all that was meant to be said the last time I talked to you. What do you want from me?" Susan glanced towards the entrance, praying that Jenny wouldn't turn up yet.

Leigh placed a hand on the button just below Susan's cleavage. "I still want you. I've had five years of regret, and I want you to truly forgive me and let us try again. I know you're not immune to me. You forgave me when we talked on the phone, and I know I can make it right. Please let me try. "

Susan rolled her eyes. *I don't need this—especially now.* Placing Leigh at arm's length, she shook her head. "This isn't the time or place. In fact, the time is long gone."

Leigh paused, then moved so fast to kiss the lips that called her name, she didn't see someone else enter the establishment. As their lips joined, she felt a rough hold physically remove her from Susan. "Hey, what the hell is your problem?"

The short walk from the subway to the corner where Delia's stood had Jenny checking her appearance before opening the door. She hesitated a few moments. Inside, her stomach trembled at seeing Stark in the flesh after an enforced absence for five months, ten days, and three hours. She scrunched up her face at that pertinent fact. She felt like a kid counting down to Christmas.

They had talked on the phone for at least two to three hours on the weekends, catching up on each other's lives, and had e-mailed during the week in some instances just to say good night. It was a courtship in a way, but it didn't come close to feeling the warm skin of Stark holding her hand or touching her shoulder or their face-to-face confrontations. Even the non-physical communication they used still had them at odds at times. She recalled that first call when Stark was released from the hospital.

"Hi, Jenny, it's me."

Jenny smiled. She'd been waiting for the call, and although there had been numerous times when she wanted to just say *to hell with it* and take a plane to Washington and visit Stark, she hadn't. "Hey, good to hear you. Does this mean you've arrived at home at last?"

"At last is right. I thought they had me down as a permanent resident. I almost had to use my dad's strong-arm tactics to have them release me."

Jenny chuckled. "I'm sure Mr. Stark isn't into that kind of practice."

"You know my dad's a general, right? They do all kinds of interesting stuff for the government, so can you imagine what they would do for their only child?"

"You're teasing me, right?" Jenny wasn't sure if Stark was or not—she sounded serious. There was that light laugh that Jenny allowed to wash over her as Stark replied.

"Yes, I'm teasing you. How have you been?"

"I could say busy, but you knew that. Otherwise, going about my business as usual, nothing special." Jenny kept the conversation light. No way was she going to allow her emotions to get the better of her this time.

"I knew that, ever the vigilant legal eagle. Incidentally, have you caught up with Lorna? When I get back, I intend to do that article. It's just that—"

Jenny understood. "Other things got in the way. Actually, I did have a call from her a few weeks back. She's Andy's guinea pig and receives a small stipend for the research. Andy managed to secure a place at the university for her to study, too. Her life has changed dramatically, or maybe her ghostly voices are trying to make amends for her losing so much on their behalf. I read the articles."

The bald last statement even surprised Jenny as she wondered if the silence was her cue not to belabor that point.

"And the verdict was?"

"You enthralled a nation."

"Ah, but did I enthrall you?"

"Can I ask you a question?"

"Go for it. Although, as you're a lawyer, it had better not incriminate me." Susan chuckled.

Jenny was relieved. "I'm glad you can still laugh. That last story you posted was harrowing in lots of ways."

"I'm sure that wasn't the question."

Jenny felt an icy blast in that retort. "No, it wasn't. Did you mean what you said in that last story? That the world you once knew no longer existed?"

"Yes. How could it after what I experienced?"

"I guess that makes sense. Do I still exist in your world?" Jenny waited. It was the question that had been on her lips since she'd read the story.

A woman's voice calling that dinner was ready delayed Stark's reply. "You exist in my world, Jenny, you always will. Can I call you tomorrow? It's my parents' house, so I have to have dinner like a good child."

Jenny felt the tension leave her body, and she laughed at the thought of the paradigm she had of Stark sitting docilely down for dinner—it was a cute image. "Yeah, I'd like that. Want me to call you instead?"

"I'll call but then after that, we can take turns. Deal?"

"Deal. Sleep well, Stark, and enjoy your dinner."

They had gone from there, and that night was the beginning of what she hoped would enrich the lukewarm friendship they had forged in the last couple of months. She opened the door to Delia's and walked in. Her face contorted in disgust as she saw two familiar figures, and they looked less than platonic. Walking over to them, she viciously grabbed Leigh by the arm and pulled her away from Stark.

"Hey, what the hell is your problem?" Leigh spun around and glared defiantly at Jenny.

Leigh's reaction had been typical, and Jenny waited for her to say more. When she didn't, Jenny smugly said, "I don't have a problem, not now. She doesn't want you here or your hands on her." Jenny had acted on a knee-jerk impulse when she'd walked into the café and saw Leigh like a spider claiming her prey. She convinced herself it wasn't appropriate and took action.

Susan's expression gave nothing away as she looked from one woman to the other, then a quirky smile played on her lips as she caught Jenny's angry eyes. "I think I said that earlier, Leigh. Have a great night."

Jenny folded her arms across her chest in an aggressive stance.

Her lips pulled into an obstinate line, daring Leigh to cross her.

Leigh tilted her head slightly and stared at them both. "I guess I know when I'm not wanted. One day, Susan, one day, you'll come back, and I'll be waiting." Leigh winked at Jenny audaciously and walked away.

Susan and Jenny watched her go in silence.

Then Jenny caught the speculative look in Susan's eyes and felt an inner connection fit in place. *God, I've missed you so very much, and I didn't even know it.* "I think you mentioned a friendly coffee."

Susan, about to slide into the chair, nodded, then did an about turn and crossed the few paces to Jenny, hugging her tightly. "I did. It's good to see you, Jenny."

Jenny caught her breath. The hug was exactly what she needed. When Susan let her go, she whispered, "Likewise." They stared at each for a few seconds more, then Jenny motioned to the chairs.

Susan gave Jenny an intense stare and sat down.

Jenny followed suit and began to fiddle with the menu as they waited to be served. She looked across at Stark and saw a faint trace of amusement filter across her angular face. It looked the same as always—beautiful. "Hey, look, I didn't mean to intercede with you and Leigh. I'm sorry if I spoiled a reunion."

Susan took Jenny's hand to stop her from playing with the menu. "Thank you."

Jenny felt a smile curve her lips as she glanced at the much larger hand that held hers. Reluctantly, she removed her hand. Her inner impulse was to take Stark into her arms and kiss her senseless, right then and there, forgetting everything but the need that seemed to consume her. Finally, she accepted that the tall lean body, whose hand had entwined with hers, was paramount to her existence.

"You're blushing," Susan pointed out.

"Oh, it must be the heat in here. "Jenny fanned her cheeks with the menu, and the server arrived. It was the same woman she'd spoken to the last time she was there.

"Elsie May said you were here, and there was no way anyone else was going to serve you. How are you doing, Susan?"

Susan grinned and stood, hugging the goggle-eyed woman warmly. "Great to see you, Jane. I'm good. What about you?"

Jane chuckled. "You missed out on the nuptials. Janice finally caught me off-guard." Jane flashed a small diamond engagement ring and gold band in Susan's face.

"Why that rogue. I guess I have been away too long. Congratulations, Jane, and you tell that wife of yours I'll be over to the club again soon to beat her." Susan winked at Jane as she returned to her seat.

"Oh, no! She's so darned competitive, I'll never see her. What can I get you?"

Jenny listened to the conversation and wondered how chess could ever be competitive. It bored the pants off her when she watched it. Although maybe if she were watching Stark play, it would be a whole new ball game for her, so to speak. There had been many times over the past weeks of their phone calls that Stark mentioned playing chess with her dad. The subject matter hadn't registered much, but the voice had and that was all that was necessary. If she'd been talking about filleting fish, the topic would have been interesting.

A few minutes later, having ordered their coffee, they sat in silence once again. "You told me a couple of days ago you'd had a new offer from the *Washington Gazette*. How did it pan out?"

Susan shrugged, then turned her gaze to Jenny. "It depends."

Jenny decided to push further. "On what? Or is it more than one thing?"

Curling her left hand under her chin, Susan became thoughtful. "More than one, but only one is paramount."

"I can understand you going up market. It must be what serious journalists hope to achieve. I'm proud of you." Jenny was unable to ask what the most pertinent point was. Her mind was going through scenarios of how they could possibly have a relationship a thousand miles apart if Stark took the job.

Susan chuckled. "Ah, at last you think I'm a serious journalist." She tilted her head slightly. "Thank you."

Jenny smiled back at the teasing. "Are you kidding me? After the articles I read, no one could doubt it."

Their coffee arrived at that moment, and Jane whispered something to Susan, who warmly replied, "I'll be there. Can I bring a friend?" Jane nodded.

"Do you need to go?" Jenny was annoyed that Jane had claimed the closeness to Stark that she desperately craved.

Susan shook her head. "Oh, no, Jane asked me over to dinner. I think it's a belated celebration of her and Janice's nuptials. I'm all yours." Susan's brow puckered as she asked, "Did you receive a letter that I sent you when I was away?"

Jenny frowned and shook her head. "No, I've received nothing from you."

"Ah, that explains it. Interesting." Susan seemed preoccupied.

"What's interesting? Did you send me a letter? What did it say? Why haven't you mentioned it before?"

Susan chuckled. "Oh, it doesn't matter."

"It matters to me," Jenny said softly before she caught Stark's piercing gaze.

"In that case, I'd written to ask if you were still waiting for me. Dumb question, huh?"

Jenny was at a loss for words before she allowed a smile to brighten her pensive features. "Is that why you contacted other people after you returned and not me?"

Sheepishly, Susan sipped her coffee. "Yes, I figured you might have changed your mind. After all, our relationship wasn't exactly smooth. Tempestuous covers it better, I think. When I woke up in the hospital and knew I wouldn't be coming back here for a while, I thought I'd best let you get on with your life."

An incredulous look came over Jenny's face. "I regretted the bitch I'd been, Stark. I thought of you every day. For the record, I wasn't interested in anyone else. All I wanted was you back and for us to try to be friends at least. I figure over the last couple of months we've proved that, don't you?"

Susan's expression became serious. "I wasn't fair to you, though…was I? Talking to Leigh and not even contacting you. I had this weird image in my mind that I needed to be walking before I saw you again. There were some dark thoughts going through my head those first weeks at the hospital. One good thing kept me going when I was at the bleakest point and my nightmares at the most potent."

Jenny hardly took a breath. "What was that?"

Stark looked slightly embarrassed as she pulled at her napkin. "You."

Jenny was speechless, her fingers lifeless as she held the menu more for something to ground her than anything else.

"Jenny Price, would you allow me to take you out on a proper date?"

Jenny heard the words and her gaze caught Stark's. Her eyes had that amused quality about them that she missed when they had talked or e-mailed. With a deep smile that made grooves in the side of her mouth, she said, "I'd like that. What about dinner?"

Susan hesitated for a fraction, then with a self-conscious expression, nodded to a discreet booth. "I actually booked a table and hoped."

Jenny laughed. "Then I guess we'd better go sit and begin this date in earnest. You do appreciate I'm not cheap to take out, don't you?"

Susan grinned widely. "I was going to say the exact same thing to you. I guess we'd better share the bill."

Teasing banter followed as they made their way to the table. Taking a seat opposite each other, they fell into an awkward silence.

Finally, Jenny decided that since Stark had done the hard work by asking her out, the least she could do was get the date going. "You know, we really have only scratched the surface of what we know about each other. I'm glad in a way that we've done that, but now I want to know the real Stark in the flesh. What makes you happy and sad? How can you drive that beast of a Jeep instead of something like my Daisy? You know the whole *how we react to each other on a personal level* thing."

Susan threw back her head and laughed heartily. "You're absolutely right." Susan held out her hand to Jenny. "Hi, my name's Susan Stark. I'm thirty-two, and I work as a journalist."

Jenny giggled at the formal introduction as she shook Susan's hand. "Hi, I'm Jenny Price. I'm thirty-eight and a lawyer."

They both laughed at the absurdity. It did break the ice. As they stared into each other's eyes, Jenny drank in the fact that they could equate an expression with an action—it was wonderful. They began their dinner date.

"I've got to ask, you call your BMW Daisy?"

"Yes, what's wrong with that? It's a very respectable name and she likes it." Jenny wagged her finger, a teasing expression on her face.

Stark shook her head. "She likes it? Does she speak to you?"

Jenny giggled. "Of course she does. And I'll have you know she has a very sexy voice, too."

Stark scratched the back of her head. "You're joking, right?"

"Wrong. I have a modern vehicle with a computer voice onboard." Jenny winked and burst into laughter at Stark's incredulous look.

"Wow, I always thought lawyers made a ton, now you've just proved it. There's something else I wanted to ask you, and I kept forgetting when we talked."

"Go ahead," Jenny said, unsure if her supposed wealth threatened Stark in any way. The truth was, it wasn't her job that made her wealthy, it was her trust fund.

"I read your profile on the Internet when I met you, and it said you wanted to be a ballerina, not a lawyer. However, it said you suffered an injury that prevented your dream." Susan sank her teeth into a piece of chocolate mud pie.

Jenny contemplated her answer. "You looked me up? Well, I did some research on you, too, but I could only find the professional information. For the record, I did want to be a ballerina, and I was good, if I do say so myself." She buffed her nails on her shirt with pride.

"So what went wrong?"

"The guy who was my partner pulled a groin muscle when he had me over his head and dropped me. I landed awkwardly. That was the end of that career choice." Jenny held up her hands.

Susan drew up her eyebrows in sympathy. "I'm sorry," she

said sincerely. "What about now? Do you have a dream that you'd like to have come true?"

Yes, you. Jenny tossed the question back. "Fair is fair. What was your childhood dream or ambition?"

"I thought you might ask me that." Susan nodded as her eyes narrowed in a teasing gesture.

Jenny picked up her fork and sank it into the cheesecake she'd ordered for dessert. "I have, now please tell me. I promise not to laugh, cry, or anything other than listen and nod sagely."

"That I'd give my next paycheck to see." At Jenny's quick glance, Stark chuckled. "Okay, I wanted to be a novelist."

"Oh, really? What type—fiction, romance, history, current affairs? How cool. You'd be great at it, too, if your other writing is anything to go by. I know I'd buy a book written by you." Jenny could have pitched her fork in her hand to stop her babbling. *What on earth has gotten into me? I sound like a fawning idiot.*

Susan allowed a ghost of a smile to grace her lips. "Thank you. I might need to hold you to that."

Jenny looked up at that second and found serious hazel eyes reflecting into hers. She held her breath and felt her heartbeat increase as they exchanged a long moment of silence. "You've started it, haven't you?"

A nerve flickered on the left side of Susan's face like a piece of elastic that stretched and snapped back to its original size. "You are very astute, my dear Jenny. Yes, I have. In fact, I finished the first edit only yesterday. It kept my mind off things that I'd rather not remember in such vivid clarity."

Jenny didn't need to ask what those memories were. They'd briefly skimmed the surface of the subject several times over the months, but nothing significant revealed. "You were injured, Stark. When you were incapacitated, the memories were bound to take hold from time to time."

"It was nothing, really…not compared to some of the other guys."

The solemn statement had Jenny reaching out to place a hand on Stark's resting on the table. "If you don't want to talk about it, that's okay…I know it must be hard."

"Normally, it is." Susan looked at the dainty hand that touched hers, and she gave a small smile. "It was pretty much what I said in the story I wrote. The armor plating provided protection for my chest, although it caused severe bruising, but they healed quickly. My back bore the brunt of the weight. I tore several muscles, and there was talk of a bone or two broken. They were amazed I walked out of there, which in fact, I didn't. Someone was pushing me all the way."

Jenny watched Stark's expression change, probably a bad memory, she concluded, as a slight grimace showed on her face. "Didn't they carry you on a stretcher? Did they think that you'd broken your back?" Jenny asked.

"No, though when they shipped me from the battle zone to the field hospital, they had me strapped down and prevented me from moving for almost a month as a precaution. The medics at the time I was rescued were otherwise engaged with more severe casualties. They operated when I got home, which is why I didn't come back here immediately. Call it needing my mom. You know all that, though…it's old news." Susan laughed self-consciously.

"I can understand that…wanting your mom," Jenny said with empathy.

Susan leaned back in her chair and furrowed her brow in concentration. "I was absolutely petrified out there, Jenny… especially on that last day. I felt like a child who had lost sight of her parents on a trip to the mall. I was so damn helpless. I'd never felt like that before in my life, and when I looked for Cathy as my base of familiarity, she was…dead." Susan swallowed hard as the horror of her memories seemed to show up on her face.

Jenny was glad they'd left this conversation until now. This was how you knew a person. It wasn't as much the words as their expressions and the tremor that she saw in Stark's hands as they lay on the table. "Don't. It's okay, Stark. You don't have to do this. Some things are best left alone for a while so you're allowed to heal." Jenny took hold of Stark's trembling hand, desperately wanting to hug her tight. She didn't, fearing Stark might misconstrue her action as pity.

Susan gave Jenny a grateful smile. "I know, and that's why I wanted you to know that I'm not as fearless as I thought."

Jenny heard the bitterness and wanted to make Stark feel better but didn't know how. "We all have fears. Take me, for instance."

Susan directed her gaze quizzically at Jenny.

"Now you'll think I'm a wimp. You remember that night I went with Lorna and Andy to the cemetery to conduct that experiment?"

Susan nodded.

"I was scared out of my wits when I thought someone was whispering in my ear, and there was no one there. I was screaming in fear like a banshee." Jenny smiled as she recollected where she'd flown to Stark's arms.

Susan smiled. "I remember that you thought I must have been a ghost. You almost deafened me with that scream."

Jenny caught Stark's gaze. "And there you were—no phantom—just a wonderful safe haven. I don't think I ever thanked you for stopping me from making a complete fool of myself."

Susan scratched her nose. Her expression was bland when she looked at Jenny. "Then I guess you'd better stay away from whispering ghosts, and I'd better be more careful next to crumbling walls. Deal?"

"Deal."

"Jenny?"

"Yes?"

Susan smiled. "You're not a wimp." Her fingers entwined with Jenny's, and they sat there smiling in a dopey way until someone cleared her throat to ask, "Are you finished?"

Susan unlocked her fingers with Jenny. "Sure."

Jenny watched Stark for a few seconds. *We've only just started.*

Chapter 19

Jenny glanced around Stark's apartment. "This is so minimal."

They'd had busy days at work and decided to catch a movie and a pizza at home, and Stark's place was closer. After a tense day, Jenny followed Stark's directions and felt herself relax at the sight of Stark framing the doorway when she'd arrived.

Susan shot Jenny a teasing look. "Is that a bad thing?"

Jenny laughed. "Sorry, no. It's merely an observation after my place. I'm one of those people who collects things."

"I have a collection. Come over here and see." Susan pointed to the room where a red leather sofa ran along one side of the room, which could seat about six people. A glass coffee table almost as long as the sofa ran in the middle with a fifty-inch TV mounted on the wall. Next to that was a music system.

Jenny looked around. *Still minimal.* "Ah, you're a vinyl fan. Not many people have a turntable these days." She looked at the humongous collection and her eyes widened. "Wow, you have a lot of them."

"Yes, I do. When I have the chance, I peruse the markets on the weekend for any that might be of interest." Susan grinned as she knelt in front of the system and opened the cupboard below to show another massive storage of records.

"How many are in your collection?" Jenny moved to stand behind Stark and watched her flip through several albums.

Susan looked up enthusiastically. "Probably around a thousand or so by now…I inherited my parents' collection."

Jenny's eyes flared open. "Inherited? I don't understand.

Your parents are alive. I know that I've briefly talked with both of them."

"They wanted a permanent home for them when I was in college, and well…" Susan chuckled, and with her hand to her mouth, she whispered, "I didn't want to give them back."

Jenny laughed. "Okay, what are we going to listen to?" Jenny moved to sit on the comfortable sofa at the end closest to the system and sighed in delight as the leather enclosed her after a hard day.

"Let me see now." Susan flipped a few covers, then grinned. "Here you go…let's see what you make of this." She cued up the album and pressed the button to begin the turntable. She moved to settle next to Jenny.

The eerie strains of "Funeral for a Friend" by Elton John began to fill the room.

Puzzled, Jenny asked, "Okay, who and which album?"

Susan turned to Jenny with a slight frown. "It's classic. You mean you don't know? Oh, I have my work cut out educating you. I can see that now."

"Hey, I've had a hard day, and thinking right now will bring back the headache I've had all day," Jenny said with a pout.

Susan smiled and reached across the sofa, and her arm easily encircled Jenny's shoulders. "In that case, Elton John, album *Goodbye Yellow Brick Road*, track 'Funeral for a Friend.' I wouldn't want a repeat of the headache."

Jenny slipped naturally into the crook of Stark's arm and let out a sigh of contentment. "Now this I could get used to after a long day at the office," Jenny whispered.

"Me too." Susan kissed the top of the blond head.

After listening in silence to a couple more tracks, Susan stood. "I'll order that pizza before you're too tired to eat it."

Jenny halfheartedly smiled in agreement. "Lots of pepperoni."

"You got it." Susan sauntered off to the kitchen. A few minutes later, she walked back to the room as the first side of the album finished. "Want more?"

Jenny grinned. "Sure, anything softer?"

"The Carpenters?"

Jenny laughed. "Hey, Stark, thank you."

"For what?"

"I needed to lighten up and you made it happen." Serious blue eyes caught hazel.

Susan didn't reply immediately. She turned her back to change the music. "Well, you do the same for me, Jenny. Any chance you want to volunteer to go on another ghost hunt with Andy and Lorna Saturday night?"

Surprised, Jenny moved her legs to sit forward. "They're going on another cemetery trip? Wasn't once enough, or did you instigate it? I remember our conversations. You were fascinated, so don't lie to me."

"I do believe from what Lorna told me, there have been others." Susan laughed. "Nevertheless, you got me. It was my suggestion. Besides, I needed to refresh my mind on what I was going to write. After six months, you tend to forget things, and I want a fully rounded story. Are you game? I promise to hold your hand every second."

Jenny found that part quite appealing and the other less so. "Remember, I have a Little League game Saturday morning. It's the next to last game. So don't be surprised if I fall asleep on you with an all-nighter thrown in."

Disappointment flooded Susan's face as she glanced at Jenny. "Ah, yes, the Little Leaguers. You love doing that, don't you?"

"Yes, it's one of those things in life that is satisfying. I love to see the kids' faces light up when they win and…oh, I don't know, it's just a good feeling. You should drop by one morning. Although you'll have to be quick since only one game is left after Saturday."

Susan moved back to sit with Jenny and smiled. "I'd be happy to watch a game. Why didn't you ever mention it before? You in Little League gear—wow, that's an image." Her gaze roamed the expensive clothes Jenny wore. "You haven't exactly said no to my proposal of holding hands through Saturday night."

It was a temptation…a gloriously giddy one, too. "Hey, be careful, you might blow your *take it easy on the romance* front with thoughts like that." Stark looked positively chastised, accompanied by a beguiling grin. "Hmm, I'm not sure about Saturday night. It creeps me out going to graveyards."

"Scout's honor I'll ensure nothing ghostly happens to you." Susan gave a short salute.

Jenny chuckled. "You can't be a Scout that salutes…it has to be a Brownie or guide."

Susan wriggled her eyebrows. "Tch, details, details. Are you game?"

Jenny began to feel warm under the intense gaze of Stark's eyes on her body. "I'm game. The Carpenters, huh?" she said, changing the subject.

Susan chuckled. "Yeah, take your shoes off and I'll massage your feet. You know I'm pretty good at painting toenails if you ever need that therapy."

"Now that is something I'd pay to see."

They laughed as Susan moved to pull Jenny's silk-clad legs on her lap before proceeding to massage her feet.

Jenny wiped the sleep from her eyes as Stark pulled the car up to the steps of the university building where they had arranged to meet Lorna and Andy.

"Are you sure you can stay awake? I can take you home and meet the others at Centenary Cemetery."

Jenny exhaled a deep breath and raggedly said. "I'm good. I just hate it when I fall asleep in a car."

"Didn't you take a nap like I suggested after the game?" Stark shot Jenny a mock threatening look.

"It was only midday by the time I arrived home. I had laundry to do and a few chores, lunch, et cetera, et cetera. You get the point." Jenny shrugged.

Susan moved slightly to face Jenny full on and touched her chin, lifting it slightly so that they captured each other's eyes. "Hmm, what about this evening?"

"You called, and frankly, I was wired after that, and I…"

Susan opened her mouth to say something, then clamped it shut. "Damn," she whispered.

They heard a door open along with the sound of feet running down the steps.

"We'll table that conversation for another time." Stark shook her head, opened her door, and climbed out.

Jenny shrugged. "I can wait," she muttered to the vacuum.

The door of the Jeep opened, and Lorna smiled cheerfully. "Great to see you, Jenny. I have something important to tell you."

Lorna looked like the cat that had gotten into the cream. Her eyes seemed to sparkle. "You do? Well, that's great. Can't wait to hear it."

"Well, yeah!" Lorna giggled.

"Hi, Jenny. We have the old team back together. It's good to see you again." Leigh Chambers smiled seductively.

Balling her fists, Jenny politely said, "I wasn't sure if you were still around town, Leigh."

"Oh, just because you were a little protective doesn't mean I've given up." Leigh smiled, then turned to Lorna, who was looking out the window. "That and dear Lorna here appears to be the real deal. I couldn't leave town without completing my work."

Stark climbed into the vehicle at the same time as Andy. The silence that ensued was almost as unhealthy in Jenny's perspective as the location they were about to go to.

"Hi, Jenny, good to see you," Andrea said, smiling warmly, then she cheerfully settled in her seat.

"You too." Jenny quickly switched her gaze to the rigid profile of Stark—she obviously hadn't known that Leigh was going to be there. "I guess we'd better get this expedition going then." She reached across to place a hand on Stark's leg and winked when Stark looked at her.

"Yeah, let's." Susan smiled slightly and put the car into drive. They were on their way.

Two hours later, with rain slowly coming down, Lorna was camped next to the headstone her *voice* told her was in trouble. Andy and Leigh flanked either side. So far, there hadn't been evidence of a nuisance.

Susan smiled as she watched Jenny place a hand to her mouth to stifle a yawn. If it wasn't for the odd glance Jenny gave, she'd think the woman had fallen asleep. They were, as Jenny had been on the previous mission, superfluous at this stage. Their task was to wave towards the others if they heard or saw anything. Moving a few feet with a gentle smile on her lips, Susan whispered, "Why don't you and I shelter under that tree over there and try to get out of this rain? I don't know about you, but it feels to me like a cool breeze getting up. That's a bit odd for the time of year."

Jenny closed her eyes and grinned. "Oh, am I glad you said that. After the last time, I wasn't going to move…just in case."

"Just in case what?" Susan tipped her head slightly as she took Jenny's hand and they walked over to the tree.

"I really did think I'd heard a whisper in my ear. It was eerie, especially when all those lights began to dance around Lorna's head. Would have made a great "X-Files" episode—spooky."

Susan chuckled. "Hmm, that show was over by the time I could have appreciated it. Although, come to think of it, I thought you said you never saw the lights."

Jenny whispered in Stark's ear, "I'd never admit that to anyone but you," before she shook the raindrops from her hair like a dog.

"Hey, I came here for shelter, not to have you drench me." Susan winked, then checked the boundary of her peripheral vision.

Jenny chuckled softly. "This was a great idea." She pulled the collar of her jacket around her neck tighter. "I was getting a bit cold out there. It must be because I'm tired."

Susan watched her, then in a swift movement, she wrapped her arms around Jenny's unresisting body and pulled it to rest against hers. "Are you warmer now?"

"Oh, yes…wow, you're like toast. How do you do that?" Jenny lifted her head to gaze into Susan's face.

"No idea. Probably because I'm bigger than you are. I have more fat deposits to keep me warm. You, on the other hand, are like a will-o'-the-wisp." Susan hugged her lightly.

Jenny sighed. "Maybe whoever was going to do the damage tonight changed their mind. The rain is unexpected."

"That is a distinct possibility." Her chin rested lightly on Jenny's blond head, and she allowed her feelings for the woman to encompass her.

As the silence stretched out, Susan asked, "Penny for your thoughts?" as her gaze constantly surveyed the boundary while listening intently for any odd sounds.

"Oh, I was thinking, what am I doing out here when I could be tucked up in a nice warm bed? What about you?"

A wonderful memory of the last time Jenny had gone on one of these endeavors surrounded Susan. They had spent the end of it making love, which had her sighing. *Can't go there, not yet.* "I'm glad you came."

Jenny turned to stare directly at Susan. "I am too."

There was a silence between them as they both looked into each other's eyes and Susan moved her head rapidly around. "Can you hear that?"

Jenny looked around. "Hear what?"

"There it is again. Bells, I think. Can't you hear it?" Susan looked around, and nothing had changed from her original surveying of their position.

Jenny's expression changed from confusion to understanding "I do, at least I think I do. Should we call Andy?"

Susan drew in a deep breath. She held Jenny's hand and nodded. "Come on."

They moved closer to the others' positions and saw nothing amiss. As they moved towards Andrea, she looked in their direction with a quizzical expression on her face. "What is it?"

Jenny stumbled over the words. "We heard music…at least bells…we think."

Andrea jumped up and grinned. "Where? Show me."

Susan watched as Andrea dragged Jenny off, and a tender amused smile was on her lips.

"You love her, don't you? Really love her…like the stuff they always sing about in love songs."

Susan turned to look to Leigh, who had come up beside her. "It's none of your business."

Leigh gave a barely discernible shrug in the dim light. "I know that now. I guess I always knew, but deep down, I figured if you gave me a second chance..."

"If circumstances had been different, who knows what might have happened?" Susan looked away from Leigh to the two figures next to the tree Jenny and she had sheltered under.

Leigh sighed heavily. "It was my fault and Jenny stepped in and took my place."

Susan gave Leigh a long hard stare, then coldly said, "Jenny didn't take your place. She means more to me than you ever did or could. She's the circumstance I mentioned earlier. Even if I hadn't met her, there still wouldn't be a remote chance of us trying again." Susan strode away from the woman who had her mouth open in astonishment.

"Hey, I thought you were never coming. It's stopped now," Jenny said.

Susan looked down at Jenny's face and allowed her feelings to override her annoyance at Leigh's confidence that Jenny was second best. "Well, I guess we'll just have to stay under that tree a little longer and see if it starts again, won't we?"

Jenny chuckled. "We can do that, though I think with Andy calling out, 'Is there anybody there?' they might have flown the coop."

"Oh, well, who cares." Susan enclosed Jenny in a warm hug and molded her close to her body.

"Yeah, who cares." Jenny settled into the warm body.

Eventually, Andy declared the evening a non-event after another two hours in the rain. It was four a.m., and they all looked bedraggled.

"I would kill for a cup of steaming hot coffee right now," Jenny said.

Susan didn't say anything as she negotiated the bend in the road but listened as the others all agreed. A few minutes later, she was pulling up outside Delia's Café/Bar.

Jenny grinned as they got out of the vehicle, and she hooked her arm in the crook of Susan's arm. "I guess you wanted coffee, huh?"

With a wink in Jenny's direction, Susan dropped her gaze to the women behind her. "Let's go inside and have coffee. Then, Doctor, you can tell me exactly why we were all out there soaking wet with nothing to show for it." Andy was about to stammer out an answer when Susan chuckled. "I was only teasing you. Come on, let's go have coffee…it's on me or rather the paper. They owe me for this overtime." Susan knew she'd never put it on her expense sheet because she didn't want the hassle from Daryl.

The nightshift personnel were different to those Susan usually saw in Delia's, and the familiarity she felt with the place was somewhat diminished. A young man, about college age, looked up from behind the counter, and his expression changed from boredom to life. "What can I get you?"

Susan looked to her companions and listened while they each ordered their own favorite coffee. "Anyone want anything to eat? I'm starving."

Lorna, Leigh, and Andrea chose quickly, and Susan motioned for them to stake claim to a table as she waited for Jenny's choice.

Susan gave Jenny a tender smile as she saw the tip of Jenny's tongue peep out as she thought hard about her choice. Who would have thought a snack could be that difficult?

Then Jenny made a choice and Susan began the order with an amused glint in her eyes.

When their orders came, all eyes turned to Jenny. Looking up, she smiled, then creased her brow. "What?"

Susan shook her head, and Lorna asked, "I thought you were cold, Jenny."

"Not anymore." She picked up her spoon and filled it with a liberal helping of Ben and Jerry's chocolate fudge ice cream. Once that first spoonful was in her mouth, she smacked her lips.

Leigh groaned. "My toast looks positively bland now."

Lorna and Andy agreed.

Taking a mouthful of her bacon sandwich, Susan discreetly

watched Jenny devour the ice cream. Since they'd been dating, she'd found Jenny's fondness for ice cream rivaled every other food group. Once, watching a movie at Jenny's home, she'd happen to watch in fascination as Jenny opened her freezer and revealed several cartons of the dessert in varying flavors taking over the compartment. An interesting facet of Jenny and one that brought out tender amusement in Susan's expression.

The server arrived at that moment to ask if everything was okay. Susan looked at the still goggle-eyed spectators and smiled. "We'll all have what she's having and," she paused a few seconds as Jenny looked up with a smile curving her lips, "my friend here will have a strawberry vanilla surprise."

The server went away, shaking his head.

"Doctor, what's the verdict tonight?" Susan asked as she felt Jenny's hand squeeze her leg gently in thanks. It gave her added warmth inside.

"Hmm, well, the equipment didn't pick up much, but you both had an experience, right?" Andrea's brown eyes lit up in hopeful anticipation.

Jenny raised her hand at that point, waving around the spoon that looked rather dangerous. "Sorry, but if your equipment didn't register any anomalies going on, I'm not going to admit that I heard anything. It could have been a car radio or something."

Disappointment flooded Andy's face. "That's true," she agreed. "What about you, Susan? What do you think you really heard?"

Susan looked first at Andy, then at Jenny, who gave her an interested expression. "Hard to say. However, I think the more important factor is how Lorna felt about what happened tonight."

Lorna blushed, shaking her head. "If you take it in the context that I went to save a gravestone from being desecrated, it wasn't."

"That's very true. My article will be in the *Daily Post* a week from Friday," Susan said.

Lorna looked pensive. As she picked up her coffee cup, it shook slightly. Andy leaned across and placed a gentle hand on Lorna's, giving her a supportive smile.

Half an hour later, with ice cream consumed, the party was ready to leave.

"Do you want dropped off at the campus or…?"

"Campus is great, Susan. We need to debunk our findings and the sooner the better…right, guys?" Andy said. Lorna and Leigh nodded in agreement.

An hour later, Susan turned to Jenny, who had fallen asleep on the journey home. Reaching across, she pushed away a wisp of hair that had fallen over Jenny's eyes. Jenny looked so peaceful, it was hard to wake her, but she didn't think Jenny would appreciate her neighbors waking up to collect their morning papers while she was fast asleep in the drive. "Hey, sleepyhead…it's time you went to bed."

There was no answer.

Gently, Susan shook Jenny's shoulder and whispered in her ear. "Come on, Jenny, you're home, and it's more comfortable in bed than in the car."

"Only if you come with me," Jenny mumbled in her half-asleep state.

Susan felt the raw power of that statement, and the temptation to do just that was almost irresistible. However, she drew in a deep, ragged breath and shook Jenny slighter harder. "Jenny, you're home."

Groggily, Jenny opened one eye, then the other. "Hmm, really…okay." She placed a hand to her mouth as she yawned. "Thanks, Stark. You know, I have to hand it to you. You really do know how to take a girl out on a date."

Susan smiled. "Anything to be of service, ma'am."

Almost purring, Jenny stretched her body. "Want me to make you breakfast?"

"We've just had breakfast Jenny Price-style. I think the others are all still in shock at eating ice cream so early in the morning." Susan smiled as she recalled the faces of the others who tentatively began eating the decadent fare only to smile in contentment with each spoonful.

Jenny grinned. "I aim to please."

Susan chuckled. "And you do. Now I aim to please, too, so

get to bed. You must be all in."

Jenny didn't reply immediately, then nodded. "Do you really think we heard something spooky out there?"

The slight hesitation in Jenny's voice had Susan reaching across and placing her long arms around the warm inviting body. "Nah, I think it was a car radio. Sleep well. I'll call you later."

Mesmerized at Stark's closeness, Jenny sighed lightly. "Make it late. You know I sleep like the dead."

Susan chuckled. "You got it. Pleasant dreams." Susan tenderly kissed the pliant lips next to hers and soon they lost themselves in a tired bond of passion for a few seconds. "Talk to you later."

Jenny bemusedly climbed out of the car mumbling, "Pleasant dreams, you got that right."

Chapter 20

The park in the Kennedy suburb of Merit was a lively place to be on a Saturday afternoon. People walked dogs and chatted with other like-minded dog owners. Women with strollers pushed their babies along the tree-lined walkways in the sun. Picnics where families got together seemed to be alive and kicking in the suburb.

Susan walked a little farther along, taking note of her surroundings as she glanced down at the directions Jenny had given her to attend the Little League game. Her steps quickened as she saw the field and the tiny players, not to mention hearing the yells from parents and spectators, all screaming support for their particular teams.

Agreeing that getting to know each other was equally as important on a mental level, as well as a physical one, Susan and Jenny had been on numerous low-key dates since their initial dinner six weeks earlier.

Several dinners out and at home, drinks, and the odd coffee stop at lunch along with a cinema visit or two had all been successfully undertaken. They'd even gone back to the nightclub of their first disastrous social outing. Sometimes, she wanted to simply take Jenny in her arms and love her as they had once before, but the more she got to know Jenny, the more she realized this was for the long haul. Unlike her previous relationship with Leigh, there was no way she would assume things about Jenny. Patience was going to pay dividends, and this time when they made love, it would be perfect.

The previous Saturday's cemetery shift regarding her article on Lorna had brought them even closer. In fact, today was a testament to their growing friendship. Jenny invited her to come to the last game of the season. Of all their dates, this one Susan felt could be the catalyst to a deeper understanding between them. Slowing at the small set of bleachers that held the spectators, she glanced around for Jenny, then smiled as she saw the pint-sized woman in her team gear giving instructions to a little guy waiting to be the next batter.

Disturbing Jenny while in full tactical battle mode might not be a good idea, so Susan slipped into a seat close by and watched the game. She knew if the tables were turned, she'd be distracted, too. A slim man of average height sat next to her, and she glanced at him with a slight smile as he shuffled around trying to get comfortable. Finally settling into the seat with her long legs tugged up, her eyes, hidden by designer sunglasses, never strayed far from Jenny.

"Haven't seen you around here before. Your kid on one of the teams?" the man asked with a gravelly voice.

Susan shook her head. "No, I'm here to support a friend." Her gaze constantly switched between the game and Jenny, who looked like she was enjoying herself immensely.

"Ah, now the question would be which team are you supporting?" The man pointed to the smallest kid on the field, who was holding a bat that was almost as big as she was, standing next to Jenny. "That's my kid...she's next up. I thought I was going to miss her big game. She's been a bench warmer all season, but one of the other kids has a summer cold, and Jenny is giving her the big chance."

"That's great...you must be proud of her." She watched Jenny for a few seconds. "I guess we're supporting the same team because that's my friend." Susan motioned to Jenny, who was now whispering to the girl. Susan saw the flash of a smile from the tiny girl whose red hair was visible in tufts through the helmet she wore for protection.

"Great. Yeah, I'm proud of her," he said. "Jenny's cool with the kids and they love her. I'm Roger Ackroyd. I live five doors down from Jenny." He held out his hand and Susan shook it.

"Susan Stark, pleased to meet you, Roger."

"You're Susan Stark, the reporter for the *Daily Post*?" The man sounded awestruck.

Susan smiled politely and nodded, her attention moving immediately back to the field.

Fortunately, the man didn't say anything else, and they both settled back to watch the game. When it was over, there was laughter and tears, and Roger's daughter flew across to her dad.

"Did you see, Dad? Did you see I hit the ball? Did you see?"

Roger chuckled as he swung the child in his arms and kissed her cheek. "I did, Annie. Wait until we tell your mom. She'll be upset I forgot the camera, so we could show the baby how it's done."

Susan watched the reunion and felt a tender smile tug at her lips. Then she heard a familiar voice drawing her out of her thoughts.

"You made it…I wasn't sure. Did you enjoy the game?" Jenny grinned as she locked gazes with Susan, who had removed her sunglasses.

"Certainly did. Annie was a real star, isn't that right, Roger?" Susan teased the man who scratched the back of his neck. Annie had run off to help with the collection of the equipment.

"Well, I guess I would say that's right. She's my little slugger." Roger beamed with pride.

Jenny smiled warmly at him. "I agree, she was great. Although I confess that I say that about all of them because they all are."

"I have to go. Will we see you at the barbecue later?" Roger asked as he began to move away.

Jenny turned to Susan, who had replaced her sunglasses. "Yeah, see you later."

Leaving them alone, Roger ambled off to the other parents and their kids. When he got there, they saw him point in Jenny and Susan's direction.

"You looked like you were enjoying yourself out there," Susan said.

Jenny laughed. "I was. I think because it's so different from the day job." She took a seat on the bleachers.

Susan followed suit and nodded her agreement. "Definitely different, I'll give you that. Did you ever want children?"

"Always too busy with the career...besides, I'm a firm believer in kids having two parents. I've never had that stability in any of my relationships. What about you?"

Susan considered her answer carefully, then removed her sunglasses and looked at Jenny directly. "After what I've seen today, I could be persuaded by the right person."

Jenny nonchalantly said, "I guess we both need to find the right person and quickly in my case."

Susan laughed. "You're hardly old, Jenny." Her hand moved to gently cup Jenny's cheek in a simple caress.

The action broke when a shout from the pitcher's mound called to say all the equipment was ready. Jenny disengaged with a jerk and gave a slight shrug. "I'd better do my last official duty and take the stuff back to the clubhouse."

"Hmm, I'd better not interfere with that, can't have you slacking on the last day of the season. Is it a normal ritual after a game...the barbecue?" Susan asked as she stood.

"Only the first and the last games. Now I have the rest of the year free until we start again next year." Jenny dropped down the small step to the ground.

"I guess I'll say goodbye then. Enjoy the rest of your day. I'll call you tomorrow." Susan donned her sunglasses and began to leave but stopped when a small hand grabbed her arm. To Susan, the touch felt like fire searing her skin.

"You're not staying for the barbecue?" Jenny asked, surprised.

Susan didn't say anything for a moment. "I wasn't sure I was invited."

"Of course, you are! I want you to meet everyone. Can you stay, please?"

The plea didn't go unanswered. Susan grinned. "I love barbecue. Want help with the equipment?"

"Why do you think I asked? No carrying the heavy stuff, I'll do that. I don't want you complaining of a bad back." Jenny winked as she spoke.

"Yes, ma'am."

Laughing, they headed for the field and the baseball gear.

Susan, with beer in hand, settled against a tall wooden fence, watching Jenny laughing and talking with her neighbors. They'd been very friendly. In fact, she'd felt almost fan worshipped when Roger announced in the middle of several of them that she was the reporter. It was nice but embarrassing as she'd fielded their questions.

Overall, it was an interesting experience in lots of ways. The first, she realized that seeing Jenny in this environment gave another dimension to the woman, and it filled in the empty pieces of the jigsaw puzzle in a wonderful way. The second reason, she had never fully realized what living in this kind of community was like. They had barbecues and played games and stuff when she was a child, but the constant moving from place to place as an Army brat had meant that none of the camaraderie she saw could ever have been built up. The only equivalent had been her friendship with Van.

They met at a summer school in Germany, and both were sent to the same boarding school. They quickly developed what was, until five years earlier, a strong bond. Vanessa Arlington had been simply the best in Susan's eyes. They shared their first physical relationship together but quickly realized that it wouldn't work. Yet it had led them both down the same path, and fortunately, fate, though appearing cruel at the time, was on her side. She never would have known Jenny.

She scanned the happy faces of parents talking and children playing and knew how lucky she'd been. She had forgiven Leigh and maybe she could do the same with Van. Afghanistan had taught her many things—life was too short to waste on petty recriminations.

Jenny had caught Stark standing alone with a beer against the fence and moved in her direction. From a distance, Stark's eyes seemed unseeing as a thoughtful expression filled her face. As she got closer, she noticed that etched on the rigid profile was a faint look of sadness. Reaching out, Jenny placed her hand on Stark's hand. "This wasn't all too much for you, was it? I know some of the guys have been awestruck since they found out who you are. If you want to leave now, we can…"

"The guys have all been fine…better than fine. It's a nice set of neighbors you have."

Jenny persisted. "You looked sad…I just wondered."

Susan shook her head, allowing her fingers to slip down slightly to intertwine with Jenny's. "I'm not sad…quite the contrary."

Jenny wanted to reach out and kiss Stark's hand or better yet, all of her. However, the middle of the yard of one of her neighbors was hardly a place for making out. The slow motion of their courtship was beginning to wear thin as she constantly pulled in her raging desires whenever she was with Stark. "Glad to hear it. Look, the barbecue is almost over, so we can go if you want. I need a shower. It gets quite grimy in the dugout."

Susan smiled and exaggeratingly sniffed the air. "Hmm, you do smell a bit ripe."

Jenny scrunched up her face. "Yeah, I know. Want to go to the movies later or do something else?"

"Actually, I promised George and some of the other guys at the paper I'd go for a drink with them. They think I've become a stay at home. Want me to cancel?"

Jenny didn't want the day to end. It was working out far too well. Everyone had been asking her if Stark was the one—it was the first time Jenny had ever brought a girlfriend to any of their neighborhood get-togethers. "Of course not. Besides, I owe George after our first meeting. Next time we come into contact, I want him to know I'm not a barracuda out for his blood. I think he mentioned something about an interview when I tried to ask him for contact details about you." Jenny smiled slightly as she thought about the situation at her mother's birthday party. Not to mention the strange phone call she'd had with him.

Susan frowned. "You called George? He never said. What interview was he talking about?"

Jenny shook her head. "Beats me, we never talked in detail. He said something about you asking me first…I figured you forgot."

"Ah, now I know. Brian once said I should try to get an interview with you, and I must have mentioned it in passing to George. It's his field. He probably thought I didn't want to step on his toes," Susan said vaguely.

"I still owe him for my mother's birthday party fiasco." Jenny looked down at her T-shirt that really needed changing.

"He never thinks that way. In fact, he has a birthday party at his place coming up next month. We'll go and it will prove conclusively that you've been forgiven."

Jenny smiled. "Sounds like a good plan to me. I can always play a few games on the computer this evening. I haven't since you came back." Jenny chuckled at Stark's expression regarding her choice of amusement for a Saturday evening.

"What about tomorrow?" Susan asked eagerly.

"Oh, tomorrow, I have my monthly lunch with my parents." Jenny saw Stark's look of disappointment. It was the same way she felt when Stark couldn't extend the day with her. "Come with me. I know they'd love to meet you."

Astonished, Susan asked, "Are you sure I won't be intruding?"

"Trust me, my dear Stark, you won't be." Jenny smiled and this time allowed nature to take its course as she craned her neck and kissed Stark gently on the lips. It was quick, almost a fleeting touch, although Jenny felt her heart race at the pressure. "I'll pick you up at noon."

Bemused, Susan automatically nodded.

"Did you leave your car in the drive?" Jenny asked casually.

"Yes," Susan said absently.

"Let's go. You can walk me home. I'm in need of relaxation. I love those kids, but boy, do they wear me out."

"Then may I be of service, milady, just in case you keel over in exhaustion?" Susan bowed theatrically and held out her hand.

They both laughed as Jenny linked hands. Before they ambled over to her house, they said their goodbyes to her neighbors. Jenny smiled as several neighbors gave them invitations to drop by again soon.

Arriving at the driveway of Jenny's house, Susan looked around at the neat colorful yard. "I see you have green fingers."

Jenny laughed. "Not me, unfortunately. My neighbor Harry. He's retired and potters around for me for a small fee. Between you and me, I volunteered to pay more, but he wouldn't take it. He only wanted enough to keep him in his weekly tipple."

Susan nodded sagely. "I can understand that. The older you get, the more you appreciate the little things in life."

Jenny frowned. "You're not old, you're younger than me… oh, I get it."

Susan laughed and pulled Jenny into her body. "That's my girl, the clever lawyer who understands everything…eventually." She dropped her head and kissed Jenny passionately.

Eventually, they broke off the kiss and Susan smiled. "You're a great kisser. Did anyone ever tell you that?"

"Nope, in fact, the last relationship I had, she told me I was too boring."

"She doesn't know what she's missing. Boring isn't a word that I would ever use to describe you. Stubborn, sure…"

"Okay, enough said. Enjoy your evening. Though you can keep in your subconscious that you could have spent it with me." Jenny grinned impishly.

"You are so bad." Susan pulled Jenny in for another long deep kiss, feeling the smaller body melt into hers. It felt wonderful.

Jenny dropped her head against Susan's chest when the kiss ended. "Go, before either one of us forgets we have other plans."

Susan reluctantly moved away and took out her car keys, the sound of the lock being opened brought her to earth. "Call me if your parents don't want me at lunch. I'll understand."

Jenny grinned. "No chance of that, have a great night with the guys. Don't do anything I wouldn't."

Susan winked and climbed into the Jeep. "No chance of that. See you tomorrow."

Susan debated her next step when she arrived home after being with Jenny, inwardly chastising herself over her self-doubt. She finally picked up the phone and called an old familiar number.

The phone rang and rang, then she heard Van's voice mail.

"Hi, you've reached Vanessa Arlington, please leave a message after the tone."

Considering if it was the right move, Susan sighed heavily. "Hey, Van, it's Susan. When you get this, call me…I think it's time we had coffee and let bygones be bygones."

That wasn't so hard. Susan was satisfied at her attempt at reconciliation with her old friend. Besides, she had a much bigger problem lurking—Jenny's parents. *Hell, I hope they like me.* "What am I going to wear?" Preoccupied with clothes, she headed to her bedroom wardrobe.

Jenny called her parents and asked them if it was okay for Stark to come over for lunch. There was no dissention. Her mother in particular was ecstatic. After the call, Jenny allowed her fingers to touch her lips and linger over the memory of the kisses she shared with Stark.

Breathing in deeply, Jenny murmured, "I love you, Stark… wow, did I really say that? I did and I mean it." For a few seconds, she contemplated that fact, then shouted as loudly as she could, "I love you, Stark," before succumbing to the numbing sensation of being in love.

Chapter 21

Charles Price welcomed Susan warmly when she arrived with Jenny. Almost immediately, when she walked over the threshold, Marina Price breezed forward and ignored the proffered hand and hugged Susan hard before kissing her cheek.

"Charles, a drink for our guest," Marina said while shooting her husband a teasing look.

Charles chuckled and winked at Jenny. "Yes, dear. What can I get you, Ms. Stark?"

"Susan, please…whatever you're having will be good." She wasn't sure what the man was having, but without options, she didn't want to make a fool of herself.

"Good girl, I like the way you think. Two beers coming up. Jen, what can I get you?"

"I'm driving, Dad, so I'll have juice with lunch." Jenny smiled at her father as she moved closer to Stark. "I'll just go check on Mom. Is Peter coming over today?"

"Unfortunately not, he's away at a conference and won't be back in town until later tonight." He ambled over to an ornate bar that seemed to be part of the room.

"Oh, that's right, he mentioned something like that last month. I won't be long. Dad won't bite you, Stark, I promise," Jenny whispered, and for good measure, she kissed Stark's cheek.

Susan merely nodded. She wondered if Jenny was a witch for each time she kissed her, she felt at a loss for words.

Charles Price walked towards Susan with the beers in hand. "Take a seat, Susan. Jenny's right, I don't bite. Although I think some of the people who've stood in front of me in the courtroom have had serious doubts about that." He chuckled and sat in his favorite chair.

"I'll take that under advisement. You have a beautiful home, Judge Price, the grounds are stunning." Susan drank a little of the beer. She had become inwardly like jelly, hoping the light alcohol wouldn't make her say or do something silly.

"Charles, please. Has Jenny shown you the grounds before you came inside?" Charles raised his eyebrow in question.

"No, I reported…at least took pictures for your wife's birthday party earlier in the year. It was a grand affair."

"Oh, yes, Marina is indulged in that department, but then don't we all do that for the ones we love? Indulge them, that is."

Susan bit on her top lip, feeling her body relax as the man gave her a warm smile. "Yes, we do. Take Jenny and her love of ice cream…even on a rainy day."

Charles laughed. "You know it always puzzled me, too. She's been like that ever since she had her first taste of the stuff. The stories I could tell you when she was a child."

Jenny chose that moment to step back into the room, moving to sit on the arm of Susan's chair. Her hand rested lightly on Susan's shoulder, stroking the fabric of the soft lilac shirt she wore. "Are you talking about me, by any chance?"

"Actually, it was about ice cream, darling. As Susan and I have found out, you and the wonderful creation go hand in glove," Charles said as Jenny gave him a mock frown while wagging a finger at him.

"Hey, don't let him fill you with stories of me growing up. Dad is apt to exaggerate." Her eyes crinkled with her smile. "Mom said lunch will be ready in ten minutes, and she asked for a glass of wine. Want me to take it to her?"

Charles stood and shook his head. "Bless my soul, darling. She'd throw a fit if I didn't take it to her. You know she loves to think she wraps me around her little finger." He winked and headed to the bar once more.

Jenny gazed down into Susan's upturned face, then breathlessly asked, "He hasn't been interrogating you, has he?"

Susan was entranced—it didn't take much with Jenny. She

felt wonderful and wanted to feel like that 24/7. Throatily, Susan said, "No, he was being the perfect gentleman. He told me he indulged your mom, and I mentioned that I took pictures at the party."

Jenny moved slightly to face Susan full on. "My mom is from the Margolis family. Do you know the name?"

Susan nodded. "Sure, they're one of the founding families of the state. That makes her a true socialite. Does that make you one, too?"

"I confess I did the full ten yards of balls, and the coming out party was quite literally a coming out for me. I took Gayle Harrison as my date. Actually, I enjoyed it for a few weeks. Did I ever mention I love ball gowns? All that silk and flounce. Ah, it takes me back." Jenny had a happy expression on her face.

A hand snaked out and took Jenny's hand. "Then you must accompany me to the awards ceremony in New York. I'm short-listed for an award. I wasn't going to go, but…" Susan gave a derisive smile.

Jenny squeezed the hand that held hers, and she squealed. "You're going. I saw the perfect dress a week ago at Ester's, a new fashion house. Hey, why didn't you tell me that you got the invite?"

Susan shrugged and segued into another subject. "Incidentally, what were you like as a baby? I figure that it might be important in—"

The door opened and Jenny's parents entered, suitably extinguishing that conversation.

"Okay, ladies," Charles said. "How about we take a seat for lunch? Mom has prepared the table in the conservatory, allowing us the benefit of enjoying the garden view while we eat."

The two women moved to stand and Jenny didn't drop Susan's hand. Instead, she entwined their fingers closer.

Susan didn't flinch when she saw the amused indulgent looks she received from Jenny's parents at their daughter's unsubtle possessiveness. *I wonder if my parents will look the same way. We'll find out soon enough.*

Two hours later, after lunch was over, Marina insisted Jenny take Stark for a walk around the grounds. As they moved behind an arbor where they were effectively sheltered from her parents' gazes, they both laughed. Then with a shaking head, Jenny said, "Hey, I'm sorry about that. Parents, what can I say? Are yours the same?"

Susan smiled. "Yeah, only my dad's military, so he knows how to interrogate."

"And you think a judge doesn't?" They burst into laughter again as Jenny tugged on Stark's hand and they continued their walk.

After they had been walking around for a while, Stark said, "Come on, let's take a break."

Jenny complied happily, and moments later, they settled on the glider. Looking down, Stark's legs seemed to go on forever, touching the grass, whereas hers dangled above the ground. Jenny allowed the sun's rays to warm her face as she leaned back, then with a contented sigh, Stark pulled her close so that her head rested naturally on her shoulder.

"Thank you for inviting me here today, Jenny. It was very enjoyable."

The quiet gratitude eased any particle of fear that Stark hadn't enjoyed herself, especially when her dad began to talk about her time at the war zone. They hadn't talked about that since that first official date. "You do know, now that we're together that they'll expect you every month." The comment slipped out and Jenny held her breath.

"I guess we're going to get to know each other really well. I have a feeling that I'm going to be around for a long time."

"Yes, you are."

Silence ensued for a short time, then Susan turned and kissed Jenny lightly.

For Jenny, the kiss changed almost the second their lips locked and passion flared. When the kiss was broken for air, both women were flushed and breathless.

"I figure we sealed that well and truly," Susan said, resting her chin on top of Jenny's head.

"How long have we been doing this?" Jenny asked as she played her fingers over the buttons of Stark's shirt.

"Doing what exactly?" Susan placed her lips on Jenny's hair. "Your hair smells like spring blossoms. Did you know that?"

Jenny moved slightly and pinned Stark with a questioning gaze, then kissed her. She released the lips before they could fall into the abyss of passion. "No, I didn't, but please don't change the subject. When do we move to the next level? I think we've pretty much found out that we're compatible as friends."

There was silence all around. Even the birds and general hum of the insects had suddenly seemed to hold their breaths. "If it's taking that long to answer, I think I have my answer," Jenny said with resignation heavy in the air.

Susan straightened, before leaning forward. "Sometimes, slow and easy is for the best. You know I have to go away next week…can we talk about this next Saturday?"

Exasperated, Jenny said, "Slow and easy. Is that what you call it? I'd call it a turtle pace and chaste. I know you find me attractive. Hell, we've even slept together. I know we have lots in common, but I have a feeling you're holding back. If it's about your experiences with Leigh or even Cathy, then I can…"

"Hold it. What has Cathy to do with this? She's dead."

"Exactly—you can't live in the past."

Susan frowned. "Cathy and I were never involved, if that's what you mean."

Jenny dropped her gaze as her heart raced. "I don't know what I mean…but you never speak about her, yet from what I read in your reports, she was very important to you. It sounded to me more like a lover than a friend. Besides, we weren't exactly close then. Where you were and what was happening all around you might have pre-empted a liaison for those few short months."

"I asked you to wait for me! Are you saying that even now you think I could still turn out to be a womanizer?" Susan asked sharply.

"I know I said some rotten things back then, but it's in the past, right?" Jenny stared at Stark, knowing she'd hit a nerve and not sure if she should push it. Shamefaced, she added, "I don't think like that about you."

Susan pursed her lips. "We've had a great afternoon so far… do we have to talk about this now?"

"When is a good time? We never talk about Leigh or what you feel about a long-term relationship in general. We skate around the important aspects of our relationship, calling it friendship. I doubt it will change next week. We'll do what we always do—have dinner, talk, and kiss good night." Jenny sighed heavily, then a demon inside her head, one she'd locked up for good she'd hoped, popped out and continued, "Take next week, for instance. You won't even tell me why you're going away. Whenever I ask, you become secretive. I care about you. Okay, I want you, all of you, and this slow and careful is driving me mad." Jenny jumped from the seat and paced the grass.

Susan frowned heavily. "I know you care about me."

"Then tell me what's going on in your head because if you don't want what I want, then we might as well call it quits."

"I didn't realize our friendship was so tentative. Is that what you want to do? Call it quits if I don't do what you want or explain myself fully? Love needs to be a partnership, Jenny…at least in my book." Susan stood, her jaw set. "How about we get back to your folks? I'd like to say thank you and goodbye. If that's okay with you. Obviously, lunch has ended."

"Yeah, let's do that." Jenny felt her body deflate of anger. *God, why do I do this? She didn't deserve it.* However, to apologize now wasn't going to help. As she looked at Stark's profile, she could tell there was no taking back her words. Then a thought ran through her head. *Haven't I done this once before*? "I'll drive you home."

"No, that's fine. I need to clear my head. You enjoy the rest of your day with your folks. We can catch up when I get back if that's what you want. I'll probably not be keeping office hours, so I'll e-mail you, okay? We could probably both do with some personal space to decide what we want."

Hesitantly, Jenny said, "Okay. Have a safe trip. I'll be here when you get back." Jenny felt the tears building, and inside, she cried and wondered why her love for Stark flooded her with so many emotions good and bad. *That's just the point, though...I don't want personal space from you, Stark. I want you 24/7. Why do you always keep me at arm's length?*

Jenny watched Susan leave as her long legs ate up the driveway, then as she turned a bend, she was gone from sight. She worried that her impatience may have created a rift that might end their relationship. If it did, she wouldn't blame Stark. It had never been the easiest of relationships, except for the last couple of months of the gentle courtship, which had been unbelievable. *Have I soured that in a few words?* The stupid thing was, Jenny had dreamed of someone entering her life and doing just that. Yet she'd effectively slapped down the image and turned it into something cheap.

"God, what am I going to do?"

Marina Price had watched the brisk leaving of Jenny's friend. Something had happened on the walk in the gardens, and it didn't look good. Susan Stark was exactly what Jenny needed. First, the woman loved her daughter. Only a fool would think otherwise. It was in every look and touch that they shared. And she could see that Jenny loved Susan, although she might not know it. For an intelligent woman, Jenny was apt to believe in the dream of love rather than allow the reality of the emotion to flood her life.

"You're going to apologize to your friend," Marina finished Jenny's musings.

Jenny swung around and faced her mother. "I didn't know you were there."

"Clearly. She's a lovely woman, and I think she cares about you and you definitely care about her. Why did she leave so abruptly or shouldn't a mother ask?"

"Probably shouldn't ask." Jenny moved to sit on the wall. "Stark and I shared this wall on your birthday last year. She asked if I was Humpty Dumpty. That seems like an eternity ago."

Marina rolled her eyes at Jenny's ramblings. *Here she goes again, her head in the clouds. Humpty Dumpty indeed.* She then followed suit and settled next to Jenny. For the most part, they weren't alike in any way physically or personality-wise. But she guessed that Jenny was like her in the love stakes. She'd spent so much time when she was younger dreaming of a knight on a white charger that she hadn't recognized Charles as that person for some time. Her head had been in the clouds, too, at the time. "Do you mind if I make an observation?"

"Go for it," Jenny said.

"You should go after Susan or call her and tell her."

"Tell her?"

"That you love her, silly girl." Marina shook her head and placed an arm over Jenny's shoulders.

Jenny frowned. "It's not that simple."

Marina chuckled softly. "You young people always say that. Sorry to disappoint you, darling, but it really is that simple."

"She wants to take things slow, but there's slow and there's *slow*. I wasn't very complimentary about that, but I'd rather have *slow* than nothing at all." Jenny shook her head.

Marina raised her eyebrows. "Then you definitely need to apologize. In this day and age, when sex accompanies the first date, it is so rare and rather romantic that she wants to court you. At least then you'll know if you're compatible for life. Trust me, sex isn't the sustaining quality in a relationship."

Jenny looked at her feet. "Romantic, you say."

Marina smiled at her eldest child. "As I said, dear, love is simple if you take it for what it is rather than try to create something that you think it should be."

Jenny moved and hugged her mother. "Thanks. Will you and Dad mind if I leave now? I have some thinking to do."

Marina kissed her and shook her head. "Don't think it to death or you might miss the boat."

Jenny smiled. "I promise not to do that. I'll call you later in the week. Bye, Mom."

Marina watched Jenny leave to say goodbye to her father.

Five minutes later, the BMW revved up in the drive and she was on her way.

Charles walked towards his wife. “Well, that was an interesting visit. Are you going to tell me what’s going on?”

Marina smiled. “Come here.”

Charles gave his wife a speculative look as he sat beside her. “I’m here.”

“So you are. Have I told you recently that I love you?”

Charles beamed a smile that made him look a little less craggy as he took his wife’s hand. “All the time, darling.”

“Good…I wouldn’t want you to forget it.”

“Never.”

Chapter 22

Susan mulled over Jenny's words. She had been right—they had pussyfooted around their relationship. She thought it was developing into something deeper and perfect, and she didn't want anything to go wrong. She glanced at the clock. It was eight thirty, and she suspected that Jenny would be home by now.

Since arriving home, she'd sat in front of the TV and watched every current affairs program on the umpteen channels until she was sick of the wars and the state of the global economic depression. Then it suddenly dawned on her. *I'm a damned fool. Jenny is saying, in that way of hers, that she loves me.* It was a sobering yet marvelous thought. A rush of adrenaline surged through her body with the revelation. It was so different to the world that was struggling to provide any measure of peace and happiness.

Fifteen minutes later, Susan was pulling on her socks. Waiting to speak with Jenny until the following Saturday was no longer an option. Jenny needed reassurance now—not next week. Although what she had planned next weekend would have been perfect, sometimes perfect just didn't fit the bill. Right now was the time to tell Jenny exactly how she felt. The doorbell rang. *Jenny.* She dropped one of her socks and headed for the door, totally disregarding the fact that she was in boxers and a half-opened shirt. She peered through the peephole expecting to see Jenny. Susan was surprised. She opened the door exclaiming, "Van?"

Vanessa smiled. Her perfect teeth glowed as she lounged against the doorjamb with her body clothed in a commercial pilot's uniform. She swung her chestnut shoulder-length hair away from her face. "Wow, you look as good as you did when we were in college. I probably don't need to ask you this, but how are you, Sue?" Golden-flecked grey eyes appraised Susan's body.

Susan couldn't help it and moved forward to wrap the woman in a tight hug. "I didn't expect a personal visit."

Vanessa chuckled. "You've got to be kidding me. You leave a message on my machine after five years, especially with what I did to you. Only a personal visit would suffice."

"Come on in." Susan held open the door, and Vanessa picked up a small valise at her feet and entered the apartment.

Suddenly unsure of what to say to her friend, Susan asked, "Want coffee?"

"Thanks." Van rested her valise on the floor and sat on one of the bar stools. "I'm glad you called me."

Susan glanced across at the negligent air Van had always exuded. *Some things never change.* "Yeah, I'm glad, too."

"Look, if it's inconvenient, I can come back another time."

Susan contemplated the offer, then took in a deep breath and shook her head. "No, I was just going for a walk." This would exorcise the final ghost of her past, and she could genuinely say with confidence that her past was that—gone, along with its baggage. Then she could really start a new life with Jenny.

A few minutes later, with steaming coffee in hand, Van looked at Susan as she discarded her sock. "You know, I would have given anything not to hurt you. It just happened. You know I always had a hard time reining in my libido."

Susan caught Van's eyes, and for a long moment, she stared hard into the brown depths. "You did anyway. Why?"

"Leigh was a temptation that hammered on my door from the first moment you introduced us. I'm not proud of what I did, but I have to tell you, I thought I loved her," Van said unexpectedly.

Susan was surprised at her friend's disclosure and frowned. "You in love…that's an oxymoron, isn't it?"

Van turned to face Susan. "Hey, it happens to the best of us, right?"

For a second, Susan didn't answer, then smiled slightly as she walked over to the window.

"Yes, it does. Leigh could always turn heads."

"She left me to go back to you. It was depressing and sobering at the same time. I remember the day she left like it was yesterday."

Yeah, I know what that feels like. "What happened?" Susan had her version from Leigh, but Van's would put the whole episode into focus.

Van moved from her chair and walked to where Susan was looking out onto the street below. "Leigh said she should never have left you, and I was a poor replacement. I was exciting but not you. I never had anyone say that to me before…that's usually my line. I guess your gentle and considerate loving works for the long haul."

Susan frowned at the reference to her style of courtship. *God, I hope Jenny isn't bored with me. That must be why she was so pissed off today.* "Yes, that's what she said."

"You've seen her then?"

"She's here in Merit, has been for over a year, I think. I met her by accident through a friend. She's teaching at Merit University." Susan watched her old friend's face cloud at the news.

Van didn't reply at first. "Do you have her number?"

Susan hesitated for a second. "Not her personal number, but I can give you the number I called at the university. You can track her down from there."

"Thanks, you always were way too generous as a friend and obviously a lover, too," Van quipped.

"Yeah," Susan agreed with a tight smile.

They spent an hour talking about old times. Van was forgiven. "I was sorry to read about Cathy," Van said.

Susan paused before answering. "Yes, it was a shock being there when it happened. Although you and I both know that Cathy was career military. She knew what she was going into, and she wouldn't have wanted it any other way. A part of me still grieves for her. I think I always will."

Van nodded. "Those stories you sent back were awesome. Your writing has grown. Isn't it time you wrote that book you always said you were going to write when we were kids?"

Susan chuckled. "Well, as it happens, I finally finished a novel, and the publisher rang me yesterday to confirm the book will be available next Saturday. They even set up a special book signing party for friends, family, and other interested parties around the city. I didn't think a first-time author warranted that kind of lavish expense."

Van leaned over and placed a warm hand on the tan lithe leg closest to her. "You weave words magically, Sue, and now that you've matured, the world is your oyster. They must think highly of it and you. Do I get a sneak peek for old time's sake?"

Debating the request, Susan hesitated. She had wanted Jenny to be the one she personally gave the story to. Sometimes things just didn't work out the way you wanted them to. She sighed heavily and stood. "Give me a minute." A few minutes later, she returned and gave Van a pen drive. "You can read this version. It isn't the edited one but close enough."

Van breezed confidently. "Can I stay the night? I don't need to take a flight out until noon tomorrow."

Susan laughed outright. *Van will never change.* She was always confidently sure of herself. "Sure, I just need to make a call. Knock yourself out on what you want to do until I get back."

"Oh, don't worry, I know exactly what I'm going to do." Van waved the pen drive in the air and Susan laughed.

"Okay." Susan headed for her study to call Jenny.

The call went to Jenny's answering machine, and Susan frowned. *Where is she?* She didn't leave a message and hung up. She contemplated going over to Jenny's to make sure she was okay, but with the unexpected arrival of her friend, it wouldn't be polite to leave her guest even if Van would understand.

Walking back to where she left her old friend, she watched her avidly reading the words on the screen. Van seemed completely engrossed, not knowing she was there. It made Susan think about the book she'd written when she was convalescing. Her new venture had been a gamble, especially when the publisher originally approached her to write a book. The publisher wanted a manuscript about her experiences in Afghanistan. After numerous attempts, it hadn't flowed—the memories were too painfully raw. Instead, as an experiment to see if in fact she did have a story inside her waiting to be written, she'd allowed her imagination to take free reign. When finally presenting the story to the publisher in person, she expected them to throw it back at her. She was amazed when they said they wanted to publish the book.

The most astonishing thing for her was that it had been cathartic. Since completing the novel, the heavy weight of the final day in the desert and the loss of her friend were finally laid to rest.

Van called over her shoulder, "Hey, Sue, any chance of a beer? I have a feeling this could be a long night."

Startled out of her thoughts, Susan smiled. "Yeah." Susan ambled towards the kitchen, wondering if she should call Jenny again.

Jenny had driven for miles. Her journey had pretty much circled the outer edges of the city, then she'd taken the long way home, arriving there about seven thirty. Her thoughts and emotions were in disarray as she parked the car in the drive and watched as the automatic garage door opened.

As it did, she sat with the engine turned off looking ahead. Her view was of a tidy garage space, everything had a shelf. A large tool set mounted on the wall, filled with every imaginable tool on the planet for a household. She stared ahead recalling that she never actually used most of them, but she was the envy of every other do-it-yourself enthusiast on the street. Fortunately, they were all happy to help her if she needed anything fixed. Another reason she loved living there was the friendliness and family-type connection. Somehow, living in a sterile apartment, although great for the commute to work, didn't stack with the benefits she gained by living in this community. Stark's apartment, though very modern, which probably cost a fortune to rent, didn't quite do it for her. She loved her yard and the ability to grow her own vegetables, at least the ones she liked, especially when Harry, the widowed ex-teacher who was pretty close to ninety, helped her.

He was a walking encyclopedia regarding growing vegetables and flowers. Whoever said that the *help out your neighbor* traditions had died had never visited or lived in her neighborhood.

Her fingers moved from the steering wheel she gripped and traced a line over her lips as she remembered the kisses she shared with Stark. Except for that day, all other kisses had been tender, fleeting, and friendly with no pressure attached. That day had been different. Suddenly, the sparks that had flown between them had exploded like a fireworks display, and she had lost herself in the growing feelings of love she had for Stark. *Was I wrong to want more? Perhaps what I feel is one-sided.*

Over the weeks since the renewal of their relationship, they had taken a gentle slide into friendship, and she hadn't been invasive with questions. She even held her tongue about Stark's previous relationship with Leigh Chambers. At the time, she felt that it was too early to discuss what had been painful times for Stark. She figured that one day she would just talk naturally about the things that hurt the most. *Maybe if Stark had...* There was no use speculating for Stark hadn't.

This is crazy. I need to do what my mother said, apologize to Stark, and tell her how I feel. "Damn, why is saying 'I love you' so hard for me?" She answered her own question. "Because I've always refused to allow someone that kind of hold over me. I'm such a coward deep down, I don't want to be hurt, and Stark, with a simple word, can do that to me." She switched on the ignition and glided the car into the parking spot in the garage.

A few minutes later, she walked into the house and checked her voice mail, hoping Stark had called—she had but left no message. As she listened to the next message, she groaned softly and rolled her eyes. "I'll call you back later, you're gonna want to hear what happened anyway." As she said that, she realized it also gave her the perfect opportunity to call Stark back without digging up the afternoon spat. *Oh, crap, now I really am a coward! I really don't deserve you.* Then, she turned back the way she came and headed out again.

I noticed the dedication. "Have you told her?" Van asked as she closed the screen of the laptop.

Susan knew what Van meant but delayed her reply. Then she scratched the back of her neck, slightly embarrassed. "I wanted it to be perfect…I figured Saturday as a surprise."

"Wow, that's a hell of a surprise. She must be very special."

Looking up suddenly, Susan caught Van's frank stare and gave a sheepish smile. "Yes, she is special, and that's why I'm not going to invite you next Saturday."

Van laughed softly. "I couldn't make it anyway. I'll be in Rio." A serious expression crossed Van's face. "I promise you that I'll never do anything like that again. Even now, I'm not sure how it happened."

Susan stood. "Now in a way, I'm glad it happened. If things had worked out with Leigh back then, I'd never have come here and found Jenny."

"Yeah, I remember you were going to be that high-flying reporter in D.C., and look at you now. You have the city of Merit in your pocket and you're about to achieve a childhood dream. Instead of a little fish in a big pond, you're a big fish in a small one. It works for me."

They both laughed at the path life had taken them.

"What about you? Have you settled down, or are you still footloose and fancy free?" Susan asked casually before she saw a look of sadness appear in Van's eyes.

"Oh, you know me…a girl in every stopover. I never could be faithful for longer than three months. Although, I confess, I did try hard with Leigh, and I thought maybe it might have worked out," Van said in a quiet voice. "By the way, I never said…it's a beautiful story, you brought tears to my eyes."

Susan shook her head. "Yeah, right. Look, it's late and I'm going to bed. I need to arrange some things in the morning for a trip to the West Coast. I'll be gone till Friday. Want me to take you out for breakfast before you leave?"

"Now that sounds like a good idea to me. What about

your friend? Surely, you want to be with her instead…I'd understand."

Susan pulled at her bottom lip. "We said our goodbyes earlier, it's cool." *In more ways than I wanted.*

Van stared at Susan and replied enthusiastically, "When I'm in town next, will you allow me to buy you dinner? You can bring your significant other…if you dare," Van said with a teasing quality in her voice. "I'd like to prove to you that I can keep my hands to myself and not come on to your new friend."

Susan considered the invitation in the knowledge that the tentative renewal of the friendship was still in the early stages. Susan nodded with a wry smile. "Sure and maybe my significant other won't kick your ass for what you did to me. She can be quite protective…just ask Leigh when you next see her."

Van laughed as they headed towards their bedrooms. "Now this special woman is someone I'm definitely dying to meet."

An hour later, Jenny stepped through the door of the police precinct from where she had received a call—Lorna was in trouble again.

Stepping up to the front desk, she waited as the sergeant finished his call. "Why, Ms. Price, what are you doing out this late on a Sunday?" The officer, a stocky man with a mass of thick black hair, gave her a friendly smile.

"Hi, Joe, you have one of my clients in the cell. Lorna Hirste. Why are you holding her?"

Joe frowned and checked the log. He had only just begun his shift and hadn't been there when the officer brought the woman in. "Let me check for you."

"Thanks. How are the grandkids? Did Jack make the Little League team this year?" Jenny asked as she waited for the information.

Bushy eyebrows matching the hair rose and the lined faced warmed with a wide smile. "He did and they're all well. Thanks for asking. Ah, here it is, Lorna Hirste. We caught her and another woman in the Park Cemetery early this morning around two. They became, according to the officers who brought them in, abusive, refusing to leave when asked. They're charged with disturbing the peace, and I think one of them hit an officer."

Jenny bit down on her lip. "Who's the other party?"

He looked at the log again. "Andrea Campbell, she was the one who hit one of my officers."

Jenny didn't allow the officer to see her surprise as she calmly replied, "I guess I'm going to be busy then. Can I see my clients?"

"Oh, you really did catch the short straw if you have the two of them." He motioned to the door at the side of the building. "You can have interview room three. I'll have someone bring them to you."

"Thanks, Joe." Jenny moved towards the room and opened it. "God, what have they been doing now?" she muttered as she took a seat and waited.

Ten minutes later, the two women accompanied by the police officer walked in the door. Their expressions were doleful until they saw Jenny, and both seemed to beam a smile of thanks at her.

Jenny smiled at the police officer, and two minutes later, she was alone with her clients.

"Jenny, I'm really sorry…"

"Jenny, it was all my fault…"

"Hold it, the both of you, sit down and let's start from the beginning." Her tone was authoritative and brisk—she meant business. The upside of that mind-set was it took her mind off Stark. "Doctor, why don't you start?"

Andrea paused a second and gave Lorna a supportive glance. "Lorna had another name floating in her head like the last time we went to Centenary Cemetery. Only this time, it wouldn't give up. She was getting headaches, and my readings were off the chart. It was an impromptu visit, and I didn't get permission. I wanted to help Lorna because she was in so much distress. We weren't doing anything wrong."

"Really? You call slugging a police officer nothing wrong? Okay, so what happened next?" Jenny frowned and made a few notes.

"We set up the equipment and waited. Sure enough, people were coming, but it wasn't who we were expecting. It was the police. Lorna kind of freaked, and my equipment began taking readings that were off the scale. Bright orbs were dancing like a halo around Lorna. The police thought we were doing a light show and told us to move on or they would arrest us. I tried to explain what we were doing and why we were there…they wouldn't listen," Andrea finished.

Jenny nodded. "What you describe would be seen as skeptical from the authority's point of view."

"They should never have manhandled Lorna. That was why I pushed the officer. It wasn't my fault he fell over the headstone we were protecting," Andrea wailed in self-defense.

A smile tilted Jenny's lips at the description of the event, and she wanted to laugh. However, her professionalism won as she gazed at Lorna. "Is this how it happened, Lorna?" She gave Lorna a serious look and waited. She noted that she'd changed her hairstyle to a more fashionable one and her once sallow complexion was replaced by a healthy tan. Her whole face seemed more alive somehow. Funny, she hadn't noticed all that the week before, but then, she had Stark and everything paled into nothingness when the woman was near.

"Andy was protecting me, Jenny. We didn't do anything wrong. The police said they knew I was going to do this again, and this time, I'd never get out of the institution."

Jenny's eyes flew open at Lorna's explanation. "Hang on a minute. They said what and when?"

Lorna repeated her original statement adding, "When they locked me up."

Frowning, Jenny made a few more notes, then turned to Andrea. "Did you get footage of any of this?"

Andrea angrily said, "Probably all of it, but the pigs have my equipment."

Scraping back her chair, Jenny picked up her notes and went to the door. "I'll be back shortly." She gave them a stern look. "Behave yourselves until I get back." She rolled her eyes as the two women giggled at her request.

Jenny walked to the main desk and spoke to the man sitting there. "Sergeant Lucas, I need to speak with the officer in charge of this case."

Joe Lucas looked up from his paperwork and saw trouble with a capital "T" staring at him. The formal title and the tone of Jenny's voice indicated she wasn't happy. "That would be Lieutenant Fane, Ms. Price. He's back on duty in the morning."

"Well, he'll have to get his butt here then, won't he? I want to see him. Better yet, is Captain Randal on duty? Either way, I'm going to wait to see someone, and trust me, I won't be happy if it takes until morning." She glanced at her watch, noting that it was after nine.

Joe scratched the stubble on his chin and frowned. "I'll call the lieutenant."

"I'll be with my clients." Jenny stomped off towards the interview room, then turned back. "The equipment my clients were using had better be in perfect order and not tampered with, or whoever took it into custody will wish they hadn't been working early this morning." She pierced the sergeant with her eyes. "Do you get my meaning?" Jenny walked to interview room three, opened the door, and entered.

Joe Lucas made two phone calls.

Captain Daniel Randal steepled his pudgy fingers together as he looked at his lieutenant, then to Jenny. "How did the erasure of the material transpire, Fane?"

Lieutenant Clive Fane's deep set eyes glared at Jenny. His thin body seemed swamped by the tracksuit he wore. "No idea, boss. That doesn't take away that they were trespassing or that one of them attacked an officer."

Randal looked at Jenny. "He's right, Ms. Price."

Jenny snorted. "Have you seen those two women? Between them, they couldn't take on one of your officers, never mind attack one and be successful. If you take that to court, who's going to be the laughingstock? I know it won't be my clients. Besides, one of them is a celebrated researcher at Merit University, who in her haste omitted to inform the appropriate authority and get permission to do something she does frequently. I suspect you all know that." With a faint smile, she continued, "What do you call the people who do this from the university…ah, yes, *crackpot ghost busters*. I think the mayor isn't going to be pleased with the wonderful police work this weekend when the full extent of the story comes out. I wasn't aware Merit had taken bullying tactics into mainstream policing these days. I know a journalist who would love this story."

Uncomfortable with the line of questioning, Lieutenant Fane shifted in his seat before his captain dismissed him.

"Don't go far, Fane, I'm not done with you."

When he'd gone, Randal turned to Jenny. "Okay, Ms. Price, point taken. What do you want?"

"An apology to my clients for a start, then I want this expunged from their records. I also want whatever detrimental information you've tagged Lorna Hirste with taken off. She paid her dues and now she's working with the university. Everything she's doing is legitimate."

Randal looked down at his desk. "She did kill a man once. We can't forget that…we shouldn't forget it."

Jenny sucked in a deep breath. "Yes, she did, but I figure spending fifteen years in a mental institution on a manslaughter charge that was more self-defense and ended up a shambles of an investigation is enough. I wanted to reopen the evidence and ask for a retrial, but my client didn't want that. All she wanted was to go forward with her life. You were here then, Captain, you knew the score. Just how successful do you think I'd be?"

"You can't dictate what a jury will do. You know that more than I do."

"Exactly, and I think with the right evidence and an unbiased jury, we both know she wouldn't have spent a day incarcerated."

"I'll take care of everything," Randal said gruffly.

Jenny nodded. "Thank you." She stood and moved towards the door. "Oh, if I were you, I'd let Lorna and Andrea continue their work. You never know, the graffiti problem we have in town might begin to disappear without using the taxpayers' money."

Fifteen minutes later, Jenny was driving the two women to

their respective homes. At least that was what she thought when she stopped at Andrea's condominium complex. They both got out of the vehicle.

"Don't you want to go home, Lorna? Won't your parents be worried?" Jenny frowned at the two women who gave each other amused looks.

Then Andrea answered as she took Lorna's hand. "We're a couple, Jenny. Lorna lives with me. I guess your talk with me that day about living in a dream world opened my eyes to other possibilities." Her gaze caught Lorna's, and she gave her a tender smile.

Jenny watched them and saw Lorna's expression become almost beautiful as she gazed adoringly at Andy. "Well, I guess congratulations are in order. I'm pleased for you both. Now stay out of trouble, okay?"

They both nodded and headed up the steps to the condo.

Jenny watched them go, and although it had been a very long day, her eyes caught the time on the dashboard—quarter after midnight. There was some satisfaction in what had happened that night. Not only that, what she had just heard made everything clear to her. Just as her mother said—*love is that simple*. She switched back on the ignition and drove away.

Hopefully, she could catch Stark first thing in the morning, and they could have an early breakfast together. She really did need to apologize and explain.

Jenny peered at the clock. It was six thirty. At least she'd managed a couple of hours of decent sleep, and the only thing keeping her from dreading the rest of the long day ahead was the thought of seeing Stark. She climbed out of bed and showered and changed. At seven, she decided it was okay to make the call.

Nervously, she dialed Stark's cell and waited. When it went to voice mail, she was bitterly disappointed but decided to try the land line. Once again, she waited.

This time, the answer was a sleepy "Hi."

Jenny felt her brow puckering. It didn't sound like Stark. "Stark?"

After a few seconds of silence, the tired voice casually said, "Nope, she's in the shower. Want me to get her for you?"

"No, it doesn't matter. I'll call back at a more convenient time. " Jenny disconnected the call abruptly.

In a daze, Jenny picked up her jacket and automatically made coffee and drank a few mouthfuls before leaving an almost full mug on the counter. Did all her ranting finally make Stark decide to switch away from her? Who could blame her? The reality was too horrendous to consider.

"I will not do that. I will not let my imagination run away with me. She and I have a deep friendship and it's solid. There has to be an explanation." Her demons whispered, *Yeah, but who does she know that could interrupt a shower?* Suddenly, that day and the rest of her life had become a mammoth task of putting one foot in front of the other.

Chapter 23

Jenny stopped in front of her hall table and looked at the gold envelope that enclosed an invitation for a book review and signing the next night. It was unusual for she'd never requested to be on any list and certainly hadn't joined a book club that might have her name associated with it. When she'd receive it on Wednesday, her first instinct was to drop it in the garbage, but for some reason, she had placed it on the hall table in clear view when she came home.

The phone rang and she automatically picked it up. "Hi?"

"Jenny?"

That voice, with all its baggage both real and imagined from Jenny's point of view, was unmistakable. "Stark, this is a surprise."

There was a clearing of a voice at the other end. Jenny could faintly hear other voices in the background. *Things never change.*

"I know we haven't caught up with each other since Sunday, but I figured we both needed a little personal space. Did you receive the invitation to the book review for tomorrow evening?"

Yeah, right. You mean you *needed space!* Automatically, Jenny looked at the envelope. "Yes, I thought it was junk mail."

"I see. I guess you ditched it in the trash." Jenny remained silent and Stark continued. "I was going to offer to pick you up. We could have a bite to eat, then go from there."

This time, Jenny heard a note of impatience, which was something Stark rarely showed. "I've never heard of the author, and to be honest, it isn't my scene. I read e-books these days.

When did you get back? I thought you might have called me earlier." She glanced at the clock. It was five fifteen.

"I came back later than expected. It's been a hectic schedule."

Jenny felt her lips curl sardonically. "Well, if I knew where it was you went, I might sympathize. As it is…whatever."

"You don't sound very happy to hear from me. What's wrong?"

Silence dropped like a shroud, and Jenny wanted desperately to ask who had been in Stark's apartment the previous Monday morning when she'd called, but she resisted the temptation. Speaking with Stark, however acrimoniously, felt good, and the sensation was one she had been desperate to engage in since they last met. "Absolutely nothing. Are you still going to this book signing? Is it a job thing?"

There was another pause before Jenny received an answer. "It is a job thing in a way. Jenny, will you reconsider? We said we'd talk."

Jenny was in two minds, then decided irrationally she didn't want to be second best. "We are talking."

There were sounds in the background of several people talking. "Yes, we are. As ever, you are literal."

"I'm a lawyer, remember?"

"How could I forget that pertinent point?"

A knock on the door had Jenny torn between the call and the person at the door. "Stark, don't go anywhere. I just need to answer the door, okay?"

"Sure."

Jenny walked over to the door and opened it. A courier handed her a brown envelope that she signed for, and she looked at it for a second. Then she returned to her conversation with Stark, depositing the envelope on the hall table. She picked up the invitation. Retrieving the phone, she glanced down at the invitation.

You are cordially invited to the first-ever release and book signing by new author, Cathy James, for her romantic tale "Falling

Into Fate," an addictive exploration of the misunderstandings of love in the modern world.

Venue: Casters Bookstore, Meredith Street.

Time: 7 p.m., Saturday, 25 April

Drinks and buffet complimentary

"I'm back, it was a courier with the information I expected a couple of days ago. Do you know this author?" Jenny vaguely recalled the name but couldn't quite put her finger on it.

There was a pause for a few seconds, then Stark answered. "I do. Intimately."

Jenny's eyes flew open at that comment, then it dawned on her where she'd heard the name before—Stark's Army buddy. "Cathy James, your Army friend, she wrote a book before she died?"

Stark laughed. "Nope, I did. Remember I mentioned in passing I'd written a novel when I came back to Merit?"

Jenny was lost for words as she tried to equate Stark with a pen name and a published novel—it was surreal. "That was why you were so secretive? What's wrong? Are you ashamed of the novel? I think it's wonderful. I'm proud of you."

"I'm not ashamed of the novel—" A voice interrupted their conversation.

Jenny tried intently to listen in and heard the odd word but nothing definitive.

"Sorry about that. They want me to do an interview for the local TV station that will air Sunday morning. Will you please hold my hand tomorrow at the book signing? I promise you a decadent night on the town complete with chauffeur-driven limousine."

Jenny drew in a ragged breath. "If you turned up in tattered jeans on a bicycle and offered me Taco Bell, I'd take it. This is so wonderful. When will you be finished? Maybe we can catch up later tonight."

"Who knows? I'd love to catch up, but I'm not sure when that will happen, tomorrow for sure. I'll be at your place around five. Is that okay? Oh, and put on one of those beautiful dresses you love to wear. I want a distraction if the story doesn't appeal to the masses."

Jenny heard the self-doubt in Stark's voice and she smiled. "I'll do that, but I'm dressing up for you, not anyone else. Besides, I know how you write. I haven't read the story, but I love it already."

"Look, they need me...something to do with a cue or something like that. I'll see you at five." For Jenny, time seemed to stand still as she heard Stark's breathing before saying, "I've missed you, Jenny."

The phone went dead and Jenny sighed. *I've missed you, too, Stark.*

Jenny placed the invitation back on the hall table, picked up the brown envelope, and ripped it open a few minutes later. She took in the contents and exclaimed, "Damn not tomorrow, no way." Frustrated, she threw down the papers and reached for the phone.

Susan felt the tears brimming to the surface vanish like magic as she disconnected the call to Jenny. The conversation was initially distant, and her original euphoria about her book dampened at the thought that Jenny was upset about something. What, she couldn't determine. However, Jenny had been genuinely happy about the book, and that boosted her self-esteem. A hand on her shoulder brought her back to earth.

"Susan, we're all ready for you. Sorry it's taken so long."

Susan nodded at the television producer and took a seat alongside the owner of the bookstore, who was a rotund woman with bright red cheeks and a ready smile. The fact that she'd chosen to have the book released in Merit was a coup, and she suspected that the owner was thrilled. Especially since her bookstore was one of the few independents left in the city. "Hi, Chris. Is everything ready for tomorrow?"

Christine Walker grinned. "Well, like everything, there will be last-minute stuff to arrange, but the main thing is organized."

"What's that?" Susan asked with a smile as the anchorman for the TV program entered the studio.

"Not a what, a who—you." Chris chuckled, pointing in her direction.

Susan felt humble at the words but didn't reply as the director called them to mark.

Jenny mulled over her options. She'd taken an overnight flight to arrive in Salem as early as possible. She needed to take the deposition; it was paramount to a case she had been working on for months. She prayed it wouldn't interfere with her need to be home in time for Stark's big moment. There was no way on earth she was going to miss it. Except right now, it had. She was still in the airport waiting for a delayed flight that looked like, with the best will in the world, she'd arrive in Merit with only an hour to spare before the book signing.

Dragging her cell out of her pocket, she found Stark's number and called it.

Several rings later, a sleepy voice said, "Hello?"

"Hey, you sound as if I've woken you. Have you been burning the midnight oil?" Jenny felt her smile automatically replace the tight-lipped expression she'd had with the waiting game for her flight.

"What time is it?"

Jenny chuckled and looked at her watch. "A quarter after three." Incredulously, she continued, "You were asleep, weren't you? My, how decadent. What did you do—stay up all night with the TV folks?"

There was faint clearing of a voice, then Stark throatily replied, "Tonight when you meet Chris, you ask her why I need to have a nap in the afternoon. I thought only old people did that."

"That's my Stark," Jenny said with a lilt in her voice. "I will, whoever Chris is." She meant the words innocently, but Jenny had a niggling doubt that perhaps Chris was the woman who had been at Stark's apartment that Monday morning.

"Oh, I'm sure you will, my intrepid lawyer friend. Anyway, I'm glad you called me, or I'd be late to pick you up."

Jenny sighed heavily. "That's exactly why I called. You remember last night I had a courier arrive?"

"Sure. It wasn't bad news, was it?"

"No, no, nothing like that. A case I've been working on for months hinged on a witness who finally agreed to testify."

"Hey, that's great, means we have a double celebration tonight."

Jenny frowned. "She would only testify on video, and I needed to be there to verify the authenticity."

"And?"

"It was in a place called Sweet Home. Cute name, huh? I'm at the airport in Salem."

There was quiet at the other end of the line.

"I guess that means you won't be coming tonight."

The despondency in Stark's voice had Jenny almost crying. "No, I took a red-eye flight out last night. I have everything, but my return flight is delayed, something about a baggage handlers dispute."

A metallic voice sounded behind Jenny. "Stark, I'm going to be there. I can't make dinner or arrive at your side, but I will be there, I promise you."

"If you can't, you can't, Jenny, I understand that work takes priority."

Jenny shook her head. "I can, I will. Don't count me out. I'm going to be there come hell or high water."

"Okay, so what does this mean…you'll meet me at the bookstore?"

"Yes, absolutely."

"Jenny, safe journey."

Jenny grinned. "I…never mind. Hey, the flight is finally being called. Talk to you soon, bye."

David and Sheryl Stark jumped out of the taxi outside the bookstore, complete with overnight bags. The rain that had been threatening all day began to pound the ground and every other surface within its watery reach. David gallantly held the door for his wife to rush out of the taxi and straight into the building with little or no effect from the sudden deluge. Sheryl smiled her thanks and surveyed the room for Susan.

David was about to step inside after his wife when a petite

woman almost cannoned into him. Her outer clothing, which was hardly rain-worthy, was soaked and molded to every curve of her body. Her blond hair was sticking out in all directions while rivulets of water dripped from her chin. He held the door for the young woman and smiled at her reassuringly.

"Thanks." The woman flashed him a grateful smile. "I bet I look a mess. Damn, now I don't think this was a good idea."

"Are you meeting someone?" David asked with a flash of a wide smile.

"Yes, although looking at me now, I think she'll look the other way."

David gave her a friendly once-over and winked. "I have a feeling that if she cares, she won't mind what you look like. By the way, I'm David, and that's my wife, Sheryl." He pointed to a woman holding a bag similar to his, who was looking around the throng of people.

"Hi, David, I'm…" Jenny stopped in mid-sentence when someone coming in the door bumped into her.

"Sorry." She moved to one side to allow the person entry, then was swept up in a wave of people turning to the woman at the podium advising the crowd that they were about to start.

"David, you'll never believe who had the audacity to turn up here tonight of all nights."

David Stark frowned and looked in the direction his wife pointed. "Ah," he said as he recognized the person. "Let's find Brian. He promised to hold a seat for us. We can cross that other bridge if we need to." He took Sheryl's hand and glanced around for his old Army friend. He located the man easily on the front row of chairs placed around the room. He was sitting in the middle and flanked by two empty seats. "Let's go. I've seen him. Hey, our girl looks great up there."

Jenny sighed heavily as the crowd finally stopped pushing her along. She eventually stopped next to a support column that held a slim mirror, and when she caught a glimpse of her appearance, she groaned. So much for dressing up for the occasion. There had been no opportunity since she went directly from the airport. Her clothes were expensive but casual. Hardly fitting for this event. If her mother could see her now, she'd have a fit.

Glancing around, she was sure there were people she knew or at least had seen. In the far corner of the room, with seats at the front, were Andy and Lorna. *Oh, Stark, you're such a softy.* Stark's article had been unbiased and surprisingly good about Lorna. It didn't make her out to be a weirdo or someone who needed pity. It was thought-provoking. Then she stood on tiptoes and tried to seek out Stark—she couldn't. A very tall woman and several of her friends obscured Jenny's view. She resigned herself to standing behind one of the large bookcases and listening to the proceedings until she could find Stark at the end of the formalities.

"Welcome, everyone. We're here tonight to celebrate the publication of a new book by an esteemed member of our community. Many of you will know her under another name and for her reporting prowess. However, it isn't for reporting that she's being fêted tonight. She's here for the release of her first novel, *Falling Into Fate*. Having had the privilege of reading it ahead of tonight, I can tell you it's a wonderful read. Without further ado, let me introduce you to the author herself, Cathy James."

There was a loud crescendo of applause and again people jostled and pushed Jenny in an attempt to get closer. She felt like a sardine at the bottom of the can. Then Jenny felt her pulse react as a familiar voice began to speak.

"Good evening, everyone. Thank you for coming…although I didn't give some of you a choice." Cat calls and whistles along with applause heralded the remark.

"The first question most people want to know is why I wrote a romantic novel instead of a grittier thriller or a true event piece. The simple answer to that is I needed to write something that was gentle and sweet after my experiences in Afghanistan. I was laid up in the hospital with a back problem for weeks, so what else could I do—twiddle my thumbs?" Laughter ensued for a few moments, then Susan continued.

Jenny felt her eyes flare at that comment. She always felt the same gut-wrenching pain in her stomach whenever she thought about what she could have lost.

"Anyway, I had a notion in my head that falling in love wasn't less gritty. If you allow, it certainly can be explosive. Therefore, it had the makings of its own war zone. However, the only important reason I wrote the story was for the woman I dedicated it to. I will be forever grateful for her part in my life. I'll attempt to give you a reading now, then we can socialize and you can all buy the book." Susan grinned slightly. "Hey, they paid me to say that." Applause and groans greeted the comment.

For the next half hour, Susan read partial chapters and paragraphs that gave a flavor of the book. When she'd finished, there was more applause, including from Jenny. Stark was fabulous in her eyes. How could she deserve a person like Stark?

Jenny had the opportunity to move into a bay window that had a bench and she stood on it, looking over the throng of people, hoping Stark would see her. She didn't. Jenny stepped off her perch and tried to get closer.

As the food was served, it gave Jenny time to stare discreetly at Stark, who was smiling and thanking people as they came up to her. Then, when Stark was alone for a few seconds, her façade dropped and Jenny saw a fleeting sadness cross her face. It was gone almost immediately as the very tall man named David, who had opened the door for her, engulfed Stark in a hug. "Oh, my god, I bet that's her dad. If I bothered to pay more attention earlier, I would have seen that she looks like him. Crap, when he finds out who I am, he'll wonder who his daughter is involved with. Turning up on a special event like this looking like I do."

A man to her left heard her and winked. "You look pretty good to me. Any chance I could buy you a drink so we can get to know each other?"

It was one of the oldest chat-up lines in history, and it was lousy. About to decline, Jenny felt someone staring at her—it was a familiar connection. She switched her glance to the front of the room. Sure enough, Stark's gaze caught hers, and by the frown on her face, it didn't look like she was happy. *What have I done?*

"What do you want to drink?" the immaculately dressed man asked again in annoyance. "Hey, I'm over here." He moved his muscled body to obscure Stark. When Jenny looked at the man, the leer that curled his lips said he expected more. He was good-looking if she liked that side of the fence.

"Thanks, but no thanks."

"Oh, come on, a pretty thing like you needs someone to take care of her. Bet I can guess the drink. Hmm, let me see now." The stranger pulled at his lower lip in concentration. Then he yelped as someone elbowed him in the back. He turned to glare at the offender and his lips curled. "Oh, it's you, Susan…or should it be Cathy now? You had your chance at me and now I'm interested in this beauty."

Susan crossed her arms and gave the man a long intense look. "Take your interest elsewhere, Mr. Daryl. She's taken."

Luke Daryl gave Susan a hard look, then smiled. He moved to within an inch of Susan's body as his arm snaked out to rest on her waist. "Always knew you had a soft spot for me, Susan. When you're done here, we can take the party to my place." He leaned in, attempting to snatch a kiss. Susan deftly sidestepped the action. "Oh, don't go all shy on me. We both know you want it." Then he felt a sharp pain for the second time that evening.

Jenny glared at him, willing him to say something as he rubbed his ribs in annoyance. "She's taken, too."

"By whom? Stark hasn't had a date in years," Luke said loudly. Several heads turned in their direction.

"Then you have no idea because I know personally she's been dating someone for a while now, and that person doesn't take kindly to you muscling in." Jenny ignored the increased tempo of her heart and steadfastly refused to look in Stark's direction.

The obnoxious man glanced around. "Yeah, like who? If he cared that much, why isn't he here?"

Susan intervened as her hand shot out and roughly grasped Daryl's arm. "Take a big hint. This is a women's bookstore, the book is a romance about two women, and it's dedicated to someone who isn't a man."

Jenny heard anger simmering in Stark and turned to catch the glint in the hazel eyes and the set of the firm mouth. Then Jenny made a decision. She moved towards Stark and pulled her hand away from the man's arm. She replaced him as the body closest to Stark before reaching up and soundly kissing the stunned woman.

Peripherally, Jenny heard a groan and "I want to be sick." Then she lost herself in the lips that moved sensuously over hers. The feeling, that this was the right place at the right time and nothing else mattered but the two of them, washed over her.

When they came up for air, there was loud applause, and several calls of "get a room" from people close by who had witnessed the scene.

Susan gazed into Jenny's flushed face. She traced a finger down her cheek. "You finally got here. I'm glad."

Jenny nodded and turned her face to rest against Stark's white silk shirt. "I couldn't keep away. If they hadn't worked out a flight plan, I'd have hired a private jet."

Susan smiled tenderly. "Now this evening is perfect." Susan released Jenny slightly when a voice cleared behind them. Turning, Susan saw her parents looking at them with amusement etched on their faces. "Jenny, I'd like you to meet my parents."

Jenny grinned at the couple and moved forward to shake David's hand. "We've tentatively met. Hello, David."

Stark's father ignored the outstretched hand and hugged her. "It's good to finally meet you, Jenny. I told you she wouldn't be disappointed."

Sheryl chuckled as she watched her husband. "Hello, Jenny, I've heard a little about you, which is amazing. Susan doesn't give much away on the personal relationship aspect."

Jenny felt herself blush. Stark had spoken to her parents about her. *Wow.* "Hello, Mrs. Stark."

"Away with the Mrs. Stark, my name's Sheryl." She hugged Jenny in response.

There was a call for silence, then Christine Walker announced that the book signing would be under way when she could find her star of the evening.

Virtually everyone around gave up Susan's position as she smiled at the bookstore owner, mouthing, "two more minutes."

"Looks like I have more work to do." Her gaze didn't leave Jenny's face.

"We were going to find the buffet and a drink. Want to join us while Susan is basking in the glow of her fans, Jenny?" David asked as he took his wife's hand.

Jenny smiled warmly. "Thanks, I'd like that. I guess I need to buy her book and have it autographed."

Stark's parents gave each other a surprised look, then chuckled. "We'll be over in that corner. I think I can command us a seat as I'm the father of the star of the evening."

Susan virtually ignored her parents except for a brief nod in their direction. Her gaze fixed on Jenny. "Don't buy the book, Jenny. I have a copy for you. I'll give it to you later, okay?"

Jenny felt the heat of Stark's intense gaze and grinned. "Sure, thank you."

Susan nodded and saw Christine shuffling agitatedly at the front of the room. "At least I can take you home in a limo afterwards."

"I came in my car," Jenny said automatically.

Disappointment flooded Susan's expression until Jenny reached up and stroked the lines that appeared at the corner of her eyes.

"I could take you home instead."

Susan smiled. "You have a deal. I'll be as fast as possible." Bending her head, she fleetingly captured Jenny's lips and reluctantly returned to the front of the venue.

Chapter 24

Susan finally looked pleadingly at Chris for a break from the signings. She'd spent the last hour signing her life away, or so it seemed. "Any chance of a break?"

Chris nodded. "The rest of the evening actually. We've run out of books. I call that a success. How do you feel?"

Susan smiled and looked over to where her parents and Jenny were talking. "Perfect," she whispered. "If you need me, I'll be over there." She pointed towards the people she loved and let out a gasp.

"Is that Jenny? What an exotic-looking woman," Chris asked with interest.

Scraping back her chair, Susan ignored the question and moved like lightning to the table where Jenny looked small and vulnerable. "Why did she have to come?" Susan muttered bitterly.

As Susan moved within a few feet of the table, a fan forestalled her. Politely, Susan nodded at the woman's words, rather than listened, her ears tuned to Leigh and her mother's conversation, which she could just hear.

"You're not welcome here, Leigh."

There was a short laugh from Leigh. "It's a public place, Mrs. Stark. Besides, Susan and I have sorted out our differences. It's all cool. Isn't that right, Jenny?"

Susan sucked in a silent breath, waiting for Jenny's reply.

"I wouldn't know any of the details."

"Oh, please, Jenny, we both know that you've taken my place in her affections."

"That's enough, young lady," David said forcibly. "Now go before Sue gets here. I don't want this evening spoiled for her by having to deal with you."

Susan couldn't help it. She grinned widely as her dad interceded.

"Do you think it's funny? I had the impression that you had more depth…you wrote the articles that way."

Susan frowned and looked at the woman who was speaking to her. She looked annoyed. *Damn, I didn't hear what she said.* "I'm really sorry. I didn't mean to offend you. Do you know Chris, the bookstore owner?"

"Of course, she's the best."

"Wonderful. I have a private drinks party at the Waldorf in two weeks for personal guests only. Tell her I said to put you on the list, Ms.?" Susan smiled at the woman, who was constantly looking back and forth between Susan and the family scene enfolding a yard away.

"Rose Lester. You really want me at the party?"

Susan winked. "Sure I do and bring a friend. I'm sorry, I have to go. My parents…you know how it is." She smiled politely again.

"Wow, do I. Thanks, you're awesome."

Susan shook her head as the woman headed off happily towards Chris. Then she walked the few steps that took her behind Leigh. "Leigh, have you bought a book? I assume that's why you're here…for me to autograph it."

Leigh turned away from the table and stared at her. "Actually, not yet. I was hoping as an old friend you might pass me a free copy."

Susan drew in a deep breath, her lips twisted into a cynical smile. "Something for nothing as usual with you, Leigh. Some things never change."

"Oh, that's rather cruel. I can remember lots of occasions when my *nothing,* as you call it, appealed to you big-time."

Susan stroked a finger down the side of her face as she contemplated what to say next. Then she looked at Jenny and saw an amused expression on her face. It really didn't matter what

Leigh said or thought because she wasn't important, and that was the bottom line. "Well, if you can find a book to buy, get in line, and I might autograph it for you." She winked at her parents, who gave her a nod of approval. Just as she was about to sit next to Jenny, who had snorted a soft laugh at her response to Leigh, a hand caught her arm.

"Hi, you don't know me, but I read your articles, and they were so exciting. I expect the book will be the same. Will you sign it for me?"

The woman who latched onto her arm like a limpet prevented Susan from sitting down, thereby obscuring Jenny from the stranger's view as she turned to confront the woman. She was about as tall as she was with dark brown hair tinted at the back with red, as thin as a rake, and a hard pretty face that was heavily made up. "Sure, who do you want it made out to?"

"Sheila West." The woman's voice had lowered seductively.

Susan was about to sign the book when she heard Jenny gasp behind her. Quickly shifting her gaze to Jenny, she saw a surprised expression on her face.

Her movement brought Jenny into Sheila's view.

"Jenny, I didn't expect to see you at this kind of event."

Susan watched Jenny place a hand over her mouth before she slowly said, "No, I guess you wouldn't. You look well, Sheila. How have you been?"

"Wonderful, I'm footloose and fancy free again. We can hook up for a night out. Drinks at our old haunt Kincaid's. Have you been to that great nightclub Crescendo? I know we had VIP tickets given before we split, but I expect you never used them. You're not exactly the most adventurous person alive. Although you look like you've let yourself go a little since we were together. What would your mother say if she saw you?"

Susan felt her hackles rise at that comment about Jenny's personality, not to mention her appearance. *This woman has no idea.* Then her expression softened as Jenny spoke.

Jenny retorted calmly, "Actually, I did go to the club for the record, and I met someone very special that night."

Sheila appeared to ignore Jenny's comment as she spoke

again. "Now this woman is a different entity altogether. She is just so exciting. If you're free, I'd be happy to show you a good time."

David Stark cleared his throat and whispered to his wife and left the table. Susan closed her eyes briefly. That was way too much info for her dad. Her mother cast her a quick fascinated glance. Jenny looked mortified. *Okay, that has to stop right now.*

"Jenny, come here, please." Susan smiled at Jenny, who stood and was by her side in a few seconds.

"Oh, so you know each other..."

"Intimately. Isn't that right, darling? We met at that club you mentioned." Susan didn't give Jenny time to respond as she dropped her head and began a slow and enjoyable exploration of Jenny's pliant lips.

When they came up for air, Susan rested her forehead briefly against Jenny's. No one in the room mattered except for them. Then in a voice loud enough for those standing close to them to hear, she said, "I love you, Jenny, you are the most exciting woman I've ever met, and who cares about clothes, right?"

"Jenny, exciting? Oh, please, you haven't lived."

Susan was about to allow her pent-up anger at this woman spill out when she was saved by an unexpected quarter.

"Hey, girl, come on. We're not wanted here, and trust me, we never will be."

Susan watched as Leigh placed a commanding hand on Sheila's arm and dragged her away.

"That's about the only thing that woman has done that's good for you."

Susan grinned at her mother. "Yeah, she isn't all bad."

"Perhaps not. Look, I'll catch up with your dad. If he and Brian begin to swap stories, I'll never get us home at a reasonable time." Sheryl smiled warmly at them and left to find her errant husband.

"Well, that was interesting and unexpected. I have to admit, she has a point, I do look a mess." Jenny's words tumbled out as she inwardly basked in Stark's admission of love.

Susan shook her head as they sat down, and she placed her

arm around Jenny's shoulders. "Never to me." She moved to place her lips on Jenny's in a tender kiss. "Hell, who would have expected both of our exes to turn up? Though I'm grateful."

"Really, why?" Jenny asked.

Susan caught Jenny's puzzled expression. "Because maybe they might find a mutual bond and leave us alone."

Jenny frowned. "You'd have no problem with Sheila. She doesn't find me exciting. I think her last words when we split up were that I was boring and she needed more excitement."

Susan saw the distress in Jenny's eyes, and she tilted her chin to stare into them. "Leigh left me because she thought I was boring, too. I guess that makes us the perfect match then. Although, I'd never say you were boring. Quite the contrary."

Jenny laughed, then her features became serious. "I love you too, Stark. Thank you for being you, and most of all, thank you for being in my life. I've wanted to tell you that for months now. I realized when you were away how much you meant to me."

Susan allowed a tender expression to cross her face, then she touched Jenny's cheek gently. "I guess I should have told you sooner how I felt. I fell in love with you from the first moment I saw you standing up for Lorna. I guess after my experiences abroad, I wanted everything to be perfect. I had a feeling I'd almost blown it for good at your parents' house. At the end of the day, Jenny, I'm here for as long as you want me."

There were no words but the gentle pull of Jenny's hand on her face initiating a long and passionate kiss.

The bookstore finally closed around midnight. With the sales of the book being better than expected, they took more than a few back orders.

Jenny pulled the car up to the pavement and waited for Stark and her parents. They had protested, but she had insisted that they take the lift offered. After all, they were staying with Stark. She'd enjoyed their company, and although she'd liked nothing better than to have Stark alone, it wouldn't have been right.

On the ride back, Sheryl casually said, "I suppose you must be thrilled about the book, Jenny."

Jenny considered the remark carefully. "I am, you must be very proud of St…Susan." Jenny turned to Stark, who sat next to her with her eyes closed. Jenny was certain she was asleep.

"Oh, we are. But the dedication, it isn't every day a book is dedicated to you, and it's so lovely."

Jenny frowned. "I haven't actually seen the book yet. In fact, until a few days ago, I didn't even realize that Susan had been given a contract to publish her novel. Are you saying she's dedicated it to me?"

"Oh, my goodness, she didn't tell you? Sometimes I wonder about that girl of ours." Sheryl shook her head.

"I don't understand," Jenny said.

"Susan will explain it all to you, Jenny. Won't you, Sue?" David asked.

Jenny shot him a look through her rearview mirror. "I think she's bushed. She looks asleep to me."

David nodded. "Yeah, it's been a tough week of traveling and preparation."

"She didn't elaborate what was involved last week, to me at least," Jenny said.

David shrugged. "Susan isn't much for letting people help."

The rest of the journey turned out to be relatively quiet as Jenny watched Stark's parents doze in the back. The prime thought in her head—*She dedicated her book to me. Oh, my god.*

The car slowed and stopped outside Stark's apartment building. The lack of motion made Stark's parents wake up and apologize profusely for nodding off. Jenny waved away their embarrassment with a smile.

Then Jenny gently prodded Stark. "Hey, sleepyhead, you're home."

A groggy, half-asleep answer had Jenny in shock. "I am… with you."

As Stark's parents retrieved their bags from the trunk, Jenny bent closer to Stark. "Come on, Stark, you need to go to bed."

This time, the answer was much clearer as a piercing gaze caught hers. "Is that an invitation?"

Jenny pulled back and shook her head reluctantly.

"Call me tomorrow, honey, and I'm sure we can work something out."

Susan whispered, "Tease."

"Caught me." Jenny leaned over and kissed Stark, lingering over her lips as her heart hammered in her chest.

Susan blew out a slow breath. "You take my breath away. You always have. Thank you for coming this evening, for driving us home, and for being you."

Self-consciously, Jenny answered, "Any time. Good night, Stark. Call me."

Susan moved to extricate herself from the passenger seat. "Good night, Jenny. I will."

A few minutes and several goodbyes later, Jenny's car moved away.

Jenny drove home in a daze. *Stark dedicated her book to me. How cool is that?* The whole evening had been surreal. Stark's secret writing career had been well and truly discovered from Stark's parents, who had happily waxed lyrically about her convalescence before she came back to Merit. Her father had even moaned good-naturedly over the fact that their chess game had to take second place. It was the most natural thing for her to listen and enjoy finding out snippets about Stark that she knew would have been like pulling teeth to find out from her.

Then there had been the confrontation of their exes, which had been weird. Who would have thought Sheila and Leigh would arrive at the same time? One thing she and Susan had in common was that the exes meant nothing in their lives anymore.

Half an hour later, she opened her front door and was about to kick her shoes into a corner of the hall when she saw an envelope on the floor. She picked it up curiously and looked at the envelope that looked like it had traveled the world several times over. On the front scrawled in pencil was a note of apology from her next door neighbor, who had been away visiting relatives for over six weeks. It was delivered to her by mistake.

Jenny took off her coat, kicked off her shoes, and walked farther into the house before she sat in her favorite chair. She was tired but intrigued by the contents of the letter. She looked at the neat handwriting on the back and knew it was from Stark. The postmark was an APO.

She recalled that Stark had said she sent a letter. *This must be it.*

Breathing in deeply, she carefully ripped open the envelope and lifted out the letter.

Dear Jenny,

I know I asked you to wait for me, and that being said, I wanted to apologize for leaving so dramatically without explaining earlier, not that I knew myself. That night, early morning, whatever you want to call it, had been like glimpsing my dreams in your arms, then I had to leave. It was like all my hopes and dreams finally coming together but all converging at the same time. Who would have known that fate could be so cruel? I chose, perhaps unwisely, to take this assignment and leave behind what I know in my heart is the best thing that has ever happened to me...you.

As I sit in this hammock thousands of miles from you, I can almost picture your expression. You screw up your eyes and your nose goes all pointy. Hey, I'm not being critical, far from it. It's those little things that have made me love you more and more since the first moment I saw you. I sometimes wonder what you feel about me, and after that last night, I hope that you might at least be open to pursuing the relationship further—you said you'd wait for me.

I want to show you that I'm not the womanizer you think I am. All I need is the chance to prove to you that it's not true. Please give me that chance. Call me when I get home. Yours is the only voice I want to hear when I get back.

Tomorrow, I go on my last maneuver. I've arranged to meet a few Afghan women and children to give their take on the war zone they live in day in and day out. I'm glad it isn't me. This is one scary place to live. I always thought nothing could make me afraid, and that mostly applies, except for one thing—the thought of losing you now that I've found you.

If you can find a place for me even as a friend in your life, I'd take that. Please call me when I get home so we can talk. I made a promise to myself that I will not contact you unless you make the first move.

I have to get some sleep. Tomorrow is probably going to be an exhausting day. Hopefully, you'll receive this around the time I come home. If you can't reach me on my cell, my parents' number is at the bottom. I promised to stay with them for a few days when I return. They want to assure themselves that I'm back in one piece.

Take care of yourself. Whatever you decide, please know that I understand.

All my love,
Susan

Jenny held the letter limply in her hand as she read it. It took a while for the contents to make any sense to her tired, emotional mind. Stark had loved her all along. *Oh, my god.* Tears fell as she looked at the letter and the reality sank in of what could have happened if she hadn't decided to call Stark.

Trembling with emotion, Jenny whispered, "I love you so much, Stark. I think I always have."

A short while later, Jenny climbed the stairs to her bedroom. With the letter clutched to her breast, she fell asleep knowing that her next meeting with Stark would be the best yet.

Chapter 25

Sunday morning arrived and went. Jenny groaned when she heard someone ringing her bell insistently. She glanced at the clock and frowned. It was one in the afternoon. "Damn, where did the morning go?" She grabbed her nightgown, and as quickly as her lethargic body allowed, she ran down the stairs and checked that it was someone she knew—Stark.

Pulling open the door, she threw her arms around the woman and was duly raised off her feet and thoroughly kissed.

"Now that's what I call a welcome, darling." Susan grinned as she dropped Jenny gently on the ground, then took in her apparel. "Did you just get up?"

Jenny rolled her eyes. "Worse than that…you got me out of bed."

"Really."

That one word sent shivers down Jenny's back, as she moved to allow Stark inside. "Yes, really."

Susan walked inside, and when she did, they looked at each other for several long seconds. With a shrug, Susan held out a small parcel. "I figured you'd want to see what you inspired."

Jenny felt her throat constrict as she took the package and peeled off the paper. "Do you want coffee…maybe I can make you something to eat…have you eaten…what about your parents?"

Susan moved forward and placed a finger over Jenny's lips. "I'm fine."

"A bit over the top, wasn't I?" Jenny said sheepishly as she looked at the book in her hands. "It's a great title."

Susan smiled. "Thank you."

Jenny flicked open the first few pages and came to the dedication.

For Jenny, from the first moment we met, I began to fall. As long as you're there to catch me, I know I'll land safely. You inspire me in everything I do. Then Jenny read the personal inscription, it was simple—*I love you.*

The book felt leaden in her hands as she read the words. Then with tears close to falling, she looked at Stark. At the back of her mind was the letter she'd read early that morning. "You dedicated this book to me, even before we got to know each other properly. Why?"

Stark chuckled and wiped away the few tears Jenny shed. "Because everything I wrote there is true. From the first moment I met you, I began to fall. Defending Lorna from god knows what you thought I was…ah, yes, a sleazy, good-for-nothing reporter."

Jenny groaned in distress. "Please don't remind me."

"Oh, I don't know. As soon as I saw you, I felt quite sleazy." Stark kissed her nose that had wrinkled in response. "All I wanted to do was make love to you. Incidentally, I still do, if you had any doubt." Susan winked.

"I don't have any doubts about you at all, Stark. I can't believe that after all I put you through, you still wanted me." Jenny's face looked glum as she recalled all the hurtful words and thoughts she'd had about Stark—even recently that phone call to her apartment and the mystery woman who answered.

Stark bent her head and whispered, "Simple…I love you." She captured the pouting lips in more than a fleeting kiss. The kiss conveyed all the pent-up passion and longing Jenny felt.

"I love you so very much," Jenny said breathlessly as their lips unlocked for a few short seconds.

Susan placed her arms around Jenny and lifted her easily into her arms. "I think you said something about bed."

"Oh, my god, yes." Jenny kissed the collarbone that was directly in front of her.

A few minutes later, Susan lay Jenny on the bed and tenderly removed her nightgown, allowing the garment to pillow around her as she stared at the naked body on view. It was just as she remembered. Perfectly proportioned breasts, each one the perfect handful as her body reacted to the taut stomach and the enticing glimpse of a blond triangle of hair that held the ultimate prize.

"I love you." Susan lowered her own fully clad body onto the bare skin of her lover, and she heard Jenny moan as she continued to assault the lips that called her name. Then her hands began to move, sculpting each crevice with gentle fingertips until she reached an erect nipple that asked to be pinched, and she did as Jenny moaned louder and her blond head moved in a delirious motion.

Jenny felt her body betray her as it allowed Stark's fingers to do their magic on her body. She was past thinking coherently. All she cared about was the emotions that flooded her body and knowing that this was what she'd been waiting for—to join completely and love the woman above her. Then her back arched as she felt kisses move over her breasts fleetingly as a hand once again massaged first one breast, then another.

The kisses moved to her stomach, then to the apex between her legs. Her legs automatically opened, and she allowed Stark's dark head to move between them and take what she wanted. With the touch of Stark's tongue and lips on her engorged clit, she was lost in the land of hedonistic pleasure and wanted to stay like that forever. When Stark made the final commitment and thrust into her, Jenny knew only one thing—this was exactly where she wanted to be with the right person. This was as Stark said in her dedication—falling. With Stark there to catch her, she was going to be safe for the rest of her life.

Her guttural moaning and pelvic movements came in unison with the thrust of Stark's fingers, and Jenny allowed a powerful orgasm to overtake her as she began the descent from the heady heights of passion to the plateau of a sensual haze.

Susan watched Jenny's face transform. She was thrilled that

she had the woman screaming for release. Rolling away to give Jenny a chance to catch her breath, she kissed the lips that had taunted her for so long. "How are you feeling?"

Jenny smiled. "Oh, I think you could call it loved, satisfied, and now insatiable." Jenny began to peel off Stark's clothes, and before long, she was naked. Then as Susan moved fractionally, her back was exposed and Jenny exclaimed, "You have scars?"

"Well, that doused my passion. Yes, I do. Why—does it turn you off?" Susan asked, sure it wouldn't, but with Jenny's habit of strange conclusions when it came to her, she couldn't be sure.

"Does this give you any indication?" Jenny asked huskily as she traced the scars first with her fingers, then with her lips. She kissed the line that went from one side of Stark's body to the other.

"Oh, yes," Susan said, allowing herself the indulgence of Jenny's caress. She'd waited long enough to sample it again. Then those lips moved sensually over her body until they went for the main prize. Susan lost herself as she felt Jenny gently open her legs and repeat what she had done to Jenny.

Her groan of pleasure spilled out as a tongue instead of fingers entered her, and she knew the muscle would send her over the edge quickly.

Jenny softly chuckled as she felt the control surging through her body as she glided up Stark's body. Her lips mapped every inch and spent a long time over the full breasts. Then as she lay over Stark, she gave a wicked smile, and her fingers moved back south. She took her lover again but spent longer taking her to the brink, then dropping back until Susan screamed her name. Then Jenny thrust deeper and longer, allowing the muscle wall to tighten around three fingers until Susan bucked for the final time as she sank into the aftermath of her orgasm.

Some time later, Susan kissed Jenny's head and sighed deeply.

"Are you okay?" Jenny felt the chest under her head heave.

"Couldn't be better, and you?" Susan moved to cradle her head against her chest.

"Oh, I can't think of a better place to be right now than up close and very personal with you, Stark," Jenny purred.

Susan chuckled as her fingers threaded in the blond hair. "You do know that you'll have to consider calling me Susan? Especially when we visit my parents."

Jenny moved slightly, looked up into Susan's hazel eyes, and giggled. "I can do that, but do you mind when we're at home if I call you Stark? I've kind of gotten used to it. Although, honey, lamb chop, luscious lips could all work."

Home. "I can accommodate that." Susan winked and kissed Jenny long and hard. "Lamb chop and luscious lips, really?"

Jenny giggled and didn't want to move, but her stomach began to rumble loudly. "How would it be if I made some lunch? I know people say you can live on love, but I'm afraid it hasn't convinced my stomach."

"Oh, you mean I have to try harder." Susan tickled Jenny, and the smaller woman giggled

"Stop, I can't breathe."

"Okay, you have a reprieve for now. Just remember, I'm going to keep trying to convince your stomach." Susan stopped her wandering fingers and allowed Jenny to move.

"I'll hold you to that." Jenny picked up her robe to cover her nakedness. A smile of pleasure highlighted her lips as she saw Stark's spellbound gaze watching her as she headed for the bathroom. "By the way, what about your parents? Where are they?"

"They took the midday flight home. Dad needs to be at work first thing tomorrow." Susan leaned back on the bed, her arms resting behind her head. "They like you."

Jenny returned to the room with a T-shirt and shorts replacing the robe. "I liked them, too. What can I get you?"

Susan cast Jenny a sultry look and smiled.

"Not that. For now anyway." Jenny laughed as she headed out the door.

"Spoilsport. I'll get up. I don't want you out of my sight." Susan moved from the bed and began to collect her clothes.

Jenny allowed the shivers to run down her back as Stark

bent over to retrieve her clothes. "See you in the kitchen. I'll get started." She rushed out of the room, knowing if she didn't, she'd ravish the woman all over again.

An hour later, they sat together at the kitchen table drinking the last of the coffee after a makeshift Caesar salad and cold chicken.

Susan leaned on one arm and gazed at Jenny.

"Have I spilled something on me?" Jenny asked with a grin and proceeded to pick up the napkin and dab at her face.

"Nope," Susan said softly as she kept staring.

Jenny laughed. "Okay, why the intent look?"

"Because I never thought I'd be in this position. Sitting here with you over the kitchen table knowing that if I reach across I can touch you, and you won't be a figment of my imagination, darling," Susan said seriously.

Lost for words, Jenny remained silent.

"Have I said too much?"

Jenny shook her head. "I've never met anyone who is so generous in their love and isn't afraid to say so." Jenny hesitated a few seconds, then blurted out, "I finally received your letter. It was on the floor when I arrived home last night."

Susan looked down at her plate as her cheeks took on a tinge of red. "I guess you know my guilty secret then."

Jenny took a deep breath. "We have the same one, I think. I can't imagine my life without you in it. From the first moment we met, my body knew instinctively you were my lover inside and out."

Susan chuckled as she reached across and took one of Jenny's hands in hers. "And they call me the author."

"Just how did you fall in love with a grouchy lawyer?" Jenny shook her head again as she felt the reassuring warmth of their joined fingers.

"It was a challenge to my womanizing ways."

Jenny caught Stark's gaze, lost herself in all her previous doubts, and realized that they were a figment of her fevered emotional response to Stark. Now it was all irrelevant except for one thing. "I called you last Monday morning and someone else answered. It was early."

The fingers that held hers tightened slightly and Susan understood. "You recall that Leigh left me for my best friend Van?"

Though they had never discussed the breakup in depth, she did remember the name of Stark's ex-best friend. "Yes."

"It was Van. She was in the city. She's a pilot. I wanted all the old baggage sorted out. I called her, and instead of returning my call, she turned up on my doorstep. We talked, and I think we can go back to being friends. Not like before, but at least there isn't any animosity," Susan said.

"After what she and Leigh did to you!" Then Jenny realized she was irrationally angry on Stark's behalf again. "Here I go again, and yes, I know intimately that you're a big girl and can take care of yourself."

Susan winked. "I love the way you defend me. No one has ever done that before…except for my parents."

Jenny felt vindicated for her instinctive defense of Stark. "Get used to it. I'm going to be your defender for the rest of your life, honey."

"I think that's a rather wonderful thing to say. Thank you. I accept you as my defender. To be honest, I'm glad that episode happened back then. As it turns out, fate decided I needed to fall, otherwise how would I have found you?"

Jenny gave Stark a strong steady stare, then smiled. "Maybe I won't kick your friends' asses. I have a lot to thank them for."

Susan laughed. "We both do. For the record, I didn't know you'd called. Van didn't say. I'm sorry."

"No, it wasn't her fault. Call it jealousy. I had some evil thoughts you'd taken someone else to bed when I offered myself on a plate to you and you refused. You know me. I jump to conclusions when you're part of the equation."

"For the record, since I met you, I've not been out with another woman or been to bed with anyone. You captured me that day at Lorna's home. All I wanted to do was be with you. Everyone else pales in comparison."

Frowning and surprised, Jenny asked, "What about the club and the bartender?"

Susan laughed and shook her head. "We talked, that's all. I just let you believe what you wanted. After all, you had a pretty poor opinion of me, and I needed to rectify that if I had a chance at all of winning your affections."

"What's your book about? I wasn't really listening to what you said last night." Jenny's face reddened. "I was just so darn glad to get there before it was over."

Susan cocked her head to one side and with a wry smile said, "You read it and see. I have to tell you that the ending isn't as satisfactory as some would like."

"What do you mean?"

"Because I left it where the two lovers might go in different directions…it was based on my experiences."

Jenny's eyes flared. "Is it a love story about you and me?"

"Ah, my perceptive darling, it most certainly is. I guess if they ask for a reprint, I can add an epilogue. In fact, I could let you write it." Susan grinned as she saw Jenny's surprised expression.

"I can't write…I'm too logical."

"Logical and you say the most eloquent things, and I quote, 'From the first moment we met, my body knew instinctively you were my lover inside and out.' If that isn't worth putting on paper, I don't know what is. How do you think it will end?"

"Hmm, let me see now." Jenny grinned and continued. "They got married, had ten kids, and lived happily ever after."

Susan stood, walked around the table, and pulled Jenny up. "I think I can accommodate most of that. But ten kids! How about a cat and a dog for starters?" She didn't allow Jenny to answer as she smothered her lips with her own.

When they did come up for breath, Jenny replied huskily, "Can we live here?"

Susan laughed. "Wherever you are, I'll be. Now come on, I have a stomach to educate." She lifted Jenny in her arms and once more headed for the bedroom. This time, food of another variety called their names.

About the author

JM Dragon, born in England and now a New Zealand citizen, lives in the beautiful countryside area of North Canterbury with her family.

She has a passion for stray animals and shares her life with a multitude of chickens, two alpacas, and Molly the cat, not to forget Shadow, the stray black cat at the bottom of the garden.

She loves to write, garden, and travel.

Visit her Web site at www.jmdragon.net.

You may also enjoy...

Echo's Crusade
by JM Dragon
ISBN: 978-1-935216-02-5
Price: $16.95

Echo Radar is outgoing and happy, working as an advertising executive in a reputable firm with a bright future for promotion. Karen Thompson, from a poor unstable background, works at the same advertising firm as Echo. Where Echo prefers a relaxing environment in her free time, Karen helps others through the Greystoke Project, which caters to the very people she had once been—destitute and down on her luck.

Two women form a bond and look forward to the prospect of a romantic relationship when the disturbing events of a Thanksgiving holiday bring the walls tumbling down around them.

Echo is now on a quest, and with the help of Detective Roan Keating, searching for justice becomes Echo's crusade.

AlsoFrom Intaglio Publications

Of Course It's Murder
Book Five: Kate Ryan Series
By Kate Sweeney
ISBN: 978-1-935216-11-7
Price: $16.95

Kate Ryan is sent to New England on a photo assignment. Seems her editor's ex-cousin, the hapless flamboyant Simon Merriweather needs photos of his new inn for the local travel guide. It was to be a nice quiet week of reflection for Kate. What could go wrong?

Enter Kit Parker, Emily Masterson, and Rebecca Townsend. Newport, Rhode Island's old, very old money... The irresistibly delightful elderly friends of Simon arrive for the grand opening. All hell breaks loose one stormy night and what happens?

Of course... It's murder!

Murder In City Hall
By Mary Jane Russell
ISBN: 978-1-935216-13-1
Price $ 16.95

Molly Hamilton is a dedicated public servant. She consistently out-thinks the men she works for and with. As Molly's department director, Jack Sampson is a boss from hell. Jack routinely abuses the tightly knit group of men and women who work behind the scenes in local government.

Christine Miller meets Molly by chance while struggling to find help in City Hall. As a police investigator, Chris finds Molly to be a person of interest personally and professionally after murder is committed in City Hall. Was Molly involved? Will Chris be able to save her new relationship with Molly by solving the crime? Or is Molly fated to be yet another victim of City Hall?

Rebecca's Cove
by LJ Maas
ISBN: 978-1-935216-12-4
Price: $16.95

Chicago native BJ Warren travels to the Florida island of Ana Lia to care for her grandmother's house after she has an accident and breaks her hip. Nothing and no one on the island is anywhere near what BJ would call normal. The island inhabitants exist in a world that cares little for what folks do on the mainland. The center of activity for their society revolves around a diner called Rebecca's Cove where the self-centered BJ alienates just about every member of the small community. But she meets her match in a local woman—Hobie Lynn Allen.

This is not a "love at first sight" story as both women find the other completely annoying and self-righteous. However, the island—and Rebecca's Cove—have an odd way of changing the way folks view their world and the people around them. Sometimes it's not a matter of what you're seeing but rather the position from which you see it.

Sea Of Grass
by Kate Sweeney
ISBN: 978-1-935216-15-5
Price $16.95

Professor Tess Rawlins spent the last twelve years teaching agriculture in California, away from Montana and her heart. When she's called back to the sprawling Double R cattle ranch and her ailing father, Tess is thrown back into the world she had nearly forgotten since the death of her brother two years earlier.

Unsettling memories boil to the surface for Tess, and her only pleasant distraction is the new cook Claire Redman and her son Jack. However, there is more facing Professor Rawlins than dealing with the memory of her brother or her attraction to Claire. Tess must figure a way to save the Rawlins's five thousand acres of rich grassland. It has thrived for five generations, when her great-grandfather started the dynasty in the 1880s; now she may lose it all to an unscrupulous land developer.

Set in the foothills of the Bitterroots, Tess and Claire find themselves in the fight of their lives—for love and the sea of grass.

Collide
by Maria V. Ciletti
ISBN: 978-1-935216-14-8
Price $16.95

Sometimes you have to shed the identity of who you think you should be to live your true life. Sometimes that identity gets ripped right out from under you.

Renee Cardone and Anna Maria Castrovinci had been best friends since kindergarten at St. Vincent's School, but when they were fifteen, their friendship turned into something more. Even though their attraction felt genuine and pure, guilt hovered over them. Although Renee loved Annie, she was afraid about the unnatural relationship, according to her Catholic upbringing, that she and Annie had fallen into.

Annie, intent on living a life acceptable to society, began to date Tom Del Fino, which broke Annie's heart. Renee tried to explain that what they had together was nice, but it wasn't real. She knew Tom could give her what she needed.

Renee and Tom married and built a respectable life together. They had a good marriage and two beautiful daughters. Then fate slapped them in the face and flipped Renee's life upside down. That's when she met Dana Renato.

Dana had it all. A lucrative career as a writer, a home she loved and a partner she adored. Then all of it came crashing down around her. She loses her partner to breast cancer, and the home they shared is threatened by her partner's estranged family. The only thing she has left is her writing, which takes her away from home and puts her in a small town in Northeast Ohio. There she meets Renee and their lives *collide*.

Clarity
by Jocelyn Powers
ISBN: 978-935216-07-0
Price: $16.95

Frustrated by a boss who continually passes her up for promotion, Chicago-based network producer Andrea Payton decides it's time to take back control of her career. She accepts an executive producer position with Resort TV's fledgling affiliate station KCOR in Summit County, the heart of Colorado ski country. The move from big city to small community affords her the opportunity to put some distance between her aching heart and constant reminders of the woman she loved. A romance was not in her plans.

Enter Snow Cap marketing exec Julianna Stevens. Julianna's beauty and sweetness take hold of Andi's bruised heart, and Andi is about to break the lesbian golden rule: no straight woman. While Andi tries to avoid falling deeper for the woman she deems "terminally hetero," Julianna secretly wrestles with her perplexing feelings for the alluring new producer.

Through a haze of confusion and doubt, Andi and Julianna search for a moment of clarity.

Love's Someday
by Robin Alexander
ISBN: 978-1-935216-08-7
Price: $16.95

Ashleigh Prather committed the sin of omission when she failed to reveal secrets of her past to her lover of five years. Her relationship becomes the casualty when the past and present collide. Erica Barrett's world is turned upside down when she is forced to watch Ashleigh confront old demons and become someone she doesn't recognize.

Is love worth fighting for when you realize that you never truly knew the person you've shared five years of your life with?

Survive the Dawn
by Kate Sweeney
ISBN: 978-1-935216-04-9
Price: $16.95

With the serum now in her bloodstream, Dr. Alex Taylor must find a suitable laboratory to continue her work to help the woman—well, vampire—she loves, Sebastian. Together they travel to Devon, England, where Sebastian hopes her old, old, friend, the flamboyant vamp Gaylen Prescott will assist them. All the while, they try to keep one step ahead of Nicholae, the elder in the hierarchy, who wants Sebastian destroyed.

They find themselves deep in the catacombs of Guys Hospital in London and to Kendra, a sultry vamp who knew Sebastian quite well a century before, too well for Alex. Kendra is conducting similar experiments of her own.

Alex becomes a reluctant comrade to this sexy vampire, and together they find a way for Sebastian and her world to survive the dawn.

Clinical Distance
by Maria Ciletti
ISBN: 978-1-935216-03-2
Price: $16.95

In the sequel to The Choice, Clinical Distance begins six years later with Mina Thomas, who has finished medical school. After divorcing her husband, Sean, and losing Regan Martin, the love of her life, Mina sets out on a quest to make her way in the world and to find the love she lost. Mina dates—a lot—but after many meaningless rendezvous with nameless women, Mina decides to give up on finding love and devotes her time solely to her career as chief resident at City Hospital.

However, one night after having dinner with her best friend Mina discovers that the love she was searching for might possibly have been right under her nose all along. That's when Regan steps back into Mina's life.

Forthcoming in 2010

Taking Flight
by Laurel Mills
ISBN: 978-1-935216-18-6
Price: $16.95
Release Date: September 2010

Librarian Sydney Burke is an avid birder and outdoorswoman. She has been single for several years after a longtime relationship ended. She meets Michelle and falls in love with her. However, Michelle is married to Robert, an abusive husband, and is afraid of him. She wants out of the marriage to be with Sydney but fears what Robert will do to them. Will the women be able to break free from the dangerous Robert and build a loving relationship with each other? Can Sydney help Michelle take flight to a new and safe life?

Liar's Moon
by Kate Sweeney
ISBN: 978-1-935216-19-3
Price: $16.95
Release Date: October 2010

In the sequel to Residual Moon, Grayson MacCarthaigh stays in Ireland, struggling with her destiny as the true descendant chosen to protect the ancient power of the fabled Tuatha De Danann. Her logical world is now replaced with Celtic legends and myths, goddesses, and immortals.

As Grayson comes to grips with all this, someone or something is doing his or her best to see that she fails in her role of protector of the ancients. Is it her new archenemy, Phelan Tynan the ancient wizard, or Elinora, the beautiful but enigmatic immortal sent to help Grayson? Grayson soon realizes everyone has something to hide. Mendacity runs amok at St. Brigid's Monastery, but all will be revealed under the Liar's Moon.

Jaded
by Jocelyn Powers
ISBN: 978-1-935216-20-9
Price: $16.95
Release Date: November 2010

Prominent New York acquisitions attorney Courtney Wilhelm had her entire life carefully planned...or so she thought. When Courtney's half sister, Marissa, is found dead from an apparent overdose, Courtney assumes guardianship of Marissa's daughter, Jade.

Courtney knows nothing of children and struggles to find balance as the custodian of a minor, while trying to maintain a high level of expertise expected by her clients and the firm. When she is confronted by Jade's new teacher Lauren McCallum, sparks fly in more ways than one.

Can Courtney let go of the life she has planned so meticulously—and clings to so stubbornly— to have the life with Jade and Lauren that awaits her? Or will the fear of failure keep her from the love and happiness she didn't even know she wanted?

Pitifully Ugly
By Robin Alexander
ISBN: 978-1-935216-21-6
December 2010

Shannon Brycen has decided to enter the dating world again after taking a hiatus from love. There's only one problem—well, many—but her reclusive personality and her sister's disastrous attempts at matchmaking force Shannon to try a different approach.

Hiding behind the online persona of Pitifully Ugly, Shannon finds the confidence she needs to pursue women, and the hunt is on. Many humorous lessons are learned along the way to her perfect match.

Published by
Intaglio Publications
Walker, La.

Visit us on the web
www.intagliopub.com